THE EVE OF SAINT HYACINTH

THE EVE OF SAINT HYACINTH

Kate Sedley

HEADLINE

First published in 1995
by HEADLINE BOOK PUBLISHING

10 9 8 7 6 5 4 3 2 1

British Library Cataloguing in Publication Data

Sedley, Kate
Eve of Saint Hyacinth
I. Title
823.914 [F]

ISBN 0-7472-1357-7

Typeset by Keyboard Services, Luton, Beds

Printed and bound in Great Britain by
Mackays of Chatham PLC, Chatham, Kent

HEADLINE BOOK PUBLISHING
A division of Hodder Headline PLC
338 Euston Road
London NW1 3BH

THE EVE OF SAINT HYACINTH

Chapter One

It was the eighth of June, the Eve of the Feast of Saint Columba, and in less than seventy-two hours it would be the longest day of the year, when the bright, dewy mornings and the seemingly endless evenings made it a pleasure to be on the road.

I had set out from Totnes at the beginning of May in that year of Our Lord 1475, and spent the intervening weeks selling my wares in as many hamlets and villages along the south coast of England as I was able to reach in comfort, without the expense of hiring a local guide. Such men were apt to overcharge for their services and, for all I know, still do. But I am old now, in my seventieth year, and no longer stray far from my native Wells. Almost half a century ago, however, I was young and vigorous, six feet tall and strongly built, and had chosen the freedom of a pedlar's life in preference to entering the Benedictine Order, which had been the dearest wish of my dead mother's heart.

But I had been made to pay a price for flouting her wishes. On four occasions during the past few years God had used my talent for unravelling mysteries to bring to justice a number of villains who might otherwise have escaped the consequences of their evil deeds. After the last unpleasantness, in the town of Totnes, I had argued with

1

God that enough was enough; I had paid my debt to both Him and my mother for abandoning the religious life. But my experience of the Almighty is that He has a deaf ear, which He conveniently turns towards those He does not desire to hear; and attempting to thwart Him by an act of defiance is worse than useless. As was soon to be proved to me yet again.

My act of defiance this time had been the decision, after leaving Devon, to go to London, with no other object in view than to indulge myself in the pleasures of the capital. Conscience told me that I should return to Bristol, where my widowed mother-in-law lived with my motherless daughter, little Elizabeth, six months old. But instead, at Exeter, I had found a trustworthy friar – at least, I judged him to be trustworthy, although I could not help recalling the saying that 'friars and fiends are but little asunder' – who was travelling northwards, and entrusted to him a sum of money, along with Margaret Walker's direction in the weavers' quarter of the city.

'Commend me most heartily to her. Say that I promise to be with her before the beginning of winter and ask her to give my child a kiss from its loving father.' And I had added a generous bonus for the friar's own use.

He had nodded merely, taking it for granted that my journey to London was necessitated by the need to earn more money in a lean and hungry year, when taxes had been raised to help fund King Edward's proposed invasion of France, for which the levies were even then massing in Kent. (I had met many men on the march during the past two months and most were bound for Canterbury or its neighbourhood.)

Increasing my fortune, however, was not my main object

in going to London and I felt a stab of guilt in deceiving not only the friar, but my mother-in-law as well; for the holy man would undoubtedly pass on his own conclusions with the other messages I had given him for Margaret Walker. But the truth was that a goodly sum of money had been pressed on me before I quit Totnes, in gratitude for all that I had done, and for once in my life I was plump in the pocket. No, my reason for visiting the capital was purely a whim; a desire to experience once more its numerous fleshpots and, on this occasion, with a little loose change jingling in my purse.

All the same, I had not disdained making what extra I could during my journey and had proceeded at a leisurely pace, with the result that, on this eighth day of June, as the summer solstice approached, I had just spent a profitable morning in the port of Southampton, and was now, at ten o'clock, thinking about my dinner. As I walked along High Street, away from the quayside and its huddle of dwellings, my nose scented the rich aroma of pig's trotters and gravy, causing my stomach to rumble hungrily. I was always hungry in those days and no matter when, or how much, I had last eaten, I was forever ready for more. I had a big frame and it demanded constant nourishment.

The town's butchers' and poulterers' shops bordered that stretch of High Street just north of Saint Lawrence's Church, although one or two were to be found in the alleyways and courtyards which opened between the houses. Southampton was as busy then as it presumably still is today and was always full of sailors, both native and foreign. The streets – and very bad streets they were, with broken paving stones and holes in the road to trip up the unwary – echoed with a babel of different tongues and there was much jostling and pushing from the various tradesmen as they vied for custom in front of their booths. I have seen unwilling customers lifted bodily off their feet and forcibly carried to the opposite side of the road by an over-zealous shopkeeper, determined on making a sale. Not that I ever suffered any such treatment. Even the most foolhardy would not dare to harass me. One glance at my height and girth and they all turned away with a shrug, content to let well alone.

The gabled ends of many of the houses faced on to High Street, with small courtyards to the side and rear, an arrangement which formed narrow passages between them. And it was along one of these, close to the public latrine, that my nose led me in search of food. It did not deceive me. Twenty paces in, set at right angles to its neighbours, was a butcher's shop which also, judging by the number of people sitting around outside busily eating, sold some of its wares already cooked. The smell of pig's trotters was overwhelming, although mixed with it was the equally delicious scent of freshly baked pies and pasties and the mouth-watering aroma of newly boiled tripe. A large trestle table displayed various cuts of meat, which two thrifty housewives were carefully prodding before making up their minds to buy, watched by the butcher, who occasionally offered his expert advice.

He was a large, jolly man, as those of his calling so often are, although I have never quite understood the reason why. Behind him, suspended from hooks set in the ceiling of the covered booth, hung the eviscerated carcasses of a pig and a sheep, not long slaughtered and still dripping blood. The trotters, then, would be fresh and tasty. I went forward to the trestle, where the goodwives continued to haggle over their purchases, and lowered my pack to the ground. The butcher's round, weather-beaten face split into a grin and the hazel eyes kindled with laughter as he eyed me up and down.

'And what can I do for a big fellow like you?' he demanded good-naturedly. 'That belly of yours takes a deal of filling, I'll be bound!'

'I can smell trotters and gravy,' I answered. 'A bowlful wouldn't come amiss.'

He chuckled. 'I'll lay it wouldn't. If you go to the back of the booth you'll find my cottage. Knock at the door and my wife will attend to you.' He turned to the two women, a shade of impatience creeping into his tone. 'Goodies, if you prod that meat any more it won't be fit for man nor beast. Make up your minds, now. What'll it be?'

There was laughter and a good deal of chaff from the other diners as the women refused to be hurried and retorted in kind, but I was too hungry to stop to listen. I picked up my pack and did as the butcher instructed me, making my way to the back of the shop, where a timber-framed cottage stood with its door wide open and the hole in its thatch belching forth steam. This was the source of all the tantalizing smells which had been teasing my nostrils for the past fifteen minutes; where the boiling and baking was done by the butcher's wife.

In reply to my shout she appeared in the doorway, wiping her hands on a coarse sacking apron.

'And what can I do for you, my lad?' she asked.

She was as small as her husband was large, with delicate, bird-like features and soft brown eyes which regarded me straitly before shifting to my pack, which I had once again placed at my feet.

'A bowl of pig's trotters with gravy,' I answered, but for the moment she ignored my order.

'You're a chapman,' she observed. 'Now there's a lucky chance. I've just broken my last good needle and I've also run out of thread. Can you help?'

'Willingly. I've both in my pack. Shall we do barter?'

She smiled. 'Why not? I'll get you your victuals first, however, for you look half starved. Then you can show me what you're hawking. You might as well come in and eat in the house; then, when you've finished, we can complete our business.'

I was somewhat reluctant to obey, it being a fine, sunny morning, and I should have preferred to remain out of doors, chatting to my fellow diners, but I could tell that the goodwife wanted to keep me under her eye until I had completed my side of the bargain. I therefore followed her into the kitchen and sat down at the table close to the oven, which was set in the wall behind me. Two big cauldrons bubbled over the fire on the central hearth, one of which contained the pig's trotters. My hostess ladled some of these on to a wooden platter and set it in front of me, before sinking down on the bench at my side and wiping her forehead on the back of her hand.

'Have you come far?' she asked.

I spoke with my mouth full. 'This morning, from the other side of the River Test.' I swallowed and continued less thickly, 'But I've walked here from Devon.'

'You're not from those parts, though,' she murmured, cocking her head to one side like a knowing sparrow. 'Nor hereabouts, either. North'ards a bit, I'd say. Somerset, perhaps.'

6

'I was born in Wells, but my home is now in Bristol.'

She nodded in satisfaction. 'I can usually tell. Although we had a travelling minstrel stop here some weeks back who came from Yorkshire. Now that speech I couldn't recognize.' She added, 'Are you married? Do you have children?'

'I was married,' I said, 'but my wife died in childbirth. I have a daughter, Elizabeth, nearly six months old. My mother-in-law takes care of her for me.'

The butcher's wife looked sympathetic and laid a consoling hand on my wrist. I smiled as gratefully as I knew how, not wishing to betray the truth: that Lillis and I had been married only eight short months, not long enough, at least on my part, for pity and guilt to burgeon into love. Would my hostess have been as shocked as I often was myself to know that, at times, I could barely recall the details of my dead wife's face?

Perhaps not, for she said encouragingly, 'You must marry again as soon as you can. A handsome lad such as yourself should have no trouble. There's girls falling over themselves, I shouldn't wonder, to tumble into bed with you.' She paused, laughing. 'Now, what have I said to make a great lummox like you choke and blush?' She rose from her seat to fetch me a second helping of trotters, saying over her shoulder, 'A pity my own girl isn't here to take you in hand for she's a preference for sizeable men.' She chuckled, ladling the steaming food from cauldron to plate. 'Which she gets from me, I don't need to tell you. For my Amice is as small-boned and short of height as I am myself, yet out of all my suitors I picked John Gentle, and him you've seen, for he must have sent you round here.' Mistress Gentle resumed her seat beside me and smiled with satisfaction as I once again eagerly picked up my knife. 'I like a man with a wholesome appetite. Now . . . what was I saying?'

'You were – er – talking about your daughter. But,' I added hopefully, 'Mistress Amice, I gather, is away from home?'

My companion heaved a sigh. 'She is that, and I miss her sorely. But,' she went on, both voice and face suddenly full of pride, 'I've no cause to grieve for her absence, as my goodman keeps reminding me, for my Amice is well settled in life, and with a very important household.' Mistress Gentle's tone deepened dramatically, taking on a hushed and reverent tone. 'She's a seamstress with – well, do you want to guess who with?' I muttered that I was bad at guessing and desired her to enlighten me, which she was more than willing to do. 'With none other than the Duchess of York herself! *The King's own mother!* There! What have you to say to that?'

I am certain that I could have found no words sufficient to gratify her maternal pride, but fortunately my looks said everything for me. And I was indeed impressed.

'How did Mistress Amice come by such a place?' I asked, and I even stopped eating long enough to look towards the butcher's wife and pause for her answer.

She smiled fondly. 'My Amice was always a pretty behaved young girl, and clever with her needle – which is something that she *doesn't* get from me, for I've never been more than a good, plain sewer. I can set a stitch in my man's shirts when necessary, or make myself a new gown or apron, but as for anything fancy, I haven't the knack. But my husband's mother, Amice's granddam, she had magic in her hands when it came to a needle and embroidered many a cope and chasuble for the churchmen hereabouts before she was called to her Maker. She taught my Amice all she knew and my Amice was a willing pupil. I believe she's even cleverer at embroidering than her granddam was. Lady Wardroper thought so, at all events. It was she who recommended my girl to one of her friends who, in turn, put in a word for Amice with Duchess Cicely's steward when Her Grace was looking for a new seamstress and embroiderer.'

I had by now returned to my meal and was sucking the last of the bones clean of its succulent flesh and licking the gravy from my fingers. But I was interested in the little tale, having once, four years earlier, met the formidable woman who was mother to our royal princes, although I had no intention of mentioning the fact: it would have involved me in too long a story.

Instead, 'Who is Lady Wardroper?' I inquired.

'The wife of Sir Cedric Wardroper of Chilworth Manor. That's a mile or so to the north and east of the city, close by the chandler's ford. Amice embroidered an altar cloth for the Chilworth chapel and Lady Wardroper was so impressed by its beauty that she would have taken the child to work for herself, but she had no real need of her. Nevertheless, she was swift to noise abroad my Amice's talents – with the happy result that I've just told you.'

'Lady Wardroper sounds a kind woman.' I licked my left thumb clean of the last gout of gravy and rubbed my sticky hands together.

'A true gentlewoman,' my hostess agreed warmly. 'And by a strange chance her only child – as Amice is ours – her son, Matthew, set out for London this Monday past, to take up a position in the Duke of Gloucester's household. I

9

know it for a fact because I met one of the cookmaids from Chilworth Manor at Saint Lawrence's market yesterday morning, and she told me. So Amice and Master Wardroper will be under the same roof for a week or more, because it seems Duke Richard is staying with his mother at this great house of hers by the Thames.'

'Baynard's Castle,' I murmured. 'I heard along the way that the Duke had come down from the north with his levies, but my informant thought him to be at Canterbury, at Barham Down.'

Mistress Gentle shrugged. 'I know nothing of that. But Audrey was certain that it was to London young Master Matthew had gone, and to this place that you mentioned. And by another strange chance John and I had received a message from Amice only two hours previously. She'd sent it by a carter coming in this direction from Duchess Cicely's castle at Berkhamsted, to say that the household was moving to London within the next few days. The carter couldn't remember the name of the house where they were to lodge, but otherwise he'd learned everything off by heart. He was smitten with my girl, I fancy, judging by the trouble he'd taken to make sure he had her message aright. She's a good child, and even though she can neither read nor write – well, who amongst us can, eh, chapman? – she does her best to let her father and me know where she is. For the gentry are forever trotting around the countryside, like they can't be still for a second. Not that Duchess Cicely's greatly given to such junketing, by all accounts, but I dare say she feels she should be in London in time of war.'

I nodded. 'She would no doubt wish to see her three sons safely off to France. And it makes sense that Duke Richard will be staying with her at Baynard's Castle. He always does so when he's in the capital.'

'You know that for a fact, do you?' my hostess asked and, glancing round, I saw that her smile was slightly mocking.

'So I've been told by those that might be reckoned in the know,' I answered. Once again I felt that to admit to having met His Grace of Gloucester twice, and to having been of service to him on both occasions, would embroil me in lengthy explanations which, anxious to be on my way, I would rather not embark on. 'That was an excellent meal, Mistress, even better than it smelled; something, half an hour ago, I would have deemed impossible. Now, to complete our business!' And I picked up my pack, opening it and spreading its contents out on the table.

In payment for the food she chose a small, carved wooden bobbin containing three needles and a spool of fine white thread which might, I considered, have cost her somewhat more in the market-place than she would have charged me for the plate of pig's trotters. However, I had suggested the bargain and could not cavil at it now. She cast a longing eye over my other wares, particularly struck by a pair of scented leather gloves the deep, rich colour of violets. Like my warm leather jerkin, lined with scarlet, I had obtained them in exchange for more necessary goods, this time from the wife of an impoverished gentleman living in Dorset. The lady had been loath to part with one of her few remaining pieces of finery, but the family had fallen upon hard times and needs must when the Devil drives. I was pleased to think that I had dealt generously with her.

11

Mistress Gentle sighed regretfully, running one fingertip over the soft, silk-like sheen of the leather, but decided that the gloves would be of no use to her.

'John would most certainly buy them for me if I asked him,' she assured me earnestly, 'but when would I have cause to wear such things?' She regarded her red and work-roughened hands for a disparaging moment, before thrusting them into her apron pocket. 'No, they'd be laid away in lavender and never see the light of day. Put them back in your pack, chapman, before temptation gets the better of me and I persuade my husband, contrary to his good judgement as well as my own, to purchase them.' She looked on wistfully as the gloves were folded away again, before adding with sudden inspiration, 'When you leave here, go to Chilworth. The chandler's ford's not more than five or six mile north by east of S'ampton and I'd lay money you'll find a willing buyer in Lady Wardroper. Very proud of those delicate white hands of hers, she is. And she has an elderly, doting husband in Sir Cedric.'

I thanked her for her advice and took my leave. She seemed a little reluctant to let me go and, I fancy, would have detained me further but that a shout from outside warned her of the advent of yet another diner. I shouldered my pack and followed her to the door, where I made my escape. The two goodwives had by now departed and the butcher was standing in the mouth of the alleyway, touting for trade. We exchanged a few words and I congratulated him on the quality of his meat, but he was too busy watching out for fresh custom to waste much time on one already satisfied.

'Your wife advises me to make for Chilworth Manor,' I said as a parting shot and he nodded.

12

'You'd probably be wise to do as she says. Sir Cedric's very plump in the pocket. They're one of the best-known families in these parts. Honest, English-speaking people. Well, the menfolk are. Saw young Matthew only last week, just before he left for London. Said they'd been entertaining a travelling singer – same one as came here looking for food, I reckon – but as all his songs had been in French, he couldn't understand a word of them. But Lady Wardroper, now, she's different. She has a few words of the language.'

I gave him good-day, deciding that I would follow Mistress Gentle's recommendation, especially as a north-easterly direction must bring me eventually to Winchester, and so on to the London road. Moreover, I would need a berth for the night, which might well be found in the Manor kitchen. It was not long past eleven o'clock, so if I walked briskly, not stopping to sell my wares, I could probably reach Chilworth by late afternoon without much difficulty.

I settled my pack more comfortably on my back, turned my feet in the direction of Southampton's East Gate, and as I walked, began to whistle in my customary tuneless fashion. For I have never had any ear for music and don't suppose that I ever shall.

Chapter Two

The afternoon was well advanced by the time I approached
Chilworth Manor. This lay a mile or two east of the ford,
close to the banks of a small stream, tributary to the River
Itchen.

It was a beautiful day, the wind blowing fresh and sweet
across the meadows. Smoke rose from cottage chimneys
iridescent as a rainbow and the sky was a swimming lake of
deepest blue, smudged here and there by soft white clouds.
The clang of a blacksmith's hammer sounded a joyful
carillon of anvil blows and the rise of pasture, away to the
west, was rinsed by blue-veined shadows. The stream
flowed softly between its fringe of rushes and I could see
clear down to the bed of gravel underneath. Daisies and the
golden cups of celandine starred the straggling grasses.

Suddenly the flow of water began to diminish until it
dwindled into the merest trickle. Rounding a bend by some
willow stumps, I came upon the reason. A shepherd had
dammed the stream in two places to form a pool and was
washing his flock, assisted by a stout lad with hard red
cheeks and a surly, disgruntled expression. It was the boy's
job to drag the reluctant animals one by one into the water,
where the shepherd stood thigh-deep, removing the foul
and loose wool from around the udders and thoroughly

washing the fleece. When he had finished examining the beast's mouth and ears, the sheep scrambled up the opposite bank to join its fellows, where it dripped and shivered miserably, regarding him with a wide and baleful stare for having been subjected to such indignity. The lambs, separated from their dams, cried piteously.

I greeted the shepherd and his assistant cheerfully. 'God be with you both! Am I on the right path for Chilworth Manor?'

The lad made no reply, but the older man paused in his work and nodded. 'You are that. You're on demesne land now. The house is about half a mile further on from here. Are you a chapman?'

'I am. And hoping to sell some of my wares to Lady Wardroper, who was recommended to me as a likely patroness by a butcher's wife in Southampton.'

The shepherd laughed. 'Mistress Gentle, I'll be bound. A good woman, always willing to help others. Her daughter, Amice, did some sewing and embroidery for my lady at one time, before she went away from home.' He turned back to the ewe he was washing and began to prise her jaws apart. The animal, justly incensed by such treatment, tried to rear up and place her two front feet against his chest, but the man moved closer, skilfully frustrating the attempt. 'Got to watch this one,' he said. 'She's old and up to all the tricks. Many's the soaking I've had from her in my time, when she was a bit younger and spryer than she is today.' When the ewe was done and had proceeded, stately with outrage, to the opposite shore, the shepherd signalled to the boy to halt a moment and turned to face me. 'My cottage is close by here. Before you go on to the Manor House, do you have time to visit my wife? She was complaining only yesterday that we've had no pedlar pass this way for several weeks, and as a consequence she's short of various items. She's broken the blade of her kitchen knife and she's also in need of a pair of good, stout laces, if you've such a thing in your pack.'

'I have and will willingly sell them to her if you'll give me more precise directions.'

'The boy can show you,' was the answer. 'There's only these two old tups left to wash and I can handle them well enough on my own. Jed, take the chapman to my cottage, there's a good lad. But mind you return here afterwards,' he continued on a minatory note, as the boy abandoned his job with an alacrity which his master plainly found ominous. 'These beasts will need careful watching until their fleeces are dry and the yolk gets back into the wool. The natural grease,' he added for my benefit, noting my puzzled look.

I followed my guide along a narrow track which led upwards to higher ground, where the close-cropped turf would have indicated the presence of sheep even had I not already known of it. The shepherd's cottage, a rough, stone-built, one-storey dwelling, stood in the lee of a clump of trees, all now wearing their delicate, early-summer green.

'That's where Jack Shepherd lives,' the boy told me, dragging his feet at the prospect of returning to his work once his errand was done. Inspiration struck him. 'I'd best come and make you known to the goodwife, you being a stranger hereabouts.'

I placed a hand on his shoulder. 'My pack will speak for itself. You'd best run along before Master Shepherd accuses you of skiving and recommends to Sir Cedric Wardroper that he employ a new boy.'

The lad looked sullen, but finally, with a heart-wrenching sigh, thought better of any gesture of defiance which might cost him his place. He set off down the slope again and vanished from sight, with just one last, yearning glance over his shoulder. I went forward and rapped on the cottage door.

My knock was answered by a sharp-featured, middle-aged woman, wearing a dress of grey brocella, together with an apron and hood of coarse, unbleached linen. My first impression was of someone of a slightly sour disposition; which only served to demonstrate how deceptive appearances can sometimes be. For on closer acquaintance the shepherd's wife proved to be a pleasantly spoken, friendly woman about the same age as her husband, who welcomed me in with a smile.

When I had told her of my conversation with her man she urged me to one of the two seats in the room, a three-legged stool uncomfortably close to the hearth, and pressed me to take refreshment.

'I've just this moment finished baking a fresh oatcake,' she said and began scraping away the hot ashes from around an upturned pot. When she had removed the pot, she took a clean cloth and lifted the cake from the hearth-tiles, placing it carefully on the table. Then she produced butter, wrapped in dock leaves to keep it cool, filled a wooden cup with ale from the barrel in one corner and bade me draw up my stool and eat.

'And while you do so,' she said, 'if it's acceptable to you, I'll look through your pack.'

I readily agreed and spread out its contents on the other end of the table, just as I had done that morning for Mistress Gentle. The shepherd's wife, too, fondled the violet leather gloves with the same mixture of longing and regret.

'I was advised to show them to Lady Wardroper,' I said, and the woman nodded.

'Ay, she'll buy them, no doubt, and be glad of the chance, for she likes fine things and we've had no pedlar pass this way for weeks and weeks, as my husband told you. But we're off the beaten track a little here and can easily be missed by travellers. That's not to say that no one penetrates as far as Chilworth. We had a travelling musician here only last month, who entertained Sir Cedric and my lady and spent the night in the guest hall. They were especially pleased, I remember, because Master Matthew was still at home, kicking his heels and waiting to take up his new appointment in the Duke of Gloucester's household.'

'I know all about that,' I said, washing down a piece of oatcake with some ale and wiping my mouth on the back of my hand. And in answer to her inquiring lift of the eyebrows I added, 'Mistress Gentle, the butcher's wife in Southampton, told me.'

My companion laughed, much as her husband had done. 'Well, that explains it. She enjoys a good gossip, does Joan Gentle.' She threw up her hands. 'But who am I to point a finger? I'd be a rich woman if I had a groat for every time my goodman's said to me, "Millisent, your tongue will swell up and turn black one of these fine days if you don't curb your appetite for pushing your nose into your neighbours' affairs."'

I grinned sympathetically. 'My mother used to tell me much the same thing when she was alive, God rest her soul! "Your long nose will be the undoing of you, my son," she used to say.' I wet my forefinger and gathered up the last crumbs of oatcake from the board. 'That was excellent, Mistress.' Millisent Shepherd smiled and refilled my cup from the pitcher of ale which she had earlier thought to place on the table. She was still examining the contents of my pack, so I settled myself comfortably on my stool and prepared to slake not only my thirst, but also my curiosity. 'How did young Master Wardroper come to enter the service of the Duke of Gloucester, then?'

The woman paused, her fingers hovering above a length of silk ribbon, which it was obvious that she would dearly love to have purchased instead of a knife, but did not dare to do so for fear of her husband's displeasure.

'I don't know exactly all the details of the appointment,' she admitted a trifle shamefacedly, as though it were her bounden duty to be aware of everything pertaining to Chilworth Manor, 'but I believe my lady has a distant kinsman already well established within the Duke's household. I forget what position he holds, but Mary Buck, the laundress, told me that it was of some importance. And when it became necessary to find a new place for Master Matthew Lady Wardroper naturally thought of this Lionel Arrowsmith and sent a message to him. Up north somewhere. Wherever it is the duke lives when he's not in London.'

'Middleham Castle, probably,' I said. 'It's high on the Yorkshire moors, or so I believe, and it's where Duke Richard spends most of his time. Where the duchess and their little son live.'

Millisent Shepherd looked at me with sharpened interest. 'You know a lot,' she approved admiringly. 'But then, in your line of work you hear a deal of gossip I dare say.'

'A certain amount. Tell me, why did it become necessary for Matthew Wardroper to find a new place? Surely, at his age, his future must have been already secured?'

'Ay, it was. He was sent away young, as all boys of his sort are, to be brought up by a friend of Sir Cedric – Sir Peter Wells, I believe his name was. It was a fair bit up-country, a long way from here, at any rate. Near Leicester, I think I heard someone tell. But last Christmas this Sir Peter dies with neither chick nor child to succeed him. His wife retires into a convent and the household's disbanded. Master Matthew returned home to Chilworth and there he was, seventeen years old and no place in the world.' The goodwife grimaced and hunched her shoulders. 'Well! Sir Cedric's not the man to want a high-spirited boy kicking his heels around the manor. He's older than my lady by a good twenty years, if not more, I'd reckon, and it wasn't long before he and young Master Matthew were at loggerheads over one thing and another. Or so my friend the laundress informs me. Not surprising, really. From a baby, Matt was always the spitting image of his mother: eyes, hair, features. And they do say that people who look alike are alike in other ways, don't they?'

I cautiously acknowledged this theory. 'Although I have known cases where even twins, identically matched, had differing natures.'

Mistress Shepherd waved this observation aside as an irrelevance. 'Maybe, but in this particular case I assure you that it's true. Sir Cedric's a humourless man, while my lady has always liked a laugh and a giggle. She's had to school her ways, of course, over the years, to suit her husband's humour, but Master Matt felt no such need to appease his father. So it became necessary to settle him as soon as

21

maybe and away from Chilworth. My lady therefore conceived the notion of sending to this cousin of hers in the Duke of Gloucester's household, and after a few weeks, back came the messenger with an offer for Master Matt to join the Duke when His Grace came south to London – for we're off to fight the Frenchies again I understand. Ah well! That's men for you! All they think about from the cradle to the grave is brawling and fighting. Women, now, they've more sense. Girls soon learn there's better ways to go on than clawing each other's eyes out. Women generally don't like violence.'

'I've known several exceptions,' I answered grimly; but once again I did not enlarge upon the subject. 'Have you found anything that takes your fancy?' I asked to divert her.

My hostess sighed. 'It'll have to be this bone-handled knife and this pair of hempen laces. It's what I need and we've little enough money to spend on gewgaws. Tell me the price and I'll settle with you, then you can be on your way to the Manor. Those gloves'll find a good home there, for Sir Cedric, for all he's so stiff-backed and can't stand levity, is an indulgent husband.' She sighed a second, more gusty sigh. 'Some women, chapman, are luckier than others.'

I laughed and, not wishing to be the recipient of marital confidences, said hurriedly, 'I'm sure your goodman would do the same by you if it were possible.' I named as reasonable a sum as I could for the knife and laces, put the money in my purse and made the shepherd's wife a present of a reel of thread, which she accepted with gratitude.

'You're a good lad. I could see that the moment you walked through that door. Now, be off with you, for you've eaten my man's supper and I'd best make another oatcake before he comes home and demands his victuals.'

Nevertheless, in spite of the need for haste, she accompanied me to the cottage door and stood there, waving, until I had turned a bend in the downhill track and was lost to her view.

Beside the stream, the shepherd had finished his work. The boy was seated on the grass of the opposite bank, yawning with boredom and scratching his flea-bitten neck while he waited for the animals' fleeces to dry. The shepherd himself was driving the lambs across the little ford he had created to reunite them with their mothers.

'Mind you,' he told me, chuckling, 'they won't all find 'em. Stupid creatures, sheep, but it's a good thing, really. It helps to wean the little 'uns.' He picked up a spade and began to demolish the dams he had made, and the stream, which higher up had been threatening to overflow its banks, now came rushing through its proper channel. 'Did my woman find what she wanted?'

'She did,' I assured him. I thought it wisest not to mention the fact that I had eaten his supper. 'I'm off, then, to the Manor House. I've some gloves Lady Wardroper might wish to buy.'

'Good luck to you,' the shepherd said. 'Follow the bank on this side of the stream for a while until you come to a willow whose branches lean over almost to the opposite bank. Strike inland there. You'll see the track across the meadow, and on the other side of a little rise you'll see the house.'

I thanked him heartily, he bade me God speed and even the boy managed to raise a hand in valediction. On this amicable note we parted.

* * *

I had been ushered into Lady Wardroper's solar as soon as news of my presence had been conveyed to her by one of the maids. The steward, a tall, emaciated man with grey hair and a watery, suspicious eye, had looked disapproving; but my guide, who had informed me in a giggling undertone that her name was Jennet, said that wouldn't deter her mistress.

'For my lady doesn't care two pins for Master Steward, and she's as bored as she can be, stuck down here in the country all summer. Sir Cedric had promised to take her to London, but he's gone back on his word now that the King is away to France. Master says London won't be fit for a decent woman with all those men there. He says licentiousness'll be rife.' Once again she giggled. 'Don't think Mistress would have minded. She'd've been well looked after in any case, but when Sir Cedric says "no" 'e means it.'

I ducked my head beneath an arch and followed the girl up a shallow flight of steps.

'He's probably worrying unnecessarily,' I agreed, 'for most of the levies have been marshalling in Kent, at Barham Down near Canterbury. Or so I've been informed by several people coming from that direction. But Sir Cedric probably knows his own business best.'

'Ay, like I told you, no one'll budge him once 'e's made up his mind.' Jennet paused outside an iron-studded door. 'And the fact that only three days since, this Monday past, his own son rode off to London to join the Duke of Gloucester's household there is enough to convince the Master as 'e's right. For the Duke's off to France 'imself in a couple o' weeks.' She knocked on the door.

A sweet voice bade us enter.

Lady Wardroper was seated in a carved armchair beside the empty hearth, a piece of embroidery lying idly in her lap. She was a pretty woman with soft blue eyes and a delicately bowed mouth, at present pouting with discontentment. A strand of dark, almost black hair had escaped from the back of her cap and lay curling gently across one shoulder. She had very pale skin, so pale that it needed none of the white lead which fashionable ladies used to lighten their complexions. But her forehead was shaved to a high, arched dome, indicating that she had not abandoned all pretension to modishness in spite of her seclusion. She wore a loose-sleeved gown of deep-blue silk, gathered at the waist with a belt of cinnamon-coloured velvet, the tips adorned with sapphire-encrusted tags of silver-gilt. She had rings on almost every finger and an ivory rosary hung about her slender neck.

She looked up as Jennet ushered me into the room and laid aside her embroidery. Her face, a moment ago so discontented, was suddenly wreathed in smiles. She had, I noticed, the most engaging dimple.

'Chapman!' she exclaimed, clapping her hands together and seeming a little taken aback, as people so often were, by my size and youthfulness. She laughed uncertainly. 'Goodness! How tall you are. Pray sit down, there, in that chair opposite, or you'll quite overwhelm me. Now,' she went on a trifle breathlessly, 'what do you have in your pack?'

For the third time that day I emptied its contents and laid them out for inspection. Lady Wardroper carefully scrutinized every item, but I could see that her eyes were drawn back time and again to the violet leather gloves. At last she put out a hand and fingered them.

'They're not new,' I informed her quickly, before she had time to make the point herself. 'You'll note that the left thumb is somewhat rubbed on the tip.'

She gave me a smile. 'I had noticed, and wondered if you'd be honest enough to tell me, especially as the mark is so slight. So how did you come to acquire them?' When she had listened to my story she nodded understandingly. 'Many people have felt the pinch of raised taxation this year, I know. Happily, Sir Cedric – my husband – has been able to weather the storm without any fear of drowning, but others less fortunate than we are have been unable to keep their heads above water.' She studied me thoughtfully. 'You look an honest fellow so I trust you gave this poor gentlewoman a fair price?' I named the sum and she seemed satisfied. 'More than sufficient. Very well! What will you ask of me, if I decide to buy?'

We haggled a little, but in the end she professed herself happy to accede to my price. She rang the small bell at her elbow and, when Jennet appeared, instructed her to conduct me to the counting-house and tell the treasurer to pay me. And while I put the rest of my goods back into my pack Lady Wardroper picked up the gloves and put them on, holding her hands away from her so that she could admire the effect. At the same time she hummed a snatch of song, finally breaking into verse with the words, 'It is the end. No matter what is said, I must love.' She gave me a coquettish glance and asked, 'Do you like music, chapman?' adding regretfully, 'I know no man who does.'

'Unhappily, my lady, I've no ear for it at all, but the words sounded . . . sad,' I finished lamely, unable to offer any greater appreciation.

She laughed. 'It's beautiful. French. A Trouvère song

26

and, as you say, rather sad. It's called *C'est la fin*, and if accompanied by the Breton bombardt, very affecting.'

When the door had closed between us Jennet let out a snort of laughter. 'Full of airs and graces, she is! You'd think she'd be past all that nonsense at her age, wouldn't you?'

'How old is Lady Wardroper?' I asked, mildly curious.

Jennet tossed her head. 'With a son of seventeen years she can't be that young, can she? It stands to reason. Besides, you can see it by the wrinkles on her neck and the backs of her hands. Mind you, I don't say she was much more'n sixteen when Master Matthew was born. Or so I've been told. I'm too young to remember.'

'But Sir Cedric's much older?'

'By twenty-five year I'd reckon. He dotes on her, but strangely enough he don't get on that well with Master Matthew.' She led me down a narrow, twisting stair to a small, dark landing at the back of the house. 'And yet,' Jennet went on, 'the young Master's the spit and image of his mother. To look at, anyway. And he seems to have her sunny, happy-go-lucky nature. Not that I've seen that much of him, mind you. Only these past few months since he returned from up-country. Somewhere near Leicester.'

'So I was told,' I answered. 'But I suppose what appeals in the wife doesn't necessarily recommend the son. Sir Cedric probably hoped that his only child would be more in his own mould than his mother's.'

'That's possible,' Jennet agreed, coming to a halt a foot or two distant from a curtained archway. 'The Master's a bluff, hard-drinking man who would wish his son to be the same.' She indicated the leather curtain. 'Through there's the counting-house.' She laid a hand on my sleeve. 'It's getting late. Do you need a bed for the night? I could persuade Cook, I dare say, to find you a corner in the kitchen.'

'I should be very grateful,' I told her, smiling. 'I had hoped that I might find a billet here. And if you could speak for me . . .'

'Consider it as good as done,' Jennet replied demurely.

Chapter Three

At cockcrow the following morning, I sat up quietly on the pile of straw which had been allocated to me in the still-warm kitchen and glanced down at the figure lying beside me.

Jennet remained asleep, the long lashes making two half-moons of reddish gold on her creamy cheeks. Her hair, of the same colour as the lashes and now unbound, streamed across the makeshift pillow of my pack, almost concealing her face. One softly rounded arm was thrown clear of the rough grey blanket which covered us both, and which she had brought with her from the truckle-bed she had abandoned in her mistress's antechamber.

It had been no surprise when, in the small hours of the chilly June morning, Jennet had crept into the kitchen and snuggled down by my side. Her glances, the previous evening, had half-promised such a visit and she knew that the kitchen would be occupied by no one but myself. No other traveller had disturbed Chilworth's peace that day and she had herself informed me that the cook, kitchen-maids and pot-boy had sleeping quarters in the main hall, in company with the rest of the servants.

I observed her in silence some moments longer, then touched her gently on the shoulder. She was awake on the

29

instant, tossing back the blanket and sitting up to hug her knees. The mane of hair acted as a cloak, but the swelling curves of her limbs and breasts were visible through the tangled tresses.

'You must go,' I whispered reluctantly and nodded towards the cracks of light around the shutters. 'Some of the servants are already stirring. I can hear them.' I leaned across and kissed her willing lips. 'And it's almost time for me to be on my way.'

Jennet sighed, got up and draped herself in the blanket. She stood looking down at me, a slight smile touching the full, sensuous mouth, a sparkle in the grey-green eyes. Then she winked, hitched the blanket more firmly around her and padded across to the door, her bare feet slapping on the flagstones.

Left alone, I dressed quickly and went outside to the courtyard pump, splashing my face and hands with the icy water. By the time I returned to the kitchen, two of the maids had made their appearance, yawning and rubbing the sleep from their leaden eyes. I cajoled one of them into boiling water for me to shave with, having first agreed to work the bellows and blow some life into last night's embers, smouldering on the hearth. The second girl, without inducement, said that if I liked she would make me gruel and fry a collop of bacon to go with it, an offer which I gratefully accepted. I was still eating when the cook arrived, but she merely nodded in my direction, making no comment other than that she trusted I'd soon be off, as she didn't want me under her feet any longer than was necessary.

'I'm away this minute,' I assured her cheerfully, shovelling the last of the bacon into my mouth and pulling on my jerkin. 'It looks as if it'll be a fine day and I don't want to waste it.'

'Where are you heading for?' she asked, tying on her apron and wielding a massive ladle.

'Today, Winchester. But eventually London.'

She gave a throaty chuckle. 'They say the streets there are paved with gold, but I doubt it's like any other place, mostly horse-shit.'

'True enough,' I laughed. 'And dead dogs and rotting garbage and fly-blown muck. Pigs running amok when they've no right to be within city limits and various other contraventions of the law.'

'And murder,' she suggested. 'I dare say there's plenty of that.'

'Oh yes,' I agreed. 'There's always wickedness of that sort even in the smallest town.' I had spoken with more bitterness than I intended and the cook glanced sharply at me. I went on quickly, 'Is there another path to the Winchester road from here, or must I go back the way I came and return to the ford?'

'Ay, there is another path,' she conceded. 'It's a track well known to local people and you'll probably find it easily enough if you follow my directions.' She accompanied me to the kitchen door and stood looking out at the hazy morning, where the sun was just beginning to penetrate the mist. Somewhere to our right a large bird, a wood pigeon perhaps, clattered through the branches of the trees. The cook gestured with her ladle. 'When you go from here return to the stream and continue eastwards. Just after leaving demesne lands you'll come to a woodsman's cottage at the junction of another track, running north and bearing westwards. It's a well-trodden path and, if you

31

keep to it, it will join the Winchester road some mile or two south of the town.'

I nodded, picturing the triangle of roads in my mind's eye, and foresaw no problem in discovering my way. The cook, however, was not so certain.

'The first league should present few difficulties. It's well worn and will lead you directly to a hermitage in the middle of the woods. But half a mile or so beyond that, be careful. The main path thereabouts is not so easily discernible from several others which thread the denser woodland and you might get lost. It's happened to strangers on more than one occasion. Natives such as myself, who know the country-side well from childhood, never miss their way and nor should anyone else if they have been warned and keep their wits about them.' She tapped me on the arm. 'You seem a clever lad. Watch out for the signs and keep bearing nor'-westwards.'

I thanked her, humped my pack on to my shoulders and started out briskly. Although I glanced back several times, there was no sign of Jennet. I smiled reminiscently. We should probably never meet again, but just for a little while last night we had given each other pleasure and a gentle affection.

I was lost. Somehow, at some point, I had taken the wrong turning, and on reflection I thought I knew where that had been.

I had passed the hermitage, set within its neat patch of vegetable garden, a while ago, and proceeded along the track with confidence. After all, had the cook not called me a 'clever lad'? And had I not, in my heart of hearts, agreed with her? (And does it not say in *Ecclesiasticus* that pride is hateful before God and man?) It had been simple enough at first to recognize the lesser paths which began to lace the forest floor with their shady, criss-crossed lines, vanishing deep into a subaqueous gloom. But at last I arrived at a place where two tracks diverged with a stealth so subtle that it should have brought me to a halt while I considered which one to follow. Had I done so, I realized now, I should unhesitatingly have taken the narrower, left-hand path, whose distant prospect curved in a westerly direction and whose surface was beaten flatter than the one I chose. Moreover, memory told me that the overhanging branches had been cut back by the sticks and crops and billhooks of former travellers anxious to ease their way through the crowding trees.

Instead, without even pausing to think – indeed, being deep in happy recollections of Jennet – I had selected the rougher but broader track which, after some quarter-mile, gradually dwindled to little more than a trail of trodden-down grasses between encroaching brakes of elder and thrusting saplings. The trees arched and towered above my head, while sodden leaves, denied any hint of sun, squelched beneath my feet in a treacherous, slippery morass. Furthermore, I was moving inexorably, if almost imperceptibly, in an easterly direction, away from the junction with the Winchester road.

I cursed myself roundly for my foolishness and the uncaring arrogance which had led to my present predicament. Although predicament was perhaps too strong a word, for I had no serious doubt of being able to cut my way through the tangle of undergrowth to my left and rejoin the proper path whenever I chose. I decided, however, to follow the grassy trail for a little while longer, in the hope of finding another such animal track, which would save me the cost of torn hose and a snagged jerkin. Also, my bulky pack could prove a severe handicap in virgin territory, where untamed bramble thickets were as plentiful as the crop of pale blossoms that they at present carried.

Suddenly the trees drew back a little and I found myself in what had once been a small clearing, but was now knee-deep in grass and flowers. And in the middle was an abandoned shrine, the niche where once its saint had stood hollow-eyed and empty. The cracked grey stones thrust above a smother of ivy like bones from broken skin and a tangle of loosestrife, succory and tansy pushed its way through holes and crevices in the crumbling mortar. I moved closer, trampling the long grass under-foot, slid the pack from my back and examined the shrine more carefully. There was no indication as to which saint it had been dedicated to, but I did have some idea as to why it had been so thoroughly forgotten. A swift reconnaissance of the surrounding area showed me humps and bumps in the turf, together with outcroppings of stone which suggested that there might once have been dwellings around the clearing. I suspected that this could have been the site of a small hamlet; probably over a hundred years ago, before the Great Plague devastated Europe in the middle of the preceding century, wiping out whole communities.

Those of you who have read my previous chronicles will know that, although not blessed – or cursed – with the second sight, I have inherited from my mother a sixth sense which sometimes manifests itself in dreams, and at others in a kind of foreboding. It was the latter which suddenly seized me in its grip, causing me to stand stock still, every hair rising on the nape of my neck in fear, droplets of sweat trickling down my spine. I had a strong sense of evil, but whether of some past deed or one yet to come I was unable to tell. The silence was deathly; not a bird sang nor an insect hummed, whereas, seconds before, the woods had been full of such noises. The surrounding trees seemed to move closer, until I felt crushed and stifled by their menacing presence...

The moment passed. I shook myself like a dog which has at last reached dry land after treading water. The trees withdrew. There was a sudden flurry of movement as a bird winged its way through the branches to its nest, calling reassurance to its little ones. Grasshoppers and crickets once again resumed their chattering chorus. I stooped to pick up my pack, noticing as I did so a small bunch of flowers – bluebell, campion, trailing stems of ground ivy – placed at the base of the shrine. They had been torn up from amongst the grasses, some of which had been pulled up with them, and, although not dead, were wilted and faded. I stared at them with interest, wondering who had bothered to make his or her way to this isolated spot in order to honour a saint no longer represented. And why? What was the purpose of the offering?

But the flowers could provide me with no solution and I turned my attention to finding a way out of the clearing. It was then I saw that a narrow track, about the width of a man, had already been flattened through the undergrowth to my left; a rough path hacked between the trees and bushes and yellowing grasses. Using my own cudgel I was able to force my way along it and, ten minutes later, emerged on to the path which I had been travelling before I so stupidly got lost.

35

* * *

The sun was riding directly overhead by the time I once again joined the main Winchester road from Southampton. The dinner hour was long past, but thanks to my stupidity I had not eaten, so I set off towards the city, hoping to find somewhere to satisfy my hunger. A roadside ale-house, maybe, or a friendly cottage, whose goodwife would be willing to sell me victuals. I had not gone far, however, when I heard the creak of wheels behind me and, glancing over my shoulder, saw an empty cart approaching, pulled by a heavy chestnut horse and driven by a square-set country fellow dressed in a smock of grey homespun and thick, woollen hose. Stout boots of rough brown leather encased the lower part of his legs. The cart drew to a halt beside me.

'Want a ride, chapman?' the man asked laconically.

'I'd be grateful,' I answered. 'But I'd be still more grateful if you'd tell me where I can find food and drink round here. I've had no dinner.'

The man screwed up his face and tugged at the liripipe of his hood. 'Missed your tucker, have you?' He regarded me thoughtfully. 'Don't look the sort who'd forget to eat. And it's midday now. Two hours past dinnertime.'

'I made a short cut through the woods and, like a fool, took the wrong turning. You know how it is when you try to be too clever.'

The man laughed. 'Aye, I know.' He patted the empty seat. 'Jump up. I'm going to collect a load of wool from a farm near here. The goodwife'll feed you, I'll be bound. A good-hearted, if sharp-tongued soul who'll be glad, I reckon, to see a pedlar.'

I mounted to sit on the board beside him, placing my

pack at my feet. My companion gave his horse the office to start and we began to move forward.

'Are you a native of these parts?' I asked.

'Born and bred within the walls of Southampton.'

'Do you know the countryside about here? The woods around Chilworth Manor?'

The carter shook his head. 'I stick to the beaten tracks, although I know Sir Cedric Wardroper. I cart his wool to the spinners and weavers. Why do you want to know?'

'I wondered if you'd ever heard of a deserted shrine in the woods near here. I stumbled across it, quite by chance, this morning.'

The man scratched his head. 'Can't say as I ever have. But then, as I say, my home's Southampton. But you could inquire at the Catchside farm when we get there. One of the workers might know something of it. Or Master Catchside and his wife. You can but ask, if it's important to you.'

At this point we turned off the main road and rattled over a mile or two of rough track before arriving at the farm. It appeared to be of sufficient hideage to support a family and its dependants in comfort, boasting a plough and four oxen, hens, cows and a flock of sheep which had recently been sheared, and whose fleeces the carter had called to collect. Most of that particular day's activity was therefore centred on the barn, where the wool was being packed. The women were rolling the fleeces, their smaller fingers dextrously pulling and smoothing as they did so, and securing each neat bundle with a narrow cord of fine twine. In the centre of the barn a huge sack was suspended almost at floor level by ropes from the beams. Two men stood in the sack, packing and treading down the rolled fleeces as the women passed them in, the wall of wool rising higher and higher until it reached the top, when the men sat astride the sack and sewed it up. It was then lowered to the ground and knotted at each corner in order to ease the handling of such a cumbersome object.

I watched, fascinated, my hunger temporarily forgotten, until the carter hailed the eldest of the women, whose tendency to direct operations rather than participate in them had already marked her down in my mind as likely to be the mistress of the house. I was not mistaken.

'Goody Catchside, here's a chapman I picked up on the road, who'd be glad of some dinner.' The man chuckled. 'He missed his by getting lost in the woods.'

The farmer's wife clucked in a motherly fashion.

'You'd best come with me then, lad,' she said, 'and bring your pack with you. There's one or two things I'm short of, and if you have them it'll save a journey to Winchester at this busy season. Come along! Don't loiter!' She bustled ahead of me, but paused at the barn door to fling an admonition at her husband. 'Andrew! Make sure the men put aside enough wool for our own use before they go loading up the cart. I know him,' she added in a grumbling undertone as I followed her in the direction of the house. 'He'll sell far too much for the sake of an extra shilling or two and then where does that leave us? Short of winter garments and forced to buy. A false economy, chapman! A false economy.'

I was given bread and cheese and ale, together with a bowl of fish stew, which reminded me that it was Friday. I remembered guiltily the collop of bacon I had eaten at Chilworth Manor for breakfast. I must have grimaced at the memory, for the goodwife asked sharply, 'What's the matter? There's nothing amiss with that soup. I made it myself with fish caught fresh from the stream this morning.'

I hastened to reassure her and explained the reason for the face I had pulled. Mistress Catchside snorted in disapproval.

'I've always suspected that the Wardropers were lax in their religious observance. A flighty woman, Lady Wardroper, far too young for Sir Cedric. And young Matthew, as I remember, was never a reverent child. One might have hoped that his years in Leicestershire, or wherever it was, would have improved him. But since his return home I've seen him talking and walking about at the back of the nave during Mass in a very disrespectful fashion. However, I've no time for gossiping. Let me see what's in your pack and then you and the carter can be going. We need to have our wool on the way to the weaving sheds before nightfall.'

Yet again I laid out my wares, and while the goodwife picked them over I asked her if she knew anything of the shrine in the woods. Her answer was decisive.

'I've never heard anyone mention it,' she said, 'and I've lived in these parts all my life. Indeed, this was my father's farm and his father's before him. Catchside,' she added, seeming to feel that some explanation was called for, 'was from the city.' She shrugged. 'But there, I was a plain girl and had to take whoever offered. And Andrew had money which he was prepared to put into the farm. My parents thought him a good enough husband for me, at all events, and so I married him.' She pulled herself up short, turning an uncomfortable red and obviously annoyed at herself for confiding in me. 'Hmmph! I'll buy this set of spoons, for mine are worn so thin the edges cut my mouth. How much are you asking for them?'

'And you're sure,' I urged, when the transaction was completed and I had knocked a little off the price to pay for my food, 'that this woodland shrine is unknown to you? You've never heard it spoken of by anyone?'

'Oh, as to that, never is too final a word. I may, I suppose, have heard it mentioned at some time in my life. I'm past my fortieth birthday.' She frowned, realizing that once again her tongue had betrayed her into an unnecessary confidence. 'But no, not that I can instantly recall. Young man,' she added with asperity, 'I don't know what it is about you, but you have a disarming habit of making me say more than I intended and I suspect that that applies to other women. You must learn not to take advantage of us poor, weak females.'

I laughed. 'I should never be so ungallant, even if it were true. But you overestimate my powers to charm and your own weakness, I do assure you.'

Goody Catchside said 'Hmmph' again, but made no further comment, anxious not to hold up the proceedings any longer. We returned to the barn, where the last of three sacks of wool had just been loaded into the wagon. I clambered up beside the carter, thanked my hostess most heartily for my meal and was driven away along the track.

'Did you find out what you wanted to know?' the man asked me after we had gone a short distance.

I shook my head. 'Mistress Catchside was unable to recall hearing the shrine talked of, but admitted that her memory might be faulty. However, someone has been there lately and been at trouble to cut a path through the undergrowth to reach it and lay flowers at its base.'

I sighed. 'Ah well! It's of no importance, I suppose. Do you continue towards Winchester now, or return to Southampton?'

'I have one more call to make and shall lie at Winchester tonight, at a hostelry just outside the city where they know me. I can therefore take you as far as the suburbs.'

'Aren't you afraid of thieves,' I asked, 'while you are sleeping?'

The carter roared with laughter. 'Who'd be able to move one of those great, cumbersome things?' He jerked his head backwards in the direction of the wool sacks. 'And if you split one open all the contents'd come bursting out. No, no! Wool's the safest cargo anyone can carry.'

I accompanied the carter to the second farm and, when the wagon was full, helped him cover it with tarred canvas, but not too tightly. (For as my friend instructed me, wool must be kept dry, but never overheated.) By this time the city bells could be heard ringing out over the surrounding countryside for Vespers and we took leave of one another. I made my way to the Hospital of Saint Cross where free ale was always available for travellers, a great consideration with me, as you might imagine. And as I sat in the late-afternoon sunshine sipping my ale, my back against the warm stone of one of the almshouses, my mind went back over the events of the past two days.

I thought of Jennet first, her eager flesh, her passionate kisses, but I knew she would have done as much for any young man who took her fancy. She was one of those loving and giving creatures unhampered by morals. My thoughts ran on to this morning and the abandoned shrine in the woods. Who had had cause to visit it recently? Who had picked and left the flowers?

41

It was a mystery to which I should probably never know the answer and already the interest of it was beginning to fade a little. I put down my empty beaker on the bench beside me and stretched my arms and legs until the bones cracked. By this time tomorrow I should be on the road to London, selling as I went, but with my goal drawing nearer with every passing mile. It would take me well over two weeks to reach the capital, yet I could feel the excitement even now, stirring in my veins.

Chapter Four

It was a Monday morning, late in June, when I crossed the Tyburn and entered Westminster. I held tightly to the shoulder-straps of my pack, for I knew the suburb's reputation as a breeding ground for thieves and pickpockets. These men and women, so it was said, would snatch anything, even the hood from your head or the cloak from your back, and then make their escape through Westminster Gate. Indeed, although I myself was never molested in such a fashion I have seen the footpads at work, so light-fingered, so agile, so swift in their approach and retreat that the unfortunate victim stood no chance of raising the hue and cry before the thief had vanished, seemingly off the face of the earth.

I have not seen Westminster now for many a long day, but my children assure me that its sprawl of houses and shops grows greater with every passing year and surely must be half as big again as when I last set foot within its walls. All I can say in reply is that I have no wish to pay a visit. Even more than a quarter of a century ago Westminster was nearly as crowded and as noisy as London itself. The streets were full of people selling their wares; and as a large proportion of them were Flemings, the cries of 'Buy! Buy!

Buy! What do you lack? What'll you buy?' grated harshly on the ears.

That particular morning, by the time I reached the Clock House, whose great bell rang out the fleeting hours, I had been physically accosted at least three times and lost count of all the other exhortations. I had been importuned to buy a pair of spectacles, a hat, hose, shoes, gloves, pins, a belt, a crucifix made from a splinter of the One True Cross and a fly entombed in a lump of amber. It was on this sort of occasion that my height and girth stood me in good stead, for I was able to deter the would-be vendors simply by saying 'No' and drawing myself up to my full six feet. People of lesser stature were not so fortunate and I saw one small man pinned against a wall by two Flemings, who refused to release him until he had purchased a silver necklace. And this right under the noses of half a dozen of the king's Sergeants, magnificently self-important in their striped gowns and silken hoods, just emerging from the law courts in Westminster Hall. The incident reminded me of a man I had once rescued in similar circumstances: Timothy Plummer.

Westminster did hold one great attraction for me, however, and that was the cook-shops close by one of its gates. Set out on trestle tables was an abundance of food – loaves, cakes, pasties, meat pies, steaming-hot ribs of beef and several delicacies new to me, including porpoise tongues – while a nearby vintner's provided a variety of wines and beakers of hot ale, spiced with pepper. As it was close on dinnertime, I stopped and bought two of the biggest meat pies I could find which, together with a bottle of Rhenish wine, I carried to the shade of some trees where I sat down on the grass to eat and drink my fill.

It was pleasantly warm, but with sufficient breeze to make me glad of my leather jerkin and its lining of scarlet. Clouds sailed majestically across the early summer sky and, once, the transparent sheen of a dragonfly skimmed across my line of vision as it returned to its haunts by the river. A jongleur was singing in a sweet, high voice, entertaining a group of fellow diners. Having finished my meal, but not yet ready to resume the final stage of my journey, I leaned against the trunk of one of the trees and closed my eyes, first ascertaining that the strap of my pack was securely looped around my left wrist and that my cudgel lay within easy reach of my other hand. After a moment or two the voice of the jongleur faded and I slept . . .

I was awakened by the sound of shouting.

'Clear the way! Out of the way there! Make way! Make way!'

I heard the tramp of feet and the jingle of harness. Opening my eyes, I was unsurprised to see the procession of some great lord coming from the royal palace on the return journey to London. It was only when I had gathered my wits together and banished the cobwebs from my brain that I recognized the retainers' livery of blue and murrey and the banners held by the standard bearers: two displaying the emblem of the White Boar and one that of the Red Bull, both badges of the Duke of Gloucester. And there, sure enough, the still, calm centre of all this hubbub, was the young man whose birthday I shared and to whom, in the past, I had rendered two personal services. He was mounted on a richly caparisoned bay horse, the strong, mobile face partially concealed, as it so often was, by the long dark hair which swung to his shoulders. All around him the other riders laughed and joked and talked, but apart from the turn of his head and an occasional smile, Richard of Gloucester contributed nothing to the general conversation. He seemed, from the little I could see of him, preoccupied; shut in on himself and alone with his thoughts.

Riding a few paces behind him, but pressing close enough for his horse's head to be on a level with the bay's swishing tail, was another young man of roughly the duke's own age, strongly built and sandy-haired, whose eyes constantly and somewhat nervously, or so I thought, scanned the crowds. His face, which I guessed would normally be of a high complexion, was rather pale and his lips compressed as if in pain. Then I saw the reason. He was controlling his mettlesome grey mare with only one hand, his left, while his right arm, from wrist to elbow, rested in a blue silk sling. The bones of his forearm had obviously sustained a fracture not yet mended, which, judging by his expression of suffering, was of fairly recent date.

The head of the procession passed beneath the gate and was lost to view, amidst the ringing cheers and encouraging shouts of the populace at large, with whom the Duke of Gloucester was a general favourite. People never forgot that he had stood loyally by his eldest brother throughout all the vicissitudes of King Edward's reign, unlike his other brother, George of Clarence, who trimmed his sails to suit every prevailing wind.

Once Prince Richard was out of sight the onlookers, who had crowded the edges of the highway for a closer inspection, began to disperse, indifferent to the tail-end of his retinue. But from my vantage point under the trees, and because I am insatiably curious about everyone, I continued to watch – and was rewarded by the sight of a small, familiar figure, last seen almost two years ago in Exeter, but recalled to mind only that very morning, bringing up the rear and riding a solid brown cob.

Timothy Plummer seemed to have grown in stature. Not physically, but in the way he held himself, in the little air of self-importance which hung about him and suggested that he was now of far greater consequence than he had once been in the Duke of Gloucester's household. He, too, like the youth I had noted, constantly looked about him, glancing to left and right in a perpetual surveillance of the crowds. But whether he was watching them or wanted to be noticed by them I was uncertain.

It occurred to me suddenly that I had no wish to renew my acquaintance with Master Plummer. On the last occasion we had met I had become embroiled, much against my will, in an adventure which had placed me in great personal danger. I made to duck my head, but before I could do so our eyes met and held for a second. I looked away quickly. It was too late, however. I had seen his start of recognition.

I decided to sleep off my dinner for a while longer, thus allowing the duke and his retainers plenty of time to put the city walls between us. But although I closed my eyes again, sleep eluded me and so, in the end, I returned to the market and purchased several items to replenish my pack. It was almost noon and I knew that if I were to find a decent lodging for the night I should set forth without further delay. Having, therefore, attended Mass at the church of Saint Margaret, I left Westminster shortly after noon. The day had grown even warmer and I was grateful for the shade cast by the houses and trees which bordered the highway. The press of traffic passing between London and the royal palace was always heavy, but with the invasion of France imminent, it was even greater than usual. Liveried messengers from the various noble households galloped by in both directions, scattering the earth from beneath their horses' hooves, their features set in lines of rigid disdain for us lesser mortals. Two wagons, piled high with armour, trundled past and at the local smithy there was a queue of horses waiting to be re-shod.

I reached the Chère Reine Cross, where both river and road begin to veer in an easterly direction, and paused, as I had done in the past, to gaze upon that memorial of soaring, flowering stone: that monument to undying love, raised by the first Edward in memory of his first queen, Eleanor of Castile. When she died he had written, 'My harp has turned to mourning. In life, I loved her dearly, nor can I cease to love her in death.' Recalling those words, once quoted to me by someone whose name I now forget as representing the summit of human affection, I felt a pang of something very like envy. Never in my twenty-two years had I experienced any emotion so profound. (It did not occur to me that I was still young. Youth and arrogance are necessary bedfellows, or else how would we all survive that most difficult of times?)

Half a dozen crows, beating the air with the black, sweeping strokes of their wings, caused me to look upwards, then follow their flight with my eyes as they disappeared inland across the open meadows. And it was thus, as I dropped my glance once again, that I saw Timothy Plummer deep in earnest conversation with a man at the foot of the Chère Reine Cross. Nearby a small urchin held the reins of the brown cob and walked the animal slowly up and down. After a moment or two I could make out that the second man was a friar, a Dominican judging by his rusty and shabby black robe. Both were staring at the ground and the friar seemed to be drawing a diagram in the dirt with his staff. Timothy Plummer was nodding.

As I watched, a third man rode up on a grey mare and dismounted awkwardly, on account of the fact that he enjoyed the use of only one arm. The other reposed in a blue silk sling and I immediately recognized the sturdily built, sandy-haired young man who had been riding in the Duke of Gloucester's procession half an hour earlier. Having summoned another urchin to hold his horse, he joined Timothy Plummer and the friar, his head bent anxiously towards theirs. Within moments, however, the friar shrugged his shoulders, spread deprecating hands and then moved on in the direction of Westminster. It was obvious that whatever information he had had to impart was now at an end; and although the younger man ran after him, catching at his sleeve and patently asking a question, the friar had no more to tell, for he shook his head vigorously and moved away with a determined gait. The sandy-haired man and Master Plummer remained a few moments longer, talking to one another, before they both remounted their horses and trotted off along the Strand.

I now entered this thoroughfare myself, passing between the great houses of the nobles and the wealthy merchants, whose gardens and orchards ran down to the wharves lining the river's edge, and thence into the second half of that same highway which is known as Fleet Street. Long before I reached the bridge which spanned the River Fleet the noises of London reached out to greet me from beyond its walls and its pungent smells wreathed themselves about my nostrils. Once across the bridge I was hemmed in on either side by ale-houses and taverns, some old, some of recent date and yet others still in the course of construction, and all catering for the many pilgrims desirous of visiting Saint Paul's. For the church housed at that time a wondrous collection of relics, including an arm of Saint Mellitus, a phial of the Virgin's milk, a lock of Saint Mary Magdalene's hair, a jewelled reliquary containing the blood of its patron saint, a hand of Saint John the Evangelist, a knife which had belonged to Jesus Himself, used when He helped Joseph in the carpenter's shop, the head of Saint Ethelbert and fragments of Saint Thomas à Becket's skull.

As I approached the Lud Gate the noise increased a hundredfold: carts screeching and rattling across the cobbles, bells constantly chiming, summoning the citizens to prayer or to some civic meeting, vendors raucously shouting their wares. I crossed the drawbridge spanning the ditch and walked under the raised portcullis, past two guards stationed there to turn back any lepers foolhardy enough to try to gain entrance. Beyond the gate was a labyrinth of alleyways in which a stranger might easily get lost; but I had been to London before. I turned left into Old Deane's Lane, right into Paternoster Row and so into the Cheap, the capital's great market.

By late afternoon, I had sold nearly all that was in my pack and was beginning to think about finding a lodging for the night. It had been my intention to do so the minute I entered the city, but the temptation to make money while I could had proved too strong. For London, because of the forthcoming invasion, was teeming with great lords and their retainers from all parts of the country. Escutcheons hung from the windows of every respectable tavern and ale-house, denoting that their owners were in residence within; and the goodwife who bought some needles and thread from me, and whose husband was host of the Saracen's Head, near the Ald Gate, said that there wasn't a decent room to be had anywhere in the city.

'I tell my man we must make the most of it,' she added, 'for in a week or so they'll all be gone. Rumour has it that the king and his brothers cross to France next week.'

'Then I must hurry and find myself a bed for the night,' I observed anxiously, 'for I dare say the guest halls of every church and priory in the city are crammed full also.'

'Oh, aye,' the woman agreed cheerfully. 'You can be sure of that. It's not just the great lords' servants needing somewhere to sleep, but more and more people are crowding into London every day to pander to their needs and make a pretty penny on their own account into the bargain. Even our kitchens and cellars are full each night at present.' She heaved a sigh. 'But as I said just now, it can't last much above another sennight.'

'Where would you recommend me to go then?' I inquired.

She pursed her lips, considering. After a moment she tapped me on the arm. 'Follow me,' she instructed. 'I might find you a place in our kitchens, now that I come to think of it. One of our lodgers was leaving this morning. His master was bound for Gravesend today on an advance embassy, or some such thing, to the Duke of Burgundy. And mighty cock-a-hoop Master Jump-up Johnny was about it, too. You'd best come and stake a claim to his space now, before my husband rents it to another traveller.'

I gathered up the remainder of my wares from the wall where I had spread them, pushed them inside my pack along with my clean hose and shirt and shaving gear and indicated to my benefactress that she should proceed without further delay. She led me along Cornhill grain market, past the rows of bread carts whose owners drove them in daily from Stratford-atte-Bowe – and whose loaves, or so my companion informed me, were the same price but a full two ounces heavier than those of the London bakers – and past the Tun upon Cornhill, which flowed with sweet-smelling water, piped in from the Tyburn. On top of this was an iron cage where prostitutes and rioters were incarcerated each night by the Watch for drunken and disorderly behaviour; and set on a wooden platform close at hand were the stocks and pillory, both of which were fully occupied by several sorry-looking knaves, the butt and target of every passer-by.

From Cornhill, we passed into Ald Gate Street, where stood the church of Saint Andrew Undershaft, the great maypole towering above it, and so into the shadow of Holy Trinity Priory, the largest and most imposing monastery in the city. South of it, just inside the gate, was the Saracen's Head. This was teeming with visitors, as the landlord's wife had warned me, and as we crossed the courtyard I could see that the stables were equally full, every stall occupied.

'Wait here,' the woman said, ushering me inside the ale-room, 'while I seek out my husband. I must make sure he hasn't let the space while I've been gone.'

I stood obediently just inside the door, watching the

drinkers who crowded the tables. The great majority of them wore livery and it was easy to recognize the tavern's regular customers in their drab, everyday tunics and hose, huddled together round two of the benches, muttering resentfully to one another and eyeing the intruders with sullen looks.

The goodwife reappeared at my elbow and instructed me to accompany her to the kitchens. 'Bring your pack. You'll need it to stake your place. I'm afraid you won't have much room, a big fellow like you, but you'll have to make the best of it. And my husband insists on payment in advance for however long you think you'll be stopping.'

The heat in the kitchen was intense and I had to dodge the pot-boys and scullions, the maids and the cooks who, sweating profusely, were chopping and basting, boiling and roasting as they strove to prepare the evening supper. For the most part they ignored my presence, merely cursing me liberally when I got in their way. Around all four walls, in between the barrels of food and water, I saw items of personal apparel, which marked the sleeping territory of the night's lodgers.

My hostess pointed to a space flanked on one side by a barrel of what smelled suspiciously like salted herring and a table where one of the cooks was busy rolling out pastry. 'There,' she said. 'And you can fetch clean straw from the stables before you bed down. Now, note your place and then be off with you, out from under my people's feet. I don't want to see you in here again until just before curfew.'

I was loath to leave anything of value, like my pack or my jerkin, so I removed my hood and dropped it on the flagstones. Then I paid my shot for a couple of nights, determined to have found something better by the end of forty-eight hours, and took myself back to the ale-room.

Someone on the other side of the kitchen was snoring so loudly that the whole room seemed to shake with the noise. Added to this, there was an overpowering smell of stale breath and sweating feet, plus the stench of brine and herring. The straw on which I lay had quickly proved to be flea-ridden and all my twitching and scratching failed to deter the little wretches from finding me to be a tasty supper. After two hours I had not managed to sleep a wink, tossing and turning to the great irritation of my nearest neighbour, an itinerant pieman, who had been lured to the capital in the hope of making money before returning to his native Norfolk.

'But there's too many other folk as've had the same idea,' he had grumbled as we settled ourselves down for the night. 'I haven't made above half what I'd've made if I'd stayed at home. Well, good-night, chapman. Pleasant dreams.'

Now, however, close on midnight and woken more than once by my restlessness, his tone was not so conciliatory. 'For God's sake, can't you stop shifting about so?' he demanded in a sibilant whisper. 'If you can't sleep, go outside awhile and walk around.'

'I shall disturb others if I pace up and down the courtyard,' I whispered back.

'I mean right outside. It'll be cool under the Priory walls. I know, because I was forced to it myself the night before last. I admit that that fellow's snoring takes some getting used to.'

'But the courtyard door will be locked,' I objected.

He raised a hand, ghostly in the darkness, and pointed to the wall. 'The key's up there. That big one hanging on a nail beside the bread oven.' He snuggled down again amongst his straw. 'And don't come back until you're feeling sleepy.'

I rose softly to my feet, pulled on my hose, boots, tunic and jerkin with as little disturbance to my neighbours as possible, reached down the key and let myself out through the kitchen door into the deserted courtyard. A horse shifted and snorted somewhere within the stables and a faint light burned in one of the upstairs rooms, but otherwise all was dark and quiet. Clouds rode high and thin above the huddled roof-tops and there was a hint of rain in the air. The dampness clung about my face.

The outer door was in the north wall and the wards of the lock slid back silently as I turned the key. Once in the street, I was facing the southern boundary of the Priory on the opposite side of the highway. There was no sign of movement from the gatehouse to my right. The guards were no doubt wiling away a long and tedious watch with a game of dice or fivestones. I relocked the courtyard gate from the outside and crossed the road to a patch of grass and bushes, hemmed in on two sides by the Priory outbuildings and on the third by the stretch of city wall running north of Ald Gate. Here I settled myself down, keeping the Saracen's Head within my line of vision in case, by some highly improbable chance, entrance might be demanded to its courtyard in the middle of the night.

The air was cool and fragrant after the fetid atmosphere of the overcrowded kitchen and the heady scent of honeysuckle wafted from the Priory gardens, teasing my nostrils. I drew back into the deep shadow of a hawthorn bush, clasping my arms about my knees and relishing the blessed silence. An owl hooted suddenly, close at hand, making me jump, but then everything was quiet once more.

The owl hooted again, louder and more insistently. This time something about the cry made me freeze into stillness, every muscle tense with expectation. I was not disappointed. After a few seconds a man padded stealthily into view, coming towards the Ald Gate from the direction of Leadenhall and the city. He paused, glancing around, plainly in the expectation of meeting someone. There was a familiarity about the stocky figure, although I could only see his outline, but it took me a moment or two before I realized what it was. His right arm was visible only to the elbow and lay close in against his side. So would a man appear if he had his forearm in a sling.

Chapter Five

The owl's call was repeated a third time, and on this occasion evoked a response. A second man moved cautiously out of the shadows surrounding the gatehouse and raised a hand in salutation. I wondered if he had seen me, minutes earlier, crossing the road; but as he neither attempted to flush me out nor made any reference that I could hear to my existence, I presumed that he must have been waiting some way down the lane which ran behind the Saracen's Head and its neighbouring houses.

'You took long enough,' the first man hissed accusingly. 'Didn't you hear me?'

'I heard an owl screech twice,' his companion muttered, 'but I've told you before, you need to be careful in this game. It wasn't until the third call that I thought it safe to reveal myself. I had no certainty that the friar would have been able to pass on my message.'

They were standing on a level with the hawthorn bush and every word spoken, though whispered, was plainly audible. Then they moved on to the grass and into the lee of the Priory outbuildings, where the darkness was almost impenetrable. But they were now just a few feet away from my hiding place and for a moment or so my whole attention was focused on remaining motionless. By the time I was able to listen again with any degree of concentration I had missed several sentences.

'You mean you have no positive news for us?' the man with the sling was asking. I knew it to be him, for he spoke much faster than the other, who was inclined to be slow and ponderous of speech. 'For God's sake, Thaddeus, we must have a name, and soon! Time is running out.'

Thaddeus grunted. 'I can't do the impossible, Master Arrowsmith, and my informant is himself having difficulties in finding out what you want to know. His source of information is proving mute until another payment is made to him.'

The imprecation which greeted this remark was delivered with such savagery that it made me start, deflecting my mind from trying to remember where, and by whom, I had recently heard the name of Arrowsmith mentioned.

'Money! Money!' the duke's officer continued. 'A great man's life is at risk and all you can do is talk about money! I've a good mind to have you arrested. A taste of the rack and thumbscrew would soon persuade you to reveal the identity of your informer.'

There was a snort of derision. 'So it might, but the news that I'd been taken would drive the others into hiding and you'd never track them down. It would be no use asking me to put a name to any but my own men, for no one knows more than that. You'd have first to discover, then arrest, then put each one in turn to the question before you came to the end of the chain.'

There was a moment's silence while Master Arrowsmith swallowed his ire. A guard came to the door of the gatehouse and looked casually about him, before stretching his arms and returning inside. Plainly he saw nothing amiss, both the men and myself remaining perfectly still throughout his brief appearance.

'So, when *will* you have a name?' Master Arrowsmith demanded as soon as he judged it safe to resume the conversation.

'Tomorrow night, if you've brought the money with you.' A faint chinking of coins reached my ears as a purse or pouch was handed over. 'I promise that by then I'll have the information you require.'

'Very well. Where do we meet? Here again?'

'I've told you my rule, never the same place twice running. Do you know Three Cranes Quay, west of the Steelyard? It's the vintners' wharf, where the ships from Bordeaux tie up.'

'Timothy Plummer'll know it. He was born and bred in London.'

'Very well. That's where you'll find me, but it must be earlier in the evening. I have need to be elsewhere by curfew.'

'You have other business?' The hissing voice was ragged with suspicion.

'Aye. I've a woman in London who's deserving of my attention now and then. It's precious little I see of her in the normal way of things, but tomorrow night I've given my word to visit her. She means enough to me to take a chance or two.'

'Chance?' Once again the man Arrowsmith's tone had an edge of panic to it.

'It stands to reason there's more risk when it's light than when it's dark, but the meeting will be brief. One name, that's all you want and, once given, we can go our separate ways. All the same, it might be better to send a two-armed man in case of any trouble. A right-handed man who can only use his left is at a severe disadvantage in a dangerous situation.'

'Fine talking!' the other snarled angrily. 'Whom am I to trust? Tell me that! There's Timothy Plummer, but he's too valuable to imperil his hide.'

I heard the second man's impatient shifting of feet. 'You can't suspect *every* member of the duke's household, surely! It doesn't make sense!'

'Until I get a name I do, and so does Master Plummer. All right. Perhaps there is just one other I'd trust, but he's too young and too green. No, no! You'll have to put up with me. I'll be with you again tomorrow evening. What o'clock?'

'Just after Compline. There's a warehouse lying empty near the right-hand corner of the quay as you face the river. Left if you're looking inland towards the Vintry. I'll force the side door and leave it unlatched. Now I must be off. It makes me nervous standing out in the open for too long.'

'You're sure you'll have the name for me tomorrow?'

'This should smooth out all difficulties.' Once more I heard the chink of coins. 'God be with you, Master Arrowsmith.'

'And with you, Thaddeus Morgan.'

The whispering stopped. A shadow detached itself from the deeper blackness by the Priory wall, crossed the grass with a light, cat-like tread and melted into one of the alleyways on the opposite side of the road. Moments later, a second shadow, moving with equal stealth, took the road to the Leadenhall granary and the heart of the city, presumably returning by devious ways to Baynard's Castle. Although beginning to suffer cramp in legs and feet from crouching behind the brake of hawthorn for so long, I gritted my teeth and forced myself to wait for several minutes before making any attempt to rise. I wanted to give both conspirators time to get clear away.

I was just about to stretch my left leg, which had borne the brunt of my weight, when I was arrested in mid-movement by the cautious emergence of a third shadow from the shelter of a buttress supporting the orchard wall. The figure advanced to the edge of the grass and glanced furtively in both directions, before also taking the Leadenhall road, in the wake of Master Arrowsmith. Who was this man? And what was he doing there? Was he an innocent eavesdropper like myself? Someone else who could not sleep and had braved the night air? Or had he followed Master Arrowsmith from Baynard's Castle with the fixed intention of spying on him and overhearing his conversation with the man named Thaddeus Morgan?

If the latter, why had I not noticed his arrival? But on reflection, the answer to that question was simple. My whole attention had been focused upon the two central characters in the drama unfolding before me. If this third man had kept close in to the orchard wall, deep within its shadow, I would not have observed him. If the former, however, he might have witnessed my emergence from the Saracen's Head and have been aware of my presence. Yet, once Lionel Arrowsmith and Thaddeus Morgan had departed, he had given no indication of knowing that I was there, not by so much as a turn of the head in my direction. Therefore I was more inclined to believe my second theory to be the correct one: that the unknown had tailed the duke's man in order to discover where he was going and whom he was meeting.

Not that it was any of my business whatever the answer, I told myself severely. I struggled to my feet, flexed my limbs, picked up the courtyard key from the grass where I had dropped it and returned to the inn. Everything was more or less as I had left it half an hour earlier. The same horse stamped restlessly in his stall, the man on the other side of the kitchen still snored loudly and had now been joined in chorus by the pieman, while the rest of my fellow lodgers were sprawled in various attitudes of abandon on their pallets of flea-ridden straw.

I removed all my clothes except for my shirt and lay down again, but not to sleep. Oblivious now to the noises around me, I turned on my back and stared up at the smoke-blackened beams overhead. A sudden suspicion had taken hold of me and I needed to think. Why had it come to me, a few moments earlier, that Master Arrowsmith's baptismal name was Lionel? Someone had mentioned it within my hearing in recent weeks and I fixed my eyes on a knot of wood in one of the rafters, forcing myself to concentrate. Then all at once I had it. Millisent Shepherd! She had been speaking of . . . of . . . Lady Wardroper's cousin! That was it! Lady Wardroper, she had told me, had enlisted Lionel Arrowsmith's help in obtaining a place for her son, Matthew, in the Duke of Gloucester's household.

So I was right! What I had thought of as my own independent wanderings had really been part of a plan. God's plan! I had been led from Mistress Gentle in Southampton to Millisent Shepherd to Lady Wardroper and, finally, to the Saracen's Head. God was using me yet again for His purposes and my resentment rose and flooded over. 'No, Lord,' I told Him firmly, 'not this time. I've only just brought two villains to book for You down in Devon. I refuse to be pushed into a second adventure in less than three months. I came to London for my pleasure, not for Yours. Let me alone! Leave me be!'

I suppose I might have known that my arrogant demands would go unheeded. After all, I should, had I deferred to my dead mother's wishes, even then have been giving glory to God and doing His work as a Benedictine Brother at Glastonbury. Instead, I was free, roaming the countryside, selling my chapman's wares, pleasing myself. But I succumbed to the conviction that I could set up my puny will against His and that, somehow or other, He would acknowledge what I saw to be the justice of my arguments and cease to trouble me. And so, with a sigh of relief, I turned on my side, snuggled into my straw, ignoring the fleas, and was sound asleep within a couple of minutes.

It had been my intention to spend two nights at the Saracen's Head; but when, the next morning, the pieman offered to buy my space from me for twice the amount I had paid the landlord's wife I willingly agreed. I had taken an unreasoning dislike to the tavern and wished to shake its dust from my feet. Indeed, I had made up my mind to quit London altogether and was only too happy to sell my few feet of kitchen floor in order that the pieman's nephew, who was joining his uncle that day from Norfolk, had somewhere to lay his head until such time as the royal princes, noble lords and all their retinues departed for France, thus relieving the capital of their encroaching presence.

'But where will you sleep tonight?' the pieman asked me.

'Somewhere in the open countryside,' I answered thankfully. In response to his inquisitive stare I continued, 'I've decided to go home to Bristol. I'll return to London in a month or two, when it's less crowded.' And to myself I added, 'And when it's too late for whatever purpose God has in mind for me.'

'Maybe you're wise,' the pieman conceded. 'I'd probably go home today myself, if it weren't for young Thomas coming to join me.'

I wished him goodbye and good luck, sought out the landlord's wife to acquaint her with the new arrangement, treated myself to a substantial breakfast in the Saracen's Head ale-room and then set off to make my way back across London to the New Gate, and so out on to the Holborn road.

Although early, an army of rakers was busy carting away the refuse of the previous day, conveying it to specially prepared pits outside the city walls or to the wharves, where boats were waiting to ferry it out to sea. But it was a losing battle. People were already throwing the night's excrement out of bedroom windows and sweeping yesterday's rushes out of doors, along with stinking straw from the many stables. Butchers tipped pails of fresh entrails and animal heads into the central drain, where they were soon joined by stale fish, builders' rubble and feathers from the poulterers. Traffic, too, clogged the streets. Carts piled high with bread from Stratford-atte-Bowe, with bricks from the outlying villages around the White Chapel and Lime House, with barrels of fresh water from the springs at Paddington, were rumbling through every one of the city gates, soon to be followed by others from further afield. Street vendors and shopkeepers were laying out their stalls

for the start of another day's vigorous trading; a gaggle of
boys, laughing and shouting to one another in the last
moments of freedom, made for the grammar school at the
church of Saint Peter-upon-Cornhill; and sumpter horses,
laden with goods, fouled the streets with their droppings. A
couple of knaves were being set in the stocks and pillory,
while the night's drunks and bawds and general disturbers
of the king's peace were rattling the bars of their iron cage,
shouting to be let out. Barely past the hour of Prime
London was none the less fully awake and busy.

It was another pleasant early summer's day, with sunlight slanting into courtyard and alley, and a light breeze
which sent the shadows racing ahead of it in patterns of
grey and gold. Perhaps, after all, with so many people
crowding the streets, and so anxious to spend their
money, I would wait until afternoon before turning my
steps in the direction of New Gate and the long road
home. A chance to make money was not to be lightly
dismissed. Besides, why should I allow God to spoil my
plans? Why should I not remain in London for at least
another morning?

In this new mood of bravado and defiance I retraced my
steps to the Leadenhall, where strangers to the city could
rent stalls for the first three days of the week in order to sell
their wares. I set out my goods on the trestle table allotted
me by the Warden and was soon besieged with buyers. By
the time that the bells of Saint Michael and Saint Peter-
upon-Cornhill sounded the hour of Tierce-Sext, I had sold
most of the contents of my pack and was thinking hungrily
of my dinner. I was just about to go in search of sustenance
when my eye was caught by a man in the crowd around the
stall next to mine: a small man with heavily pock-marked

skin whose face was somehow familiar. I stood for a moment or two, cudgelling my brains as to why this should be, then suddenly my memory was jogged. We had met four years ago on my very first visit to London.

'Philip Lamprey!' I shouted.

I hardly expected him to hear me over the babel of voices which filled the enclosure, but at the sound of his name his head jerked round and his eyes darted hither and thither until they finally came to rest on me. Almost at once a broad grin split his features and he came towards me with the slightly military gait which was a legacy from his soldiering days.

'Roger the chapman!' he exclaimed delightedly. 'Well I never! Fancy seein' you again.'

'I'm surprised you recall me so readily,' I said, for our acquaintance had been brief.

'Cor! Anyone'd remember a gert fellow like you. And anyway, you remembered me.'

'Not immediately,' I admitted.

'Ah well,' he answered, still grinning, 'I reck'n I've changed a bit since you last clapped eyes on me.'

He was right. His meagre frame had fleshed out and was clothed in decent homespun instead of a beggar's rags. There was an air of prosperity about him which he had previously lacked.

'Yes,' I replied slowly. 'Yes, you have.'

'I'm a respectable shopkeeper now,' he confided. 'Managed to save enough from me begging to rent one o' them second-hand clothes shops west of the Tun. Tha's what I'm doin' 'ere. Lookin' fer any goods goin' cheap among you furriners.' The corners of his eyes creased mockingly. 'Married again, too. Told you, I think, that me first wife ran off up north with a butcher. Got the marriage annulled by Holy Church. Found a good woman and settled down. Bad times over at last. Which reminds me, I owe you a dinner. Promised you that four year since, when you was charitable enough to treat me at the Bull in Fish Street.'

'You've a better memory than I have,' I told him, whereupon he drew himself up to his full height and sniffed.

'I never forgets a debt. C'me on. You look like you've sold most of what you got. We'll go to the Boar's Head in East Cheap and after, you can come 'ome with me and meet my Jeanne.'

For a moment I hesitated, while a warning voice sounded inside my head. 'Stay now,' it said, 'and you may never get safely away.' But at the same time another voice whispered, 'God is not mocked,' and I heaved a sigh, knowing it to be only too true.

'Well?' Philip demanded. 'You comin'? Never refuse a debt repaid, ol' friend. It don't 'appen all that often in this wicked world.'

I laughed and stowed my few remaining items in my pack, which I then humped on to my shoulders. I picked up my cudgel and nodded. 'Lead the way,' I invited. 'I was just thinking about my dinner when I saw you.'

Over a meal of eel pies and brandy tarts, washed down with some of the best ale I have ever tasted, I told Philip Lamprey of my brief marriage and subsequent fatherhood, and of the desire to see London once more, which had led to my present circumstances.

'Aye,' he commiserated, 'you couldn't've picked a worse time to visit than now. But you should've known that, cocky, what wiv us bein' at war again with them Mounseers. And only the Lord Almighty c'n tell why! Fer I don' know of any cause they've given us, do you? But there, it's not fer the likes of us t' question. You come 'ome wiv me tonight and my Jeanne'll make you more than welcome. Then tomorrer, if you're still set on goin' 'ome, you can.'

The Lampreys' second-hand clothes shop was situated in the western reaches of Cornhill and their living quarters were a daub-and-wattle hut at its rear. There was barely sufficient room for the two of them, but neither made anything of that. As Philip had promised, his goodwife made me as welcome as he did himself, and she pressed me to remain for the rest of the day and the coming night. Mistress Lamprey was a little, round, bustling body, with bright-brown eyes and a mop of unruly black curls, imperfectly confined by a kerchief. She had a smile and a cheerful word for all their customers, but what surprised me particularly was her youth. She could not then have been much above eighteen years old, while Philip was certainly past his fortieth birthday. But they seemed to suit each other and to be fonder than many a better-matched couple as regards to age.

I spent the rest of the day helping them with their stall, my own selling skills coming in handy, after which I shared their supper before assisting them to pack up for the night.

'So,' Philip asked when we had finished, 'what'll we do, then? It won't be dark for several hours.' Without waiting for me to furnish him with an answer he continued, 'There's a tavern I know of where you c'n get the best Rybole wine you've ever drunk in yer life. You'll be all right, my dearling, won't you?' he added, kissing Jeanne ingratiatingly on the cheek. 'We'll be back afore curfew.'

'O' course I'll be all right,' she answered, laughing and giving him a playful push. 'Get along with you. But don' come back 'ere drunk.'

'I'll see he doesn't,' I assured her, grinning. When we were clear of the house, I said, 'You've a treasure there.'

'Don' I know it!' he replied fervently. 'I told you my luck 'ad turned.'

We set out briskly through a maze of narrow alleyways that had me lost and confused until we finally emerged into Candlewick Street, where the drapers and mercers have their shops and dwellings. The houses there are timber and brick and painted plaster, indicative of their owners' wealth and standing, but Philip regarded them without envy. He had everything he wanted from life.

'Where are we going?' I asked, as we passed several likely-looking ale-houses and started down Dowgate Hill.

Philip made no immediate reply. Halfway along, we swung into Elbow Lane and, moments later, having turned the corner which gave it its name, we emerged into Thames Street, still busy and teeming with people. To my left, in the distance, I could see the towers of the Steelyard rising above the surrounding buildings, while opposite lay a network of small streets leading to the wharves, and comprising that part of London known as the Vintry.

'Where are we going?' I repeated sharply.

'A tavern called the Three Tuns,' Philip answered. 'Near Three Cranes Quay. I told you, it sells the best Rybole you're ever likely to come by. C'me on, man! Don't fall be'ind. It's full o' people this time of the evening. We'll be lucky if we c'n find a seat.'

For a moment my lagging footsteps came to a halt and Philip glanced over his shoulder in surprise and irritation.

'Come on!' he reiterated impatiently. 'B' Lady, what's the matter with you? I tell you, this stuff's special.'

I hesitated a moment longer, then shrugged and quickened my pace. God had caught me in His net again. He had had no intention of allowing me to escape; and I comforted myself with the thought that had I not encountered Philip Lamprey, I should either have remained in, or returned to, London for some other reason. I had as yet no notion what to expect, but I entered the Three Tuns ale-house, reluctantly resigned to my fate.

Chapter Six

I saw Timothy Plummer almost immediately, in spite of the fact that, as Philip had predicted, the ale-room was full to capacity on this fine summer's evening. I felt little or no surprise that I should have clapped eyes on him so soon, even though he and his companion were drawn well back into a secluded corner and were partially obscured from my view by passing pot-boys, rowdy customers and the ample figure of Mine Host himself, as he moved among the tables making sure that everyone was satisfied. Nor did I feel it to be anything except inevitable when Philip seized my elbow and steered me to two seats which his penetrating gaze had spotted within a few feet of where Timothy Plummer was sitting.

'Wait 'ere an' keep my stool for me,' Philip instructed. 'One o' the pot-boys is cousin to Jeanne. I'll ferret 'im out, otherwise we could be sittin' around till curfew and not get served.'

I nodded and hooked one leg across the stool next to mine, but once Philip had disappeared into the press my whole attention was absorbed by the bench in the corner. I had suspected that the man with Timothy must be Lionel Arrowsmith, but now that I could confirm the suspicion I was astonished to note that as well as having his right arm still in its blue silk sling, the latter also had his left ankle heavily bandaged and a wooden crutch propped beside him. Somehow or other, in the intervening hours between late last night and early this evening, he had sustained a second injury; a fact which explained the worried expression on both his and his companion's faces as they constantly glanced towards the door, eyeing up every fresh arrival. It would be impossible now for Lionel to risk a meeting with Thaddeus Morgan and somebody else must have been despatched in his stead; most probably that person whom he had described as 'too young and too green'. No wonder they both looked so uneasy.

Philip returned with two beakers of Rybole wine, triumphant at having been served before the other occupants of our table, who quickly raised an outcry at such unfair treatment. Philip was unabashed. 'You gotta know someone in this place,' he told them with a wink and turned to me. 'Now, what d'you think o' that?'

He was right. I had never before tasted such richness of flavour, and afterwards I regretted that at the time I was too preoccupied to do it justice. Although I exclaimed enough to satisfy Philip, my mind was on the two men in the corner, who had suddenly stiffened to attention, their eyes fixed on the ale-house door. My own gaze shifted hurriedly and I saw that a young man had just come in.

I judged him to be not above seventeen or eighteen years of age, slenderly built with delicate, fine-boned features and dark, almost black hair, which contrasted with his very pale skin. Surely, I had seen him somewhere recently; or, if not him, someone very like. He turned his head a little, searching the crowd, so that I was able to see him fuller faced, and at once the softly bowed upper lip told me who he was. Had not the shepherd's wife informed me that Matthew Wardroper was the spitting image of his mother? Perhaps that was something of an exaggeration, but certainly this young man brought Lady Wardroper vividly to mind. Moreover, whom else but his own kinsman would Lionel Arrowsmith trust with a secret mission?

So, I thought, taking another draught of Rybole and vaguely aware of Philip babbling on in my right ear, I was back at Matthew Wardroper. The wheel had spun full circle; and if I had entertained any lingering doubt that God's finger was in this particular pie it had now vanished. I accepted defeat as gracefully as possible, and all at once I felt as though a great weight had been lifted from my shoulders.

I watched Matthew Wardroper edge his way towards the corner bench and noted the questioning, almost agonized looks which the other two men bent upon him. Nor did I miss his despairing shake of the head as he sank down beside Timothy Plummer, who shuffled up to make room for him. Lionel Arrowsmith stared at his cousin in consternation, but unfortunately, just at that moment, Philip reclaimed my wandering attention.

'You ain't bin listening to a thing I've said, 'ave you?' he demanded accusingly. 'You bin watching them three over in that corner. No good denyin' it, 'cos I seen you. What's so fascinatin' about 'em?'

As neither Timothy Plummer nor Lionel Arrowsmith nor young Matthew Wardroper was this evening wearing the duke's livery I could not claim that as a point of interest and was obliged to answer feebly, 'Nothing. I just like looking at people.'

Happily, Philip accepted this explanation.

'Ah well, there ain't no more interestin' folk to be found anywhere in the country, I reck'n, than in London, and you don' come 'ere that often. You're forgiven. 'Ow about another beaker each o' Rybole?'

I realized that it was my turn to pay and thrust some coins into his willing hand, whereupon Philip disappeared again to find Jeanne's cousin, rather than wait to waylay one of the harassed and over-worked pot-boys. As soon as he had gone I turned once more to study the group in the corner. Even had the noise in the ale-room not been deafening it would have been impossible for me to over-hear the slightest snatch of their conversation: I was too far away. But the set of their faces told me that all was not well; and when, after some minutes, Matthew Wardroper rose to his feet and again quit the tavern, I concluded that Thaddeus Morgan had failed to keep the appointment he had made.

I emptied my second beaker more slowly than the first, partly to do greater justice to the unrivalled savour of its contents, partly in an attempt to honour my promise to Jeanne that I would not let Philip arrive home drunk, but most of all because I wanted to wait for Matthew Wardroper's return. During Philip's absence I had shifted my position, so that I could both face him and keep my eyes on Timothy Plummer's table, giving as my reason that I had been sitting in a draught. I was thus able to talk and watch at the same time, but as it was at least another half-hour before Matthew Wardroper came back I had difficulty in making my wine last. Philip, indeed, had finished his long since and was set on having a third, an intention it took all my ingenuity to prevent. I was just forcibly restraining him by a hand on his arm when young Wardroper slipped in with a party of latecomers. I could tell at once, by the grim set of his mouth and the sag of his shoulders, that he had had no luck. Thaddeus Morgan had failed to keep the appointment. Timothy Plummer and Lionel Arrowsmith had no hesitation in reaching the same conclusion, a fact made manifest by the look on their faces. As Matthew slid again on to the bench beside the older man, the three heads, grizzled, sandy and black, huddled together in agitated conference.

'This stuff is too potent for me,' I said to Philip. 'I need a walk before we return to Cornhill.' And, brushing aside his protestations that he wasn't ready to go home yet, I ruthlessly hauled him to his feet and propelled him towards the door.

'You're a shpoilshport,' he complained as soon as we were outside. 'I thought a fellow's big ash you'd've had a stronger 'ead.'

'You're already slurring your words,' I admonished him, 'and it wouldn't be fair to Jeanne to have two drunks on her hands.' I gripped his arm firmly. 'Come on. I told you, I've a fancy to stretch my legs before we go home.'

It was fortunate that Philip's wits were already too befuddled to ask why the walk back to Cornhill was not sufficient for my purpose. As it was, he ambled along beside me, still muttering a little defiantly, but otherwise perfectly good-humoured, while I pointed our feet in the direction of Three Cranes Quay.

The wharf was deserted, the three great cranes which gave it its name standing silent and idle. There were a couple of ships moored alongside the wall, one of them so low in the water that it was apparent she had not yet been unloaded. There was no sign of a watch kept aboard either vessel and I guessed that the crews were swelling the throng in the Three Tuns tavern. I walked purposefully towards the other end of the quay, keeping my eyes open for the deserted warehouse.

Thaddeus Morgan had been accurate in his directions. It was at the left-hand corner of the wharf as you faced inland towards the Vintry. One or two of the shutters hung loose from their frames and there was a general air of dereliction which marked it out from its fellows. I trod warily the length of its front looking for an alley where a side door might be situated. In the end, both were located quite easily and I cautiously tested the door with one hand. It yielded at once to my touch and swung inwards with a slight groaning of hinges.

'What you doin'?' Philip's voice whined fretfully behind me. 'What you lookin' for?'

'I'm not sure,' I whispered. 'Bear with me. Stay outside if you want to.'

Philip gave an indignant snort and peered over my shoulder. Just inside the door, revealed by the triangle of fading daylight which penetrated the darkness, the dust had recently been disturbed. Somebody had been standing there for quite a while and it was not difficult for me to guess that that somebody had been Matthew Wardroper, waiting for the missing Thaddeus Morgan.

I tried to put myself in the young man's shoes. He was probably more than a little afraid and somewhat overawed by this highly secret mission, which had apparently been entrusted to him after his cousin Lionel's second mishap. He had been told that the errand would be brief, a single name breathed in his ear. He could then return to the safety of the inn. Instead, he had stood here all alone with a growing sense of unease and danger. Every sound would have made him start and in a place such as this there was bound to be the creaking of settling timbers. He would have been as jumpy as a cat and therefore disinclined to investigate the warehouse further. But beyond the immediate vicinity of the door was a vast and echoing blackness which might possibly contain some clue as to the fate of Thaddeus Morgan.

Why I considered this likely I had no idea, except for that instinct, that sixth sense, which I have always believed is God's way of pointing us in the direction He wishes us to go.

'I'm going to take a look around,' I said to Philip. 'I shan't be long. Wait here for me.'

'Fuck that,' he retorted cheerfully. 'If you're goin' in, I'm comin', too. Though why in God's name you 'ave to go pokin' around a dirty, smelly old warehouse what's been left to the rats and mice, I don't know.'

I didn't enlighten him and he was just drunk enough not to care about the answer. He followed me inside, tripping noisily over his own two feet and giggling like an idiot as he did so. When he had picked himself up I pressed a hand on his shoulder.

'Hold hard a bit, while our eyes get accustomed to the darkness.'

He did as he was bid, standing docilely at my side until the gloom began to assume form and shape, revealing the beams overhead and what looked like a ladder for mounting to the second storey in one corner. A couple of barrels stood in the middle of the floor, while a bundle of some sort lay against the farthest wall.

'Nothin' 'ere,' Philip whispered, the quiet of the empty warehouse beginning to affect him.

I, too, felt that it would be desecration to raise my voice and whispered in return, 'Nevertheless I'll just look around and make sure.'

I moved forward slowly, the musty smell of damp and disuse strong in my nostrils. Now and then I heard the scurry of a rat or a mouse as it ran for the safety of its hole. In the middle of the room I paused. Philip was right, there was nothing to be found down here and I was just considering whether, without a light, it would be wise to venture up the ladder when the sound of a groan lifted the hairs on the nape of my neck. I spun round and saw that the bundle against the wall was moving. In two strides I had reached it, ignoring Philip's startled cry of fear, and fallen on my knees. What I had thought to be some abandoned rubbish was in truth the body of a man, and of a man still living.

But not for long. Even as, with trembling hands, I lifted him in my arms, he gave one last, gasping cry and his head lolled backwards. Thaddeus Morgan – for I had not the smallest doubt of his identity – was dead.

I turned my head and looked up to see Philip, his hand over his mouth, the whites of his horrified eyes clearly visible in the gloom, standing beside me. At the same time I realized that my right hand, which was pressed against Thaddeus Morgan's breast, was growing warm and sticky with what could only be blood. Whoever had killed him had stabbed him and I wondered if the murderer's weapon might still be lying around somewhere, although it was far more likely that he had taken it with him.

'For God's sake come away!' Philip was urging. 'Leave the poor devil for the Watch to find. 'S none of our business.'

'I think I know who he is,' I said. 'I want you to do something for me. Go back to the Three Tuns and look for those men who were sitting in the corner. If by some mischance they've already gone, search the surrounding streets in the direction of Baynard's Castle. Tell them Roger the chapman sent you and that it's urgent they come at once, but make no noise about it. If they show any reluctance, whisper – and I mean whisper – the name of Thaddeus Morgan.'

Philip sniffed. 'I should've remembered you was mixed up in something fishy the last time we met,' he remarked bitterly. 'But I didn' suppose as 'ow you made an 'abit of it. All right! All right! I'll go. But 'ow c'n I be sure I got the right villains? I didn' mark 'em all that well, though I could see you was intrigued by 'em.'

'They're not villains,' I said. 'One's about your own age, the second's a youth of seventeen or so and the third, well, you can't mistake him. His right arm's in a sling and his left foot is bandaged. He's using a crutch.'

Philip, despite the fact that he was shaking with fright, gave a crack of laughter. 'A bit careless like, ain't 'e? Must be blind, too, I reck'n.'

A moment later, he was gone. I laid down my burden, crossed the floor in his wake and pushed the door nearly shut, leaving myself only the merest crack of light. I wanted no one else attracted to the warehouse. In any case, my eyes were by now so used to the darkness that I was able to move about more or less at my ease. I returned to Thaddeus Morgan and my probing fingers immediately located the wound which had killed him. The knife had entered just below the heart and the fact that he had not died immediately suggested that the blow had been delivered with less force than intended, leaving him to bleed to death.

I laid his body down again and began to prowl around the room, but there was no sign of any weapon. I acknowledged that it had been too much to hope for, but I did find, high on the ledge of one of the shuttered windows, a stump of candle in a holder and a tinder-box. How long they had lain there I did not know, but as the flint was old and the tinder damp, I suspected it must have been for some time; since, probably, the warehouse was abandoned. However, I finally managed to get the candle lit and by its pale radiance was able to inspect my surroundings more closely.

The first thing I noticed was that the dust on the floor was a great deal more disturbed than could be accounted for simply by the presence of Philip and myself. Indeed, in the middle of the room it was badly scuffed, as though there had been a struggle which, I considered, might well have been the case. Thaddeus Morgan, mortally wounded but not yet dead, must have tried to grapple with his attacker as long as he had the strength to do so. This theory was borne out when I took another look at the corpse and noted a contusion on the dead man's chin where someone had hit him. Knocked unconscious, he had then been dragged back against the wall; and by the flickering light of the candle-flame I could see, here and there, the two lines made by the heels of his boots, now obliterated in places by my own and Philip's footprints.

Further examination of the body showed me blood on

the front right-hand corner of Thaddeus's jerkin and the material was creased, as though the blade of a knife or dagger had been wiped clean in its folds. Had I been able to see this earlier, it would have saved me a fruitless search. Obviously the killer had taken the murder weapon away with him.

The door creaked open behind me. I at once snuffed the candle and reached for my cudgel, which I had earlier dropped on the floor when making my grisly discovery. But almost immediately I recognized the shapes of the two men who stood framed in the doorway against the fading daylight outside.

'Come in, Philip,' I said softly, 'and bring Timothy Plummer with you. Master Plummer, I think the death of Thaddeus Morgan will be of concern to you.' The duke's man trod across the boards to my side. 'I see you came alone. Where are your companions?'

'I've instructed Matthew Wardroper to return with his cousin to Baynard's Castle. Lionel's in no fit state to endure any more tonight. You note,' he added sardonically, 'that I am naming names on the assumption that they are quite likely already known to you. How you come by your knowledge I have no idea, but I certainly intend to find out.' He knelt down and peered through the gloom at the dead man's face. 'Yes. This is indeed Thaddeus Morgan.' He straightened up and turned to me. 'You will accompany me to Baynard's Castle. Now!'

'And if I refuse?'

'Then within a few hours you will be arrested and brought there under guard. But I would much rather that that didn't happen and I'm sure you would pre-fer it too.' Timothy Plummer jerked his head in Philip's

81

direction. 'Who's this man? And how much does he know?'

'I don' know nothin'!' Philip exclaimed in terror.

'He's telling the truth,' I affirmed. 'He has no knowledge of anything beyond the name of this man, and that I had to disclose in case he was unable to persuade you to come with him. If you let him go he'll not breathe a word to anyone, will you, Philip?'

'May I be struck dead if I do!' was the fervent reply.

Timothy Plummer hesitated, then nodded. 'Very well. I trust you, chapman. If I didn't, I'd have you both clapped in chains. Nevertheless I repeat, you must accompany me to Baynard's Castle.'

'I have to get my pack,' I protested. 'It's at Master Lamprey's shop, where I was to sleep.'

'I'll have someone fetch it for you in the morning. There's no time to waste. I want to hear now, tonight, what exactly you know and how in sweet Jesu's name you came by your information.' He swung round. 'You! Lamprey, or whatever you're called! Be off now! And forget what's happened here this evening.'

'You c'n trust me, Yer Honour!'

'And Philip,' I added, 'it would be best, I think, to tell Jeanne that I met an old friend and have accepted his hospitality in preference to yours. She'll think badly of me for it, but that can't be helped. It's kinder to her if she knows nothing. And when the messenger comes for my pack tomorrow, Master Plummer here will ensure that he's not wearing the duke's livery. You can make up what story you like to account for him.'

Philip sucked in his breath. 'Aye . . . Well . . .' He began to edge towards the warehouse door. 'I'll go now, then.'

And when Timothy Plummer made no effort to stop him, he muttered a quick 'God be with ye' and vanished into the night.

'You're sure he's to be trusted?' Timothy asked uncertainly.

'He's a man who's suffered a great deal of hardship in his life, and who has only recently found security with a good woman and his own shop. He'll not jeopardize either for the sake of a careless word on a subject about which he knows next to nothing. As for violent death, he's seen too much of it to let it bother him. He's lived among beggars and the corpsers who fish the river for dead bodies. Which reminds me, what are we going to do about him?' And I indicated Thaddeus Morgan.

Timothy Plummer shrugged. 'Leave him where he is. Someone'll find him eventually. He won't be connected with you or me. It'll probably never be discovered who he really is, for I doubt he goes by his own name. None of his kind ever does. Now then, if you're ready, we'll get going. It's close to curfew.'

I replaced the candle and tinder-box on the ledge where I had found them and followed Timothy Plummer out of the warehouse, leaving the door wide open. I hoped it might persuade some vagabond to enter and lead to the finding of Thaddeus Morgan's body. Even though, if all my companion had said of him were true, he would most likely be buried in the common grave, it was better than being left to rot or to be gnawed by the rats. I felt he deserved more than that, whatever his calling.

It was growing dark and the curfew bell was tolling as Timothy Plummer and I turned into Thames Street and headed in a westerly direction. The sky still glimmered grey, but there was a smell of tallow in the air as candles were lit. Shops were being closed for the night, goods taken indoors and stowed safely under lock and key. Voices called their valedictions amid much good-natured laughter and chaff. And rising above the roof-tops, down by the river's edge, loomed the great black bulk of Baynard's Castle.

Chapter Seven

The outer courtyard was full of people, the castle being, for the moment, home to two separate households, those of the Dowager Duchess of York and of her youngest son, Prince Richard. With the invasion of France already underway, and with the king and his two brothers making preparations to follow in less than a sennight, it was only natural that to the ordinary, everyday business of bed and board should be added the bustle of military consultation. Security was close, with double the guards on every gate to the number I recalled from my previous visit. Timothy Plummer's face, however, seemed to open each door as if by magic, and in no time at all I was shepherded along a maze of passageways, up numerous flights of narrow, twisting stairs until we reached a room high up in one of the towers, where Lionel Arrowsmith and his young cousin awaited us.

The former was seated in a carved armchair, his injured foot resting on a stool, while the latter, his features pale and drawn, prowled up and down, every muscle taut with anxiety. As I entered with Master Plummer, two pairs of eyes, one hazel, one brown, were turned towards us.

'Well?' the elder demanded brusquely. 'Was it Thaddeus Morgan?'

Timothy nodded and bade me make myself comfortable. I drew up a stool from a corner of the room while he lit another of the candles which stood in their holders on the table. 'There's no point sitting in the gloom,' he commented.

'Never mind that!' Lionel's voice was laced with panic and he pulled himself forward in his chair with his good left hand. 'How does this pedlar come to know so much that he can quote Thaddeus's name? And where's the other little runt who came to fetch us?'

'Gone home. I have Roger Chapman's word that he'll hold his tongue,' Timothy answered placidly.

'A chapman's word!' Lionel's tone was scathing. 'Have you taken leave of your senses?'

'No. Nor will the duke think so when I tell him. For the truth is that Master Chapman here is well known to His Grace and in the past has done him two great services. My lord would trust him with his life, there's no doubt of that. Which, Roger, is precisely what's at stake.'

I stared at him, frowning. 'You mean ... someone is trying to kill Duke Richard?'

Timothy sighed deeply. 'That's the long and the short of it, I'm afraid.'

'But who?'

Lionel Arrowsmith gave a snort of laughter. 'That's what we were hoping to discover tonight, but someone got to Thaddeus Morgan before us, and as a result we're as much in the dark as ever.'

'Why would anyone want to kill my lord of Gloucester?'

'If we knew that,' Timothy answered with asperity, 'we might know where the danger lies. Conversely, if we knew the name of the traitor we might have a motive for the crime.'

'But if you know neither name nor motive,' I demanded reasonably, 'how can you be sure an attempt is planned on His Grace's life?'

Timothy Plummer sat down in the window embrasure, stretching out his legs and leaning his back against the stone. 'That can wait for the moment. First and foremost, you have some questions to answer, chapman.' Lionel Arrowsmith nodded vigorously in agreement. 'How do you come to know as much as you do? What circumstances led you to connect me with Thaddeus Morgan? And how did you come by his name?'

'There's no mystery,' I answered. 'I'm quite willing to tell you.'

When I had finished the broad outline of my story, but omitting those incidents which I felt had no direct bearing upon the matter in hand, there was silence for several seconds.

Then Timothy Plummer stirred. 'A remarkable chain of events. Remarkable. Or, as you say yourself, perhaps the hand of God was here.'

But my other two listeners had different preoccupations.

'You ... you called at home and ... and saw my lady mother?' Matthew Wardroper stammered eagerly. 'How was she?'

'In health,' I answered, but was given no chance to enlarge upon the subject before Lionel Arrowsmith cut in. His voice was tinged with hysteria.

'*You overheard every word that Thaddeus Morgan and I were saying last night?* You were concealed behind a bush and we didn't even know you were there? God's toe-nails!

87

Why didn't we think to search the ground before we spoke? Why didn't Thaddeus? Surely a man of his experience must have realized the possible danger that we ran! And if you could eavesdrop, who else might not have done the same? Timothy, I'm sorry! I'm a fool! An idiot! Report me to the duke! Have me whipped for negligence! Never trust me again!'

'Hold hard, Lal,' Timothy begged him. 'It's too late for regrets and I doubt there was more than one long-nosed interloper skulking about the Priory walls at that time of night. No offence, chapman, but you do have the habit of making other people's business your own.'

'None taken,' I replied cheerfully and decided that for the moment I would say nothing of that other shadow I had seen. Master Arrowsmith was plainly in no condition at present to bear up under such a revelation and a twice-injured man, I felt, had the right to some consideration. I was longing to ask how he came by his double misfortune, but curbed my tongue, suspecting that all would be revealed in time.

'My mother, Master Chapman.' Matthew Wardroper was once more clamouring for my attention. 'You say she was well?'

'Indeed, yes,' I smiled. 'And it's true what I was told. You are extremely like her in appearance.'

He seemed pleased with this and turned to his cousin. 'I told you, Lal. It's what everybody says.'

Lionel shrugged. 'I wouldn't remember, not having set eyes on Aunt Maud for so long.' He was not to be cheered, still sunk deep in a mire of self-blame. I guessed him to be devoted to the duke. But then, so were most of Prince Richard's followers. He was a man who inspired love and affection in those privileged to know him intimately, although to those who did not, he could seem cold and withdrawn.

Timothy Plummer rose to his feet. 'Matt,' he said, addressing the younger man, 'it's time you returned to your duties. There's nothing further you can do here. You did creditably tonight and I've no doubt His Grace will thank you personally in the morning. Now, off with you. I want a word with your cousin and the chapman.'

Matthew Wardroper's face crumpled ludicrously. 'But . . . but I thought I was to help, to take Lal's place, now that he's laid up with a broken ankle. You both agreed that you could trust me; that I'm the only member of the duke's household who joined it after you knew of the threat to His Grace's life.'

Timothy clapped him consolingly on the shoulder. 'Lad, that was before Roger Chapman providentially came poking and prying into our affairs. Look at him. He's twice the size of you, great gawk that he is! There's no reason for you to risk your neck when he'll do it for you.'

I made no comment, accepting the spirit in which these words were uttered rather than jibbing at their content.

'But . . . but I *want* to help!' Matthew protested, almost crying.

'And so you will do, lad,' Timothy assured him, 'by concealing your knowledge of the chapman's true identity when he joins the ranks of the duke's servants tomorrow.'

'Wait a moment, Master Plummer!' I intervened, also standing up. 'This is going too fast. I've agreed to nothing yet. And shall not, either, until I know more about what mischief is afoot, or what danger I may be involved in.'

'There you are, you see!' Matthew was triumphant. 'You'd do much better to put your trust in me.'

'Oh, go to bed, lad!' Lionel said wearily, leaning back in his chair and closing his eyes. 'Tim's right, the chapman can make two of you, and if he's trustworthy – which I'm certain he is if he's known to His Grace – then I'd rather he ran any risks that might need to be taken instead of you. Aunt Maud and Uncle Cedric would never forgive me if harm befell their only chick. They'd be bound to hold me responsible.'

Timothy nodded. 'And in any case it's high time you were getting back to your dormitory. Your fellow Squires of the Household will be wondering where you are. Or the duke may want you to sing to him. You have a fine voice. His Grace remarked on it only yesterday within my hearing.'

'Ralph Boyse's is finer. The duke won't need me if he's around.' Matthew looked sulky, rubbing the knuckles of one hand against the palm of the other like a small child seeking comfort. It struck me that he was a little younger in ways, and less spirited, than I had gathered from Millisent Shepherd's description of him. Perhaps it was this slightly immature streak in his son's nature that Sir Cedric found it hard to tolerate. Moreover, Matthew's eager inquiries after his mother's health suggested an even fonder closeness to Lady Wardroper than I had already imagined.

Lionel gave a short bark of laughter, in which I thought I could trace a tinge of resentment. 'Ralph's not on duty tonight, so he'll be otherwise engaged.'

Matthew considered this for a moment before enlightenment apparently dawned. 'You mean with Berys Hogan,' he chuckled. He added more seriously, 'I'm never sure which of you two it is she really cares for.'

'Berys is betrothed to Ralph,' Timothy said firmly. He frowned at Lionel. 'You'd do well to watch your step there. You and she are both playing a dangerous game.'

Lionel shrugged, trying to appear indifferent, but a little colour stole into his pallid cheeks. 'You're an old woman, Timothy,' he protested. 'She and Ralph have a pact that as long as they're unwed they'll not interfere too much with one another's pleasures.'

Timothy Plummer, insulted by the epithet applied to him, retorted angrily, 'Berys told you that no doubt! And you believed her? Well, more fool you, that's all I have to say. But then, you proved yourself a deal too simple and trusting last night, Lal, didn't you?'

'Friends! Friends!' I exclaimed hurriedly, laying my hands on a shoulder of each. 'Don't, for God's sake, turn on one another at such a time as this. If Duke Richard really is in danger, he needs you to work together.'

Both men looked shamefaced.

'Aye, that's true enough,' Timothy Plummer admitted. 'The last thing we must do is squabble among ourselves. Forgive me, Lal. It was only concern for you that made me speak as I did. Ralph Boyse can turn ugly on occasions. I've seen it.'

Lionel was quick to accept the apology. 'I'm sorry, too, for what I said. I didn't mean it.'

'Then that's the end of that.' Timothy snapped his fingers with relief. 'Now, we've much to discuss with the chapman, so Matt, for the last time, be off with you! And on your way back to the dormitory, get one of those idle pages to run to the buttery and bring up some wine to us here. A good malmsey, tell him. None of that inferior stuff from Crete. That's only fit for the lower servants.' Matthew departed unwillingly, dragging his feet, but at last the tower door shut behind him. Timothy waved me back to my stool and drew up one of his own. 'Right!' he continued. 'Make yourself comfortable and let me explain.'

It seemed that in the two years (or almost two years) since I had last seen Timothy Plummer he had risen to become chief Spy-Master in the Duke of Gloucester's household. This, I gathered, was a position undefined and unacknowledged in the ducal rolls, but one, none the less, of very great importance, as everybody of any moment employed agents to spy on one another.

'For instance,' Timothy said, drawing his stool closer to mine and lowering his voice a trifle, 'I know for certain that Stephen Hudelin, Yeoman of the Chamber, is a spy for Lord Rivers, the queen's eldest brother. And through him, probably for the whole Woodville clan. I am almost equally sure that Humphrey Nanfan, also a Yeoman of the Chamber, works for my lord of Clarence, while Geoffrey Whitelock, Squire of the Household, is in the pay of the king.'

'Wait!' I protested. 'Wait! Are you asking me to believe that both King Edward and the Duke of Clarence set spies about their own brother?'

Timothy glanced at Lionel Arrowsmith with a resigned shrug of his shoulders before turning back to me. 'Chapman, can you really believe that anyone at court truly trusts anybody else? If so, you must be very simple-minded.'

'I can see that the king wouldn't trust my lord of Clarence,' I answered hotly. 'He's proved himself a traitor on more than one occasion. But His Grace would surely never suspect my lord of Gloucester of working against him!'

'You may well be right,' Timothy replied, settling his elbows on his knees and leaning forward. 'But how can he ever be certain beyond all doubt that the duke's patent dislike of the queen and her numerous family might not, some day, turn to a more active hatred? Besides,' Timothy spread his hands, 'it's only tit-for-tat, when all's said and done. We have our own agents in the king's and brother George's households.' He saw my expression of horror and laughed. 'You are an innocent, Roger, aren't you? Now, where was I?'

He went on to enumerate two more members of the duke's entourage who were suspected of being spies: Jocelin d'Hiver, yet another of the score or so Squires of the Household, who might, or might not, be in the pay of Charles of Burgundy's Spy-Master General, and the man already mentioned that evening, Ralph Boyse, whose mother had been a Frenchwoman and who could, just possibly, be guilty of a dual allegiance.

'But in God's name,' I expostulated, 'if you know, or even suspect, that these men are up to no good, why do you not advise the duke's steward to dismiss them?'

Here a page arrived with a tray bearing a bottle of malmsey and three beakers, which he placed on the table and then withdrew. Timothy Plummer poured out a measure of wine, carefully tasted it, then filled the beakers to the brim before answering my question.

'That would be very poor strategy. A foolish thing to do if you think about it carefully. At least we know who these men are and can keep them in our eye. If it suits us, we can even give them false information to pass on to their masters. But dismiss them and they would only be replaced by other agents, perhaps more skilful at concealment.'

Once before, I had been given a glimpse of the spider's web of intrigue and constant double-dealing which surrounded kings and princes and had not liked it then any more than I liked it now. Even on such brief acquaintance I could well imagine the petty jealousies, the back-biting, the factions, the whispering and the strife which tore at the very foundations of every European court, and had no wish to be part of such a world. But if Richard of Gloucester's life was truly in danger, then I had no choice except to do whatever lay within my power to protect him, however reluctant I might be to get involved. For, from our very first meeting, he had commanded my heart.

'Very well,' I told Timothy Plummer, 'I accept that the enemy you know is better than the one you don't. But you haven't yet explained why you believe the duke to be in mortal peril.'

'Thaddeus Morgan brought me the news at the beginning of May, while we were on our way south from Middleham. He was heading north to Yorkshire, when he heard that the duke and his levies had reached Northampton and were resting there for two or three days. He therefore sought me out, so as to warn me of a very strong rumour circulating among the Brotherhood that an order had gone out for Duke Richard's death.'

'Wait,' I said, holding up a hand. 'Who or what are the Brotherhood?'

It was Lionel Arrowsmith who answered. 'The Brotherhood, also sometimes known as the Fraternity, is a network of vagabonds, rogues and petty criminals from the stews and sewers of every country throughout the length and breadth of Europe and probably beyond. These men sell information for money and are invaluable as spies, provided that you pay them well.'

Timothy Plummer nodded. 'No one knows who the fountain-head is, nor even if there is one, nor where the organization begins and ends. No man goes by his proper name, and each has two other Brothers – one on his right hand and one on his left, so to speak – with whom he shares information, gathered from Heaven alone knows what sources; a rag-bag of rumour and gossip from which every man picks such items as he thinks he can sell, and for which he believes he can find a customer. And that is the sum total of my knowledge of the Brotherhood and probably as much as anyone knows. Thaddeus Morgan, or whatever his rightful name was, was known to my predecessor, His Grace's previous Spy-Master, and was necessarily made known to me. And very useful he's been,' he added bitterly, 'worth his weight in gold. He will be sorely missed.'

'Someone else will no doubt take his place,' Lionel said drily, 'once his death becomes noised abroad. You have only to wait patiently, Tim, and you will be approached. As, of course, will be the Spy-Masters of King Edward, my lord Rivers, His Grace of Clarence . . .'

'I don't understand,' I interrupted. 'You mean that all these people know that Duke Richard's life is under threat? Why then does the king do nothing about it?'

'No, no!' Timothy Plummer finished his wine and poured himself a second beakerful. 'A Brother will only approach one Spy-Master at a time, the one he thinks will be most

95

interested and who will therefore pay him most handsomely. It is a point of honour with these men never to sell the same information twice over.'

'And you trust them to keep their word?'

'Oh yes.' Lionel stretched out his empty beaker for me to refill. 'These men have their loyalties and think it bad luck to break faith.'

I twisted my own beaker, still half full, between my hands, afraid to drink too deeply after what I had already consumed that evening. I needed to keep a clear head. 'So what else,' I asked Timothy, 'could Thaddeus Morgan tell you concerning the danger to His Grace?'

'Only that rumour said it would come from within his own household and that the blow must fall before the Eve of Saint Hyacinth . . . But from which particular direction it would threaten was more difficult to determine, and there was a delay of several weeks before he could offer us any further information. Then, when finally he was able to promise us a name and with it, possibly, a motive, there was a further wrangle over the amount of gold demanded by himself and his informer. That money was handed over last night, as you know, and the identity of the would-be assassin ought now to be in our possession.'

'Instead of which,' I finished for him, 'Thaddeus Morgan is dead and you are none the wiser.' I pondered for a moment or two on all that he had told me and one fact puzzled me more than the rest. 'You mentioned the Eve of Saint Hyacinth,' I added slowly. 'That would be the sixteenth of August, about seven weeks hence.'

'So you see, chapman,' Lionel Arrowsmith said, 'that time grows pressing, particularly so since we are now completely cut off from any source of further information.'

'But why the Eve of Saint Hyacinth?' I pressed. 'By then His Grace will most surely be in France. And why should a limit be put upon the deed? What will happen on the Eve, or even the Feast, of Saint Hyacinth that makes the duke's execution unnecessary after that date?'

Timothy raised his eyes from the contemplation of his once-again empty beaker and fixed them on my face. 'Is that how you read it, chapman? That if we can keep His Grace from harm until then, his life will no longer be in jeopardy?' His voice sounded a note of desperate hope.

'I may be wrong,' I admitted, 'but for the moment I can see no other construction to be placed upon the condition. If, that is, you understood Thaddeus Morgan aright.'

Timothy grimaced. 'I didn't see him again after our first encounter, but that was the message Lionel brought me.'

'And it was what Thaddeus told me,' was the indignant answer. 'Do you think me such a fool that I could misinterpret his meaning?'

Timothy raised a hand. 'Softly, softly, Lal! No one is accusing you of anything. But it has needed the chapman here to point out its importance. Neither of us has been thinking very clearly.'

'Understandably enough,' I consoled him. 'You have both been more concerned with the threat to the duke. Sometimes it wants a latecomer to the game to see things which have been previously overlooked.' Each man relaxed a little at these words. I went on, 'Let's forget that problem for a while, however, and consider the events of the past few hours. Master Arrowsmith, you were due to meet Thaddeus at Three Cranes Wharf this evening. Why you were unable to do so is all too painfully apparent. How did you come by this broken ankle?'

Before Lionel could reply Timothy cut in with a laugh, 'The same way he came by his broken arm, by falling downstairs. And the same flight each time. The top step is badly worn and Lal is a follower of fashion. When indoors, and liable to attend upon His Grace, he insists on wearing long-piked shoes. A very stupid and dangerous fashion, as he has now proved twice over.'

'All right! All right!' It was plainly a sore subject with Lionel. 'But who could have expected lightning to strike in the same place more than once? I promise to give up my piked shoes, Tim, if it will make you happier.'

It was my turn now to get my own back for having been called simple-minded and innocent earlier on in the conversation. 'Did neither of you ever consider,' I asked, 'that the falls might not have been accidents? That some-one deliberately caused Master Arrowsmith to trip in order to try to prevent his meetings with Thaddeus Morgan?'

Chapter Eight

There was silence while I might have counted to twenty, then Lionel Arrowsmith gave a nervous laugh.

Timothy Plummer said trenchantly, 'Nonsense! No one but our two selves knew of the meetings.'

'What about young Matthew?'

'He knew only of the last. When Lal slipped a second time and injured his ankle, then plainly someone else had to be found to take his place. In view of the possible danger I could not risk my own person.' His chest puffed a little with self-importance. 'We picked on young Wardroper because he was a recent arrival and could be excluded from suspicion. He is also Master Arrowsmith's cousin.'

I rubbed my chin. 'Are you telling me that the duke himself knows nothing of the threat to his life?'

'No, no! Of course he had to be told, to be put on his guard. That goes without saying.'

'Then it also goes without saying that His Grace may have imparted this knowledge to another person, either wittingly or unwittingly. Perhaps to several other persons.'

Timothy shook his head gloomily. 'You're out there, chapman. He was angry with me for even mentioning the subject and refuses to take any unnecessary precautions. He dared me, on pain of his greatest displeasure, to discuss

99

the matter with anyone except Lionel here, his most trusted Squire of the Body, who would keep him informed of what was happening and also render me any assistance I might require. The inclusion of Matthew Wardroper in our schemes has already stretched His Grace's tolerance to its limit and what he will say when he discovers that I have now admitted you to our counsels is better left to the imagination. However' – Timothy squared his shoulders manfully – 'I shall have to face him with it in the morning.'

This time I rubbed my nose. 'You consider it unlikely then that any breach of confidence could have come from the duke. But what about you? You must have underlings.'

'They do as they are told and ask no questions. So you see . . .' Timothy shrugged and spread his hands.

'I see nothing,' I answered shortly. 'This is a household of – what? Some two or three hundred souls? And at present shares this castle with another household of similar magnitude. I do not believe it possible that secrets can be kept perfectly among so many. Backstairs whispering and gossip abound in an enclave such as this. A single glance, one incautious word, would be enough to alert a guilty man to the fact that his purpose was discovered; and his aim must then be to conceal his identity at all costs until he has achieved his object. I therefore think it highly probable that these "accidents" which have befallen Master Arrowsmith were in reality no such thing. Later, I will ask you to show me the flight of stairs where they happened, but for the moment let us return to the events of this evening.'

I am ashamed to confess that I was by now thoroughly enjoying their hangdog looks and my own sense of superiority; but on reflection, I think I may be forgiven my petty triumph. They had treated me like a country bump-kin, unversed in the ways of the world. I could hardly be blamed for taking pleasure in proving them wrong.

'What do you want to know?' Timothy Plummer asked almost humbly. 'I'll answer your questions.'

'First, tell me exactly what happened tonight. When Philip Lamprey and I entered the Three Tuns tavern, you and Master Arrowsmith were alone. Matthew Wardroper joined you a few moments later. He had presumably been sent to keep the tryst with Thaddeus Morgan. When he returned, what did he say?'

'That Thaddeus had not appeared.' It was Lionel who spoke. His cheeks were flushed and the hazel eyes over-bright, but whether this was the effect of the wine, fatigue, pain or from some other cause, I had no means of telling. It occurred to me that he had been very quiet for the past ten minutes, but again, there could be a number of reasons for leaving Timothy to do the talking.

The older man nodded. 'That's right. He had found the door of the warehouse open and waited just inside, but no one came.'

'How long did he wait?'

The two men glanced at one another.

'Maybe a quarter of an hour,' Timothy said at last and Lionel murmured in confirmation.

'Did he mention hearing anything during that time? A groan, perhaps, or someone stirring?'

'If he had, he would have told us and we should have gone to investigate.' It was Timothy Plummer's turn to score.

'So you sent him back again with instructions to keep a longer vigil. At least half an hour by my reckoning. But did the lad not think to look around him? To explore the warehouse?'

Lionel sighed. 'I suspect he was too frightened. Oh, he was anxious enough to help, proud that we had put our trust in him, but at bottom he's just a raw, green lad with no experience of danger. And we had perhaps over-emphasized the need for caution.'

'With good reason, as it turned out,' Timothy objected grimly. 'If your cousin had chanced upon the murderer, he, too, might now be lying stabbed through the heart.'

'Which brings us to the question of when the murder actually took place,' I said, refusing to let them stray into realms of the might-have-been. 'Before young Matt's arrival? During his return to the Three Tuns? Or after his final departure? It depends, of course, when Thaddeus finally kept the tryst, but that is something it is impossible for us to know for certain. Whoever killed him left him, either unaware that he still breathed, or content to let him bleed to death.'

Yet, even as I spoke, something worried me about that conclusion, but I was unable to decide just what. I yawned prodigiously and stretched my arms above my head. I had had a disturbed night and a long, eventful day. My mind felt as leaden as my body and suddenly all I wanted to do was sleep.

Timothy rose from his stool and laid a hand on my arm. 'Come along, my lad, you can share my bed for tonight. Then, in the morning, when I've made my confession to the duke and, God willing, he's given his permission for your involvement, we can resume this conversation. Lal, time also that you retired. I don't need to ask if you've taken all precautions to safeguard His Grace's rest.'

Lionel grunted wearily. 'I'll come with you to the duke in the morning,' he said, 'and confess my stupidity over that last meeting with Thaddeus. He'll be angry, but not more so than I am with myself. Than I deserve. Assist me out of this chair, Tim, and shout for one of the pages to help me to the dormitory.' And, this done, he bade us both a brief good-night.

Timothy Plummer turned again to me and refilled my beaker. 'One final draught, chapman. You'll sleep the better for it and you'll need all your wits about you tomorrow.'

Timothy Plummer jerked his head towards the door and said, 'You can enter now, chapman. His Grace will see you in a moment.'

He pulled down the corners of his mouth as he spoke, indicating that his own interview with Duke Richard, some half an hour before, had not been an easy one. Lionel Arrowsmith, it seemed, had decided to make his confession even earlier and had now been dismissed once again to his bed in order to rest his ankle until it should be mended, so I had no means of knowing how he had fared.

I had to stoop to enter the little antechamber. Through the half-open door I could see the duke, seated at a table, dictating letters to his chief clerk, and also attended by his secretary, John Kendall. I sat down on a bench running the length of one wall and occupied my eyes with staring at the tapestries illustrating the story of Dido and Aeneas, but keeping my ears pricked for anything Duke Richard might let drop in the course of his dictation. Any morsel of information would have been welcome at that juncture.

To my astonishment, however, His Grace, in the midst of all his preparations for the invasion of France and the undoubted additional aggravation caused by this threat to his life, seemed to be equally concerned with the affairs of his Yorkshire tenants. He was sending a strongly worded letter to the Bishop of Durham regarding illegal fishgarths in the waters of the Ouse and the Humber which, the duke claimed, were not only impeding the navigation of these two rivers, but also diminishing the number of fish able to be caught by rod and line.

'The bishop knows very well,' the duke remarked in an acid aside to John Kendall, 'that Parliament has strengthened the magistrates' hands in this matter, yet still his bailiffs persist in flouting the law, trusting in the fact that people will be afraid to oppose him.' The royal jawline tightened. 'Well, now His Grace will discover that he has me to contend with.'

I knew a fleeting compassion for the errant cleric who was to be the recipient of so much unbending displeasure and hoped that I would fare better at Duke Richard's hands. So, when the clerk and John Kendall were finally dismissed, I approached the table where he was sitting with what I trusted was a suitably ingratiating expression. To my great relief the duke regarded me with a glimmering smile.

'There's no need to look so hangdog, chapman,' he said. 'I'm not about to order your arrest.' The smile deepened. 'Sit down.' And he indicated the stool vacated by his clerk. 'So,' he went on, resting his chin on his clasped hands, 'here you are again, mixed up in my affairs.'

'An it please your lordship.'

'Oh, it does please me, Roger, it does, the reason being that you are one of just a handful of people I can really trust. Twice in the past you have proved yourself to be an honest and devoted servant, with no thought of gain or personal self-advancement. Don't look so uncomfortable. I'm only stating the truth. I would to God that there were more like you.'

He sounded bitter, and for the first time since entering the room I looked closely at him. He was my own age exactly, still some four months short of his twenty-third birthday. But during the two years since our last meeting he had aged faster than I had. There were fine lines around the eyes and mouth which I could not recall seeing before and the thin lips were more compressed, emphasizing the heaviness of jaw and chin. I noticed, too, the nervous way in which he twisted the rings which adorned his fingers, or fiddled with the jewelled chain slung about his shoulders. The long, slender fingers with their beautiful, almond-shaped nails were never quiet, reflecting, or so I suspected, an inner perturbation of the mind.

My heart went out to him, for I guessed that in spite of his supreme happiness with his wife and little son, maintaining the peace between his brothers must be a perpetual source of misery to him. Common gossip held him to be equally fond of both the king and George of Clarence, but with the latter constantly hell-bent on stirring up trouble, it could be no easy task to keep them friends.

'And how has the world turned with you,' he went on, 'since our last meeting?'

I told him as briefly as I could, not wishing to burden him, amongst all his weightier affairs, with my paltry concerns. But he listened intently and questioned me more closely when I would have skimped the narrative. The brown eyes lit with pleasure and tenderness when I mentioned my baby daughter and I knew he must be thinking of his own love-child, the Lady Katherine Plantagenet.

'Girls are a great joy,' he said softly. 'They wheedle, they cajole, they throw tantrums, but they have a deep and abiding loyalty towards those to whom they give their hearts. Guard your little Elizabeth well, Roger. Cherish her as you would your most prized possession.' He was silent a moment longer, staring unseeingly before him, then he sighed and addressed himself to the matter in hand. 'Timothy Plummer informs me that you have stumbled by chance upon our secret and that, in view of your past success at solving mysteries, he has sought my permission to recruit you. Before I give it, however, what are *your* wishes? You have already risked your life twice in my service. I will not imperil it a third time unless I have your consent.'

'My lord,' I answered, 'if your life is threatened then I should most sincerely wish to discover the source of the danger. His Highness, King Edward, cannot afford to lose the chief prop and stay of his throne.'

The duke pulled down the corners of his mouth. 'I doubt if the queen's family would relish that description of me, chapman. However,' he acknowledged, but simply, without arrogance, 'no doubt you're right. Very well, if you are prepared to serve me yet again, so be it. And thank you. But I must enjoin strict secrecy upon you. What we know, or think we know, must remain a confidence between the four of us. You, me, Timothy Plummer and Lal Arrowsmith.'

'And young Matthew Wardroper,' I amended.

The frown reappeared. 'Ah, yes! I had forgotten. A foolish move, that, to involve the lad. He's too young to be mixed up in such conspiracies. Why could Tim not have kept the tryst with Morgan, instead of Lionel? He thinks a little too well of himself, does Master Plummer. But the damage is done. Keep an eye on young Wardroper, chapman. I would not have him suffer injury in so miserable a cause.' He held out his hand for me to kiss, indicating that the audience was at an end. 'Timothy Plummer will keep me informed as to what is happening, should any progress be made. And once more, accept my deepest gratitude.'

I was plainly being dismissed, but there were still things, I felt, left unresolved. When I hesitated, however, the duke merely smiled briefly and said, 'Timothy Plummer will tell you all you wish to know. Go and see him now. You'll doubtless find him hovering somewhere not too far distant.'

He was right.

As I stepped across the threshold of the antechamber, Timothy was waiting and pounced on me eagerly. 'Well? Did His Grace agree? Did you agree?' And when I nodded in answer to both questions he bore me off triumphantly to the same tower room where we had sat and talked the previous evening. 'Sit down! Sit down,' he urged, 'and I'll tell you what, with His Grace's consent, I've decided for you.'

I seated myself in the window embrasure. 'I assume I'm to enter the duke's household. But how will you explain me?'

'I've been thinking about that long and hard ever since I

woke up this morning, because it suddenly occurred to me that it would be impossible to keep your true identity a secret. That was my first idea, as you know, but there are bound to be at least half a dozen, and most probably more than that, of His Grace's followers who remember you from your past association with us. My suggestion, therefore, is this. On both the previous occasions when you rendered him a service, Duke Richard offered to reward you, if you so wished it, with a place in his household. At the time you had no desire to give up life on the open road, but now you have changed your mind and you came here last night in order to acquaint His Grace of the fact. You were granted an audience this morning, with the result that you are to take up an immediate appointment as a Yeoman of the Chamber. Duke Richard is even now issuing written instructions to that effect.'

'But ... what do I have to do as a – what was it? – Yeoman of the Chamber?'

Timothy Plummer smiled, not without malice. 'You help set the boards for meals, see that the torches and candles are lit, run any messages that need taking. A fairly lowly position, as you'll have gathered. But there are some twenty or so of you, so you'll not be kept too busy, a fact which should enable you to find the time to keep your eyes and ears open.'

I think he was afraid, but had also half-hoped, that I might be offended by such menial tasks and was therefore a little disappointed by my answer. 'A sensible decision, Master Plummer, for it would have looked strange indeed had I been offered any higher appointment. And in any case, it will not be for long. The Eve of Saint Hyacinth is less than two full moons away.'

The worry-lines once more creased his face. 'God forbid,' he said, crossing himself, 'that any harm should befall His Grace. Chapman, my dependence is all on you, now that I have lost my only contact with the Brotherhood.'

'I promise to do what I can,' I replied, 'and there is something I must tell you. I believe that Master Arrowsmith was followed to his meeting with Thaddeus Morgan at Holy Trinity Priory.' And I told him of that other figure in the shadows.

He cursed roundly, demanding to know why I had not mentioned the circumstance before.

I shrugged. 'It could only have distressed Master Arrowsmith still further, and as I was unable to see the man's face it made no difference. I could not possibly identify him and it might have been no more than chance that another soul was abroad so late at night.'

Timothy snorted in derision. 'And pigs might fly, chapman! You don't fool me. You don't entertain the notion for an instant!'

I sighed. 'I admit to thinking it highly improbable. Nevertheless, there might be just the slenderest of hopes that such is the case, if Master Arrowsmith's injuries are indeed the result of carelessness on his part. You promised last night to show me the staircase where they happened.'

Timothy rose and led me out of the room, along several passages and down a flight of stairs before stopping at the head of yet another flight which I had descended that very morning, and which I recognized as leading down to the chamber where the Duke of Gloucester had been working. 'On each occasion,' Timothy went on, 'Lal had been summoned by His Grace and was in a hurry. The first time was last Friday, when he slipped on the top stair and fell to the landing below, breaking his right arm, and was very fortunate, as the surgeon needlessly pointed out, to escape so lightly.'

'And you accepted it as an accident?'

Timothy shrugged. 'Why not? The edge of the top step is badly worn, as you may observe for yourself, and, as I have already told you, Lionel favours the fashionable mode in shoes: long pikes, sometimes so long that they have to be chained about his knees, a danger to life and limb. I used to warn him – and so did the duke – that one day they could prove harmful.'

'And was he wearing long pikes when he slipped and broke his ankle some time yesterday?'

Timothy glanced at me, momentarily frowning, but then his brow just as suddenly cleared. 'Of course! You saw him on Monday night, when he talked to Thaddeus Morgan.'

I nodded. 'And then only his arm was injured. But by the time Philip Lamprey and I entered the Three Tuns yesterevening, Master Arrowsmith had sustained a further mishap.'

Timothy grunted. 'Yesterday morning exactly the same thing happened. He was again summoned to the duke and again tripped and fell, this time breaking his left ankle.'

I made no comment but knelt down and carefully examined the first tread of the staircase. The edge was indeed badly worn away by the passage of countless feet over many years and the stone was as smooth and shiny as a pebble. The light, too, was poor, what there was of it coming from a lancet window on the landing below us. On either side of the staircase the walls rose sheer to the roof of this particular storey and I peered closely at both of them. At last I raised my head to find Timothy Plummer watching me expectantly, but half-hoping, I think, that there was nothing to find. I was forced to disappoint him.

'See here,' I said, beckoning him to crouch down beside me. When he had done so I indicated two places, one on either side of the top step and both at an equal height, where the mortar between the stones had been disturbed, shedding a few loosened crumbs on the floor beneath. 'My guess is that two nails have been driven in, one here and one over there, and a piece of fine wire or twine strung tautly between them. Anyone then descending in a hurry, not looking where he was going, would trip and fall. And if the nails were hammered in only lightly, the force of the fall would pull them and the string loose, allowing free passage for anyone following. Master Arrowsmith undoubtedly set up a shout—'

'Loud enough to be heard in Hell,' Timothy murmured.

'—and the setter of the trap,' I continued, 'would have been waiting close at hand to pocket the tell-tale evidence before anyone else had a chance to notice it and draw their own conclusions. Tell me, who summoned Master Arrowsmith to the duke's presence each time, and who was first on the scene?'

Timothy shook his head, his face set in grim, grey lines. We both straightened our legs and stood upright. 'You'll have to ask him that, chapman, because I don't know the answer. Not suspecting anything wrong, I naturally didn't question him.'

'But did His Grace really summon Master Arrowsmith?' I pressed.

Timothy flung wide his hands. 'Again, I don't know the answer. No one would have asked the duke, neither would His Grace have thought to enlighten us on such a matter.

For, as I say, the falls were simply put down to Lal's own carelessness.'

'But you don't think so now?'

Timothy shivered. 'No. Someone tried to injure Lionel seriously, and when he failed, made a second attempt, with more success on that occasion.' He drew a long, shuddering breath. 'And it demonstrates one thing most clearly, chapman – that Thaddeus Morgan was correct. The assassin is already installed within our ranks and waits only for the right moment to strike at His Grace.'

Chapter Nine

'That may be,' I said, 'but I doubt our murderer will strike until he's ready. And that means until he's certain he can do the deed and get clean away, or remain without falling under suspicion. For it's my experience that people who are prodigal with other people's lives are very loath to part with their own.' I thought for a moment before asking, 'Is there no possibility of persuading His Grace to rid his household of suspected persons? Of all those you mentioned to me last night, who are thought to be in the pay of other masters?'

'None whatsoever!' Timothy Plummer was adamant on that score. 'You've seen and spoken to the duke yourself and must realize how anxious he is to keep this matter quiet. A dismissal of five or six of his followers would draw everyone's attention to the fact that something was amiss.'

'Better that, surely,' I urged, 'than finding himself at the wrong end of an assassin's dagger or drinking from a poisoned chalice!'

Timothy dragged a hand through his thinning hair. 'Try telling that to His Grace. It may seem the sensible answer to you. It may seem the sensible answer to me. (Oh, yes! It's certainly what I'd do if I were allowed my way.) But these Plantagenets are an obstinate, high-stomached race; and my lord would no more let himself be cowed by a threat from an enemy than he'd take a knife to his lady mother and hold it at her throat.' Timothy glanced around, suddenly aware that we were perhaps talking too loudly and too freely. 'Ssh! Lower your voice. Fortunately, up here it's mostly sleeping quarters.'

'Where does that lead?' I asked, indicating a door in the wall behind us.

For answer, Timothy opened it and beckoned me into a small room no bigger than many a closet that I've seen in some great houses. Inside were two narrow pallets, on one of which the injured Lionel Arrowsmith was lying. He reared up on one elbow as we entered.

'What—?' he began, but Timothy, closing the door behind him, waved him to silence.

'Better we speak in here, where no one can overhear us. Lal, I've much to tell you, but be patient a moment. As you see, chapman, this room has been put at the disposal of those two of His Grace's Squires of the Body who are not on duty. The two who are sleep on truckle beds in His Grace's chamber. You can guess that, with two households sharing the castle, arrangements tend to be somewhat cramped.'

'The other three Squires of the Body,' I demanded, 'can they be trusted?'

Lionel Arrowsmith's glance was scornful. 'They've been in the service of His Grace as long as, and in two cases longer than, I have. Squires of the Body are the most carefully chosen of all a lord's servants, whoever the master. And amongst royalty they are the scions of families who have proved their loyalty over several generations. Now, what is it that you have to tell me?'

He listened with a gathering frown as, between us,

Timothy Plummer and I told him of our discovery: how the staircase immediately outside this room, which he had to descend in order to reach the duke, showed signs of having been booby-trapped in an effort to cripple him and so prevent his meeting with Thaddeus Morgan. When we had finished he hauled himself into a sitting position and reached for his crutch.

'The duke must not be left alone for an instant,' he said. 'One of the Squires *has* to be with him, and alert for danger, every moment, day and night. I must see His Grace urgently. He must be persuaded to admit the other three to his confidence.' Lionel chewed his underlip. 'At least this proves for certain that the rumours circulating among the Brotherhood, and brought to us by Thaddeus, have foundation.'

Timothy snorted. 'I had no lingering doubts of that once Thaddeus was murdered.'

'But how,' Lionel wondered, 'does our assassin know what we know? How did he find out where Thaddeus and I were to meet yesterevening?'

Timothy jerked his head towards me. 'Tell him, chapman!'

I repeated what I had seen the night before last at Holy Trinity Priory. 'So,' I finished, 'I misdoubt me now that the man, whoever he was, was a chance interloper like myself. Rather, he was someone who had followed you from Baynard's Castle.'

The Squire took the news as badly as I had feared he might, covering his face with his free hand and sinking into gloom.

'But it still doesn't explain,' Timothy remarked, lowering himself on to the second pallet, 'how our assassin came to know of the assignation at the Priory. You and I, Lal, have been most careful not to breathe a word to another soul, apart from the duke and, eventually, to young Matthew. And even he knew nothing of that particular meeting.'

Lionel made no response, but there was a less than whole-hearted agreement in the way he nodded that worried me. Did he have a sneaking fear that he had let slip something to someone who, in turn, could have passed on the information which might have alerted our murderer? I decided to keep a watchful eye on Master Arrowsmith, for it was plain that he had no intention of owning to the fault and Timothy, equally plainly, was unsuspicious of his friend.

I wondered, with an inward sigh, how anyone so unsuited to the job had come to be appointed Spy-Master General for the ducal household; then recollected that my lord of Gloucester himself profoundly despised, and had a contemptuous disregard for, the intrigues and seamier undercurrents of political life. The duke was a man of conscience who would hesitate before any but the simplest of white lies; rigid, unmalleable, as honest in all his dealings as it was possible to be in a court where dog ate dog, and which was dominated by the queen's conniving family; a man of stern, unyielding principles and therefore one who made bitter enemies; a man who carried the seeds of his own destruction within. For it seemed to me that if the duke were ever to betray those principles then he was finished; a man who could neither forgive, nor live with himself.

I could say none of this aloud, however. I asked, 'You are both perfectly certain that young Matthew Wardroper is to be trusted?'

Lionel reared his head and replied angrily, 'He is my kinsman! Are you daring to cast aspersions on the good name of my house?'

Timothy waved him to silence. 'That has nothing to say to the matter, Lal, and well you know it. There have been houses enough divided against themselves over the past twenty years. No, the point is, chapman, as I have already told you, that Thaddeus Morgan came to me with his story at the beginning of May, while we were resting at Northampton, on our way south from Middleham. Young Wardroper did not join us until after we had reached London from Canterbury at the beginning of June.'

This was a fact for which I could vouch. Had not Mistress Gentle, the Southampton butcher's wife, informed me on Thursday, the eighth of June, three days before the longest day, that 'Matthew set out for London this Monday past, to take up a position in the Duke of Gloucester's household'?

'And Thaddeus Morgan insisted from the start that the threat to His Grace's life lay within his own ménage,' Lionel corroborated icily.

'Then clearly Master Wardroper is exonerated from all suspicion,' I agreed. 'Is there anyone else in the duke's entourage of whom you can say the same? Apart from your two good selves,' I added on an ironic note, which seemed, however, to elude them.

'I think you may forget the other three Squires of the Body,' Timothy said after a judicious pause. 'And the steward. Aside from them, it might be unwise to advance any name with total confidence, although I would stake my life on the loyalty of nearly all the duke's retainers.'

'Also,' added Lionel, 'it would be well-nigh impossible

for you, chapman, to watch every member of the household. No, you'd best concentrate on those five we mentioned yesterday.' He looked sternly at me. 'Can you remember their names?'

'Refresh my memory,' I begged, unwilling to confess that I had no recollection of any of them.

'Very well.' Timothy Plummer began ticking them off on his fingers. 'Stephen Hudelin, Yeoman of the Chamber, whom we know for certain to be Lord Rivers's man, and so a spy for all the Woodvilles. Geoffrey Whitelock, Squire of the Household, who is probably in the pay of the king. (Not that I would suspect His Highness of plotting the death of his favourite brother. The very notion is absurd. But if Whitelock is in the pay of two masters, then why not a third?) Jocelin d'Hiver, a Burgundian, another Squire of the Household, who has given us some cause to think that he could be working for Duke Charles. Humphrey Nanfan, like Hudelin a Yeoman of the Chamber, formerly in the employ of the Duke of Clarence, but who apparently deserted to our own duke after some petty quarrel with a fellow servant. (I feel he needs watching. Once or twice in the past Duke George seems to have had prior knowledge of His Grace's plans.) And finally, Ralph Boyse, Squire of the Household, whose mother was a Frenchwoman who married one of His Grace's Middleham tenants. Five years ago, when King Edward and my lord were forced to flee for their lives to the Burgundian court, Ralph was amongst those who accompanied Duke Richard. King Louis's agents are everywhere, but particularly in Flanders. It might be possible that Ralph, who made little secret of his admiration for his mother's country, was persuaded to turn his coat and spy on our royal master.'

'Do you have any reason for thinking this is so?' I queried.

'I've no proof, if that's what you're asking. It's just a feeling that his sentiments underwent something of a sea change after we returned to England in that spring of 1471.'

'In what way?'

Timothy looked nonplussed for a moment, then shrugged. 'He was quieter, slyer, less eager to jump to the defence of all things French. At times he even went so far as to vilify them in no uncertain manner. But perhaps,' Timothy admitted candidly, 'it might never have occurred to me that he was trying to throw sand in our eyes had my predecessor in this job not put the idea into my head, when he resigned the office to me. "Watch Ralph Boyse," he said, and gave me his reasons. He was a shrewd man and I respected his judgement.'

Lionel began heaving himself to his feet. I rose and offered him my arm. 'I must go and beg an audience of the duke,' he panted, when at last he stood upright, disdaining my help and leaning heavily on his crutch, 'before he leaves for Westminster.'

'You'll not get him to alter his mind and tell the other Squires,' Timothy warned him. 'He was reluctant from the first even to allow you into my confidence. It was only after much persuasion that he agreed that one of you four should know. And now that our number has been enlarged by two, he'll be even more reluctant. However, if you're set on trying I wish you luck, because you'll need it. Wait, and I'll call a page to assist you down the stairs. And keep a sharp look-out. You don't want another accident.'

'Which reminds me, Master Arrowsmith,' I said, 'before you go there's a question I must ask you. On each occasion

119

when you fell, who had brought the message summoning you to wait upon the duke?'

Lionel looked astonished. 'Why, one of the pages of course! Who else would be employed to run such errands?'

'The same page both times?'

He furrowed his brow. 'I can't remember. Probably not. I shouldn't think so.'

'Then do you know the name of one, or either?' And when Lionel expressed indignation that he should be expected to recollect the names of any of the numerous pages who teemed about the place like rabbits in a warren I went on, curbing my impatience, 'But would you *recognize* one or both of them again?'

'I dare say I might do that,' he condescended.

'Then if you do, ask who it was who gave them the messages.'

Once more Lionel expressed surprise. 'Could it have been His Grace, do you suppose?' he asked with heavy sarcasm.

'It could have been,' I replied, keeping a tight rein on my temper. 'But if that should not be the case it would be interesting to know who did. And it would be even more interesting if it were to prove to be the same person on both occasions.'

'Ah!' He looked a little sheepish and his manner became a shade less abrasive. 'I see where your reasoning is leading.' And not before time, my fine master, I thought, but was careful to let nothing show in my face. 'Very well,' he continued, 'if I recognize either lad, or discover anything of note, I'll tell Master Plummer here and he will, in turn, pass it on to you. Because from henceforth, chapman, you are a mere Yeoman of the Chamber and it won't do for us to be seen gossiping together. Now, Tim, will you please send for someone to assist me to the duke? And chapman, stay out of sight until we've gone. Stand behind the door, where no one can see you.'

I did as I was bid and waited until a page had been summoned to assist Lionel to the duke's tiring chamber where, a broken treble informed us, His Grace was changing his clothes before his daily visit to his eldest brother. I waited hopefully for some exclamation of recognition on Lionel's part, but none came. Obviously this lad was not the page who had delivered one or both of the vital messages.

When the door was shut again upon us I turned to Timothy Plummer. 'In view of what Master Arrowsmith has just said it would also be as well if you and I are not seen too often together. It will only arouse suspicions if the protocol of the household is broken.'

Timothy nodded vigorously. 'Just what I was about to point out myself. But we must have a means of communicating with one another. Therefore I suggest we enlist young Matthew Wardroper. He's already in our confidence and only too anxious to be of help, and there will be nothing improper in a Yeoman of the Chamber approaching a Squire of the Household. Moreover, no eyebrows will be raised if Matt is seen in frequent conversation with Lionel, who is known to be his kinsman. So if you have anything to impart, or a message of any urgency, you will inform young Wardroper, who will tell Lionel, who will pass it on to me. I shall reverse the process to get in touch with you. Now, is that quite clear?'

'Perfectly,' I assured him. 'But I have serious misgivings as to how I shall perform in my new office.'

Timothy dismissed my fears with an airy gesture of the hands. 'Nonsense! You'll soon learn. Just watch the other Chamber Yeomen and do as they do. And no one will expect a greenhorn to do everything right first time. Now, I'll take you to the steward. Remember, he only knows what my lord duke has told him, that you are being rewarded by a position in the ménage for previous services rendered to His Grace.'

I pulled down the corners of my mouth. 'Then I shall pray that I solve this problem swiftly, not just for Duke Richard's sake, but also for my own. The sooner I'm back on the open road again and under no man's jurisdiction, the happier I shall be.'

Timothy laughed. 'I'm not surprised you quit the cloister, chapman. A man who can't abide any discipline but what he chooses for himself would never have made a monk.' He set a hand to the door-latch. 'By the way, your pack has been fetched from Philip Lamprey's and has been stored for the time being in a closet near my room. However, before we go to France next Tuesday I'll make sure it finds a more permanent resting place until you can reclaim it.'

I stared at him, suddenly uneasy. 'Before we go to France?' I echoed.

'Unless, of course, you've resolved the mystery by then. If not, then I fear you must go with us, unless you desire to wash your hands of the matter. Which would be your right if you chose to do so.'

'No . . . no.' I shook my head slowly. I could not possibly abandon Duke Richard to his fate, as long as it might lie within my power to prevent the harm which threatened to befall him. But I had not foreseen a journey to France. Foolish of me, no doubt, for it had been repeated a number of times within my hearing that the royal brothers would cross the Channel on the fourth of July. And today was Wednesday, the twenty-eighth of June . . . It seemed highly improbable, however, that I should have found an answer to the riddle by then. Yet my time was limited. The Eve of Saint Hyacinth was only seven weeks distant.

'Very well!' Timothy sounded relieved. 'You must be prepared to cross to France with the rest of the household. Now, follow me and I'll take you to the steward's apartment.'

It was the first time that I had seen at close quarters the workings of a lord's great household or had any understanding of the vast numbers of people necessary to his welfare. The knowledge did not come all at once, and I never mastered all the intricacies, but by the end of three days I was beginning to have a rough idea of who people were and of their various functions.

The steward, who carried a white wand to signify his standing in the hierarchy, the treasurer and the comptroller were the three most important officers. After them came the Knights and Squires of the Body, companions, friends and intimates of their lord, as well as servants. The Squires of the Household, of whom Matthew Wardroper was one, rode and hunted with the duke, waited upon him at table and provided, when necessary, entertainment, either with conversation, by playing a musical instrument or by singing. Next came the Gentlemen Ushers, whose job it was to enforce protocol, and then the Yeomen of the Chamber, which now included myself among their number, and whose duties were those explained to me by Timothy Plummer. At the bottom of the heap, pages and

Grooms of the Chamber tended fires, made beds and generally kept things clean, with particular injunctions laid upon them to ensure that the rooms were free of dog droppings. I could only feel thankful that, between them, the duke and Timothy had seen fit to raise me to a slightly more elevated station.

In addition, the royal ménage boasted cofferers and surveyors; a Doctor of Physic, a Master Surgeon, a barber and his underlings; minstrels, clerks, chaplains and chapel children; a Sergeant of Confectionery, of Ewery and Napery and a Yeoman of the Laundry; cooks, bakers, butchers, spicers and attendants of the buttery, who were supposed to know all that there was to know about wines. There were others, whose names and functions I can no longer remember, but who all played their part in keeping the Duke of Gloucester's household running smoothly.

I was told that, in fact, fewer than half of the duke's lesser retainers had come south with him from Middleham, but the number was daunting, none the less; particularly when I considered that, in theory at least, the would-be assassin could be any one of them. I was indebted for the information to Humphrey Nanfan, whose acquaintance I had hastened to make after I had been left with my fellow Yeomen of the Chamber. He was, I judged, a couple of years older than myself, with a mop of thick, carelessly cropped brown hair, grey eyes and, outwardly at any rate, the jollity which is generally associated with people of his build and stature. He was not really fat, just short and rounded, girth and height together giving the impression of a greater corpulence than he deserved. I soon discovered that he was the butt of the other Yeomen, who teased him unmercifully about the amount of food he ate; again

124

undeservedly for, after observing him closely at several mealtimes, I noted that although he piled his plate high with victuals, the greater part of them went into the charity bowls for the beggars. He also gave the impression of being stupider and slower than he was and, in between bouts of good-natured clowning, would sit still and silent, forgotten temporarily by his peers, but alert and observant of everything and everyone around him. He was the man suspected by Timothy Plummer of being a spy for George of Clarence and, while I could imagine that it might very likely be the case, I could not bring myself to believe that the duke, any more than the king, would order the killing of his own brother. And for what reason?

It was true that he and my lord of Gloucester had married sisters and had a mother-in-law in common. But cautious inquiries elicited the fact that the Countess of Warwick's lands had already been divided between her daughters' husbands, just as though she were dead, the Act of Settlement having been finally confirmed in Parliament only four months earlier. And the greater share of the estates had gone to the Duke of Clarence. So there was no cause on brother George's part that I could see for resentment. Besides, why would he insist that the killing should take place before the Eve of Saint Hyacinth? There was no sensible explanation for that, and I was more than half inclined to erase Humphrey Nanfan from my list of suspects there and then. But wisdom had taught me that nothing was ever exactly as it seemed and there might well be other reasons for my lord of Clarence to harbour a grudge against his brother. It behoved me, therefore, to keep an eye out for Master Nanfan, however much I would have wagered that he was not our assassin.

125

The other Yeoman of the Chamber mentioned by Timothy was Stephen Hudelin, the only one of the five that he called a spy without conjecture. Anthony Woodville, Earl Rivers, eldest brother of the queen, was named his paymaster; and although this might, in itself, have been sufficient to make me take Stephen Hudelin in dislike, it was not necessary. I disliked him on sight, from the moment of our very first meeting.

Chapter Ten

Stephen Hudelin was, I judged, somewhere in his middle thirties, thickset without being squat, the top of his head reaching well above my shoulders. He had red hair in which there was not a trace of brown, so that his fiery pate was visible wherever he was, indoors or out, and his eyes were a greenish hazel. I soon discovered that he had the quick temper which went with his colouring, but which, in general, he was forced to subdue, a necessity which left him in an almost permanent state of truculence. It also became obvious that the other Yeomen of the Chamber, or at least those who had accompanied the Duke of Gloucester south on this expedition, did not much like him. They were wary, however, of his bouts of ill-humour, treating him with an off-hand civility which excluded him from their fellowship far more effectively than picking a quarrel could have done.

I learned from Humphrey that the Hudelins had been in the service of Sir John Grey, Lord Ferrers of Groby, the queen's first husband and sire to her two eldest sons. The Greys, and therefore the Hudelins, had supported the House of Lancaster, and both Lord Ferrers and Walter Hudelin, Stephen's father, had been killed at the second battle at Saint Albans, fighting for the late King Henry.

When, however, King Edward's fancy had settled on Lord Ferrers's widow, the Hudelins, like the new queen's own family, the Woodvilles, had found no difficulty in changing sides and becoming staunch followers of the House of York. Their loyalty, in common with that of so many, was not to a cause but to the masters they had served for generations, now embodied in the young Marquess of Dorset and his brother, Lord Richard Grey, and in Anthony Woodville, their maternal uncle.

'How does Stephen come to be in the service of the Duke of Gloucester?' I asked Humphrey as he instructed me in the laying of the dinner-table.

My mentor shrugged. 'Why shouldn't he be? There's no law of the Medes and the Persians which says a man may not move from one place to another if he so wishes. Perhaps Stephen wanted a change and Lord Rivers recommended him to His Grace, for he's a good enough worker and pulls his weight. I myself was previously with my lord of Clarence, but fell out with a fellow servant and wished to find another berth. His Grace used his influence with his brother and here I have been, very happily, ever since.'

I made no answer, keeping my thoughts to myself, and concentrating instead on Humphrey's instructions concerning the protocol of place settings. The raised dais at the end of the hall, facing the musicians' gallery, was easy: the duke and his mother, the Duchess of York, would sit beneath the canopies with other persons of note on either side of them.

'The table to the host's right,' Humphrey explained, 'the one against *that* wall, is known as the Reward, because people at the head of it are served with the same dishes as the lord and his guests. The table opposite, to the host's left, is called the Second Mess, and the people sitting there mostly get the same food as the upper servants. And in both cases, the lower you sit down the board, the further away from the dais you are and the nearer to the kitchens, the coarser the victuals. Wooden plates and spoons below the salt, pewter above it. Trenchers of bread for all, with smaller ones to heap the salt on. While we're here in Baynard's Castle, we keep the same hours as the Duchess Cicely: breakfast at seven, dinner at eleven and supper at five o'clock, although at home, at Middleham or Sheriff Hutton, the duke likes his meals somewhat earlier.' Then, without being asked, he provided the information which interested me most. 'Members of the household have their meals beforehand.'

I breathed an inward sigh of relief. The prospect of having to watch others eat whilst suffering the pangs of hunger myself would have been more than I could bear. At least now I knew that I should be comfortably replete and, consequently, alert to those scraps of gossip or information which can often be gleaned where people are gathered together and off their guard. I tried not to dwell on the impossibility of the task I had been set, nor on the vulnerability of any man in the public eye to the poisoned chalice or the assassin's dagger. I could only do my best and trust the hand of God to guide me.

There were still three other suspects whose acquaintance I had not yet made, all of whom were Squires of the Household, and in order to identify them I had to rely on Matthew Wardroper. For this purpose, we both kept an eye cocked for one another whenever we crossed a courtyard or sped from one chamber to the next, along the passageways or up and down the stairs. The first time we met, after I had been supplied with a suit of livery, he gave way to unseemly mirth.

'It's too small for you,' he hooted. 'You're bursting out of that tunic in all directions.'

'Of course it's too small,' I snapped, losing my sense of humour. 'How many men of my height do you think His Grace employs? But I've been promised that a sewing woman from Duchess Cicely's household will lengthen it and let out the seams. Now, stop that foolish sniggering and tell me what news you have, if any.'

We were standing in the inner courtyard, half concealed by one of the pillars of a colonnade, which supported part of the building's upper storeys. We drew back a little further into the shadows.

'None of any moment,' Matthew sighed, 'but by a stroke of good fortune, Ralph Boyse, Jocelin d'Hiver, Geoffrey Whitelock and myself are all four on duty tonight at supper. If you can also contrive to be on hand I'll try to point them out to you. What of your two fellow Yeomen?'

'Little enough as yet. I know who they are and am ready and willing to believe the worst of Stephen Hudelin. On the other hand, if Humphrey Nanfan were to be proved innocent of the charge of being in my lord of Clarence's employ I should be happy. I like him. However,' I added on a grimmer note, 'my judgement is not always sound. I have in the past liked – and in one case more than liked – those who have turned out to be rogues and villains. Do you have a message for me from Timothy Plummer or Master Arrowsmith?'

The dark eyes darted this way and that, making certain that no one was within earshot.

'Only that the former was for once mistaken, and the

duke, after great persuasion from my cousin Lionel, has allowed his three other Squires of the Body to be admitted into the secret. They are, apparently, considered to be above suspicion, with the result that His Grace is far more closely guarded than ever before. Master Plummer now considers it possible that, luck being on our side, we can reach the Eve of Saint Hyacinth without harm befalling Duke Richard, even if you are unsuccessful in discovering the would-be assassin.'

'Which is more than possible,' I answered gloomily. I knotted my brows. 'But why, oh why, the Eve of Saint Hyacinth? For by then the duke will be in France, fighting.'

'It was only what Master Plummer was told by Thaddeus Morgan,' Matthew pointed out. 'A rumour which, perhaps, may have been false. We don't even know for certain that there *is* any plot to kill my lord of Gloucester.'

'Then why was Thaddeus Morgan killed?' I shook my head. 'No, no! I think we have to accept the truth of the story.' I ran one hand despairingly through my hair. 'If only we could find a motive for someone – anyone! – wanting to murder His Grace! I still refuse to believe that either of his royal brothers would wish him dead for any reason. The Burgundians are our allies. And surely the French would prefer King Edward's death to that of the Duke of Gloucester. This invasion seems to be purely on his whim.'

Matthew Wardroper heard me out in sympathetic silence, but could offer no solution to the problem beyond observing that the French were unlikely to order the murder of an English monarch for such a cause. 'For every ruler of this country dreams of winning back the Norman and Angevin lands of his ancestors and no doubt will continue to do so for generations to come. To assassinate King Edward might scotch the snake, but would not kill it, and the French are surely clever enough to know that. But in any case,' he finished with a shrug, 'it's not His Highness's life that's threatened.'

Sadly I agreed, and we parted to go about our various duties. 'I shall look out for you tonight in the great hall,' I called over my shoulder.

And thus it was, not watching where I was going, that I bumped into a young woman who had just emerged from an archway on my right and who was breathless from hurriedly descending a steep flight of stairs. I turned quickly to apologize and found myself looking down into a pert, rounded face with the complexion of a peach, widely-spaced hazel eyes, at present brimming with laughter, and a good-humoured mouth which curled up naturally at the corners. She was small and delicately boned, with little hands and feet, and her features reminded me of someone; someone, moreover, whom I had met not all that long ago.

'Forgive me,' I said. 'I wasn't watching where I was going.'

To my surprise, she continued to clutch at me. 'The fault was mine,' she insisted. 'But please don't run away, because I think you must be the man I'm looking for. With that height and these clothes, you can only be Roger Chapman, my lord of Gloucester's new Yeoman of the Chamber.'

I acknowledged the fact cautiously, particularly as I suspected that I was an object of some amusement to her. 'Who are you and why should anyone give you my description?' I wanted to know.

'My name is Amice Gentle, sewing-woman to the Duchess of York, and I was told that your tunic is in need of alteration.' She gurgled with laughter. 'And indeed, I can see that it is. I must take some measurements. Come with me to the sewing-room so that I can see more easily what needs to be done.' And so saying, she turned and whisked away again, up the stairs.

Gentle; Amice Gentle; I said the name over to myself as I followed in her wake. Then, of course, I remembered. She was the daughter of the Southampton butcher and his wife.

The room into which she led me was lit by a generous number of candles, for the daylight, even at the height of summer, was poor, filtering in through three small, unshuttered windows, set only in the outer wall. Five or six other young women, some sitting, some standing, were busy at two long trestle tables which ran the length of the room. Two were working on an elaborate piece of embroidery which, at a cursory glance and judging by the subject matter, I guessed to be an altar cloth. The rest were stitching away at various garments, mending rents, darning holes or resetting hems; the sort of good, plain sewing which is a necessity of every household, however humble, but especially in one as large as Duchess Cicely's was in those days.

Several of the women glanced up from their work as we entered, at first with indifference, but then with growing hilarity as they took in my height and the shortness and tightness of my azure-and-murrey tunic. I tried to make myself as inconspicuous as possible, but with little success.

Amice introduced me. 'My lord of Gloucester's new Yeoman of the Chamber. The Sergeant of Livery had nothing that would fit him, and as the duke has brought no sewing-women in his train we've been asked to help. Take the tunic off, Master Chapman, and sit down if you can spare a moment, while I begin unpicking the seams and hem.'

I did as I was bid and seated myself on the end of one of the wooden benches. I knew that I should probably have been helping to oversee the laying of the dinner-tables, or on call in case the duke desired a message to be run; but I was in no fear of dismissal for my negligence, however vociferously my fellow Yeomen might complain. Whatever excuses were needed to explain my behaviour, they would be found.

One or two of the girls eyed me flirtatiously, but the arrival of the head seamstress quickly put paid to all such nonsense, for which I was very glad.

'Was that Matt Wardroper you were speaking to?' Amice Gentle asked, the point of one of her scissor blades slashing at the threads of the tunic's hem and seams.

'Yes,' I said. 'Of course, you know him. I was forgetting.' And in answer to her inquiring stare, I explained how I had eaten at her parents' shop some four weeks earlier, adding, 'While I was still a pedlar. Before I decided I had had enough of life on the open road and came to beg a return of favour from the duke. Your mother spoke of you and her pride in your situation. She also spoke of young Matthew Wardroper.'

'Well! Fancy that, now!' she exclaimed. 'It's a small enough world, I reckon. But as for knowing Matthew Wardroper well, that I don't. But I've heard him talked about since my youth. There were always servants from Chilworth Manor in and out of Southampton and many of them came to Father's shop, both to buy and to fill their bellies. Naturally, they mentioned Master Matthew, as well as Sir Cedric and his lady.' She ripped out a final piece of thread and held the tunic up to the light of the nearest candle. 'I'm ready to start restitching when I've measured you. I'm afraid you'll have to stand up, or I can't do it.' When I had complied, Amice passed a narrow strip of material around my body, first around my chest and then my waist, snipping each piece off at the requisite length. While she did so she went on chatting. 'Of course, I've seen Sir Cedric and Lady Wardroper many times when they've visited Southampton, but Matthew I never saw as a child. He was sent away soon after he reached his seventh birthday.'

'To somewhere in Leicestershire, I understand.' Obediently, I raised an arm on her instructions.

Amice hunched her shoulders. 'I dare say, although I honestly can't remember. In fact, I'd forgotten all about him until we came here from Berkhamsted with my lady. Quite by chance, I heard a member of the duke's household mention his name one day.' She began to pin up the dismembered tunic and I resumed my seat on the bench. 'Later, I got someone to point him out to me.

'Would you have recognized him anyway, do you think?'

'There was something familiar about him. He has the same delicate features and dark colouring as his mother, although he has his father's eyes. Sir Cedric is much stouter.'

I nodded. 'Yes, you're right. At least, about Matthew resembling Lady Wardroper. I haven't met Sir Cedric.' Once again, Amice sent me a glance of interrogation and I had to explain my visit to Chilworth Manor. A sudden thought occurred to me. 'Do you know the lands thereabouts?' I asked her.

Ignoring my question for the moment she bade me rise once more while she fitted me with the loosely pinned tunic. At last, satisfied, she eased the garment from my shoulders and laid it out on the table, then broke off a length of linen thread and inserted it into the eye of her needle.

'Can you remain while this is done?' she wanted to know. 'Or are you needed?'

'I'll wait for you to finish,' I said boldly, although uneasily aware that the head seamstress was watching us, suspicious of my protracted stay.

The needle whipped in and out of the cloth, making a row of tiny stitches, exquisite in their neatness and precision. After a moment or two I repeated my question. The hazel eyes opened wide and the soft mouth was pursed in consideration.

'Around Chilworth Manor?' Amice shook her head. 'I never went there above a couple of times, to help out with the sewing when one of the women was sick. True, I've made the journey between Chilworth and Southampton, but I couldn't describe it to you. Now if you asked me about the town it would be a different matter.'

'No,' I answered. 'I wanted to know about the land to the north of the manor. Have you ever at any time heard mention of a deserted shrine in the woods? Think carefully.'

She did so, even pausing momentarily in her sewing and frowning. But the result was merely another shake of the head.

'Never,' she answered. 'But I don't suppose such things

are uncommon. I've heard my granddam say that whole villages were wiped out by the Great Death and that the buildings fell into decay. Some were never rebuilt, while others were built again in different places. Why do you want to know? Is it important?'

'No,' I said, recalled by her question to a realization of just how unimportant and irrelevant was this petty, personal concern. Indeed, looking back it was difficult to understand the sense of evil which had gripped me in that woodland clearing. So much had happened since that it had almost faded from my mind.

'You could ask Matthew Wardroper,' Amice suggested, snapping the thread between strong, white teeth.

'So I could,' I agreed. 'And so I might, if I remember.'

Our conversation languished as she bent again to her task, a fact which appeared to please the head seamstress, who now withdrew her gaze and went to oversee the work on the altar cloth. I debated with myself whether or not to return to my work without the tunic, but finally decided against it. Surely I should not be welcomed on duty only half dressed and in any case, Amice would soon be finished. I had never before met anyone who could sew so fast.

'What made you give up peddling?' she asked suddenly, completing the second seam and turning her attention to the hem.

'I – er – just tired ... of the wandering life,' I lied and swiftly changed the subject. 'Does the duchess remain here long?'

'Only until next Wednesday, the day after the king and his brothers leave for France.'

France! I had temporarily forgotten that dread word and

the prospect of accompanying the duke across the Channel. It was more than I had bargained for when I had let myself become entangled in this mesh. That I could unmask our villain within the next few days, provided that he himself did not strike first, was an impossible dream; and yet again the futility of searching for a needle in a haystack struck me most forcibly. There was nothing to confirm that any one of the five men named by Timothy Plummer was the would-be killer. How foolishly optimistic our assumption suddenly appeared. But what else had we to go on?

'You've grown very serious,' Amice remarked, looking up from her sewing with a friendly smile. 'Do you find the duties of your position so weighty?'

I returned the smile, realizing all at once how pretty she was.

'Your mother,' I said, 'didn't oversing your praises.'

It took her a moment to catch my meaning, but when she understood she laughed and blushed with pleasure.

'Oh, you don't want to take any notice of Mother!' she disclaimed hastily. 'She's very partial.'

'Not without good reason. You're like her,' I added.

'So people say.' We were both talking at random now in order to cover our embarrassment, as we became aware of the flowering of an unexpected mutual attraction. Amice hurried on, 'I can't see it myself. Oh, I'm small, as she is, but I've always thought I have something of my father in me.' In her sudden agitation she pricked one of her fingers with her needle, exclaimed with annoyance and sucked away the tiny bead of blood.

I had half reached out for her hand, to reassure myself that she had done herself no lasting injury, when I recollected how foolish I was being and withdrew it. Amice quickly fastened off her thread, stuck her needle, alongside several others, in the bodice of her gown, stood up and shook out my tunic.

'There,' she said, handing it to me, but avoiding my eyes, 'see if that's any better.

The tunic, if not a perfect fit, was certainly more comfortable than it had been before and would make me look less ridiculous in the eyes of my fellow Yeomen.

'Thank you,' I said simply.

The colour crept into her cheeks again. 'Bring it back if you have time to spare before next Tuesday and I'll lengthen the sleeves.' Again I received an unpleasant jolt at the reminder of my journey across the Channel and an even greater one when she went on in a subdued tone, 'War is a fearsome thing. God keep you safe.'

Until that second it had not entered my head that I might be called upon to fight and it only required another moment or two before common sense told me that it was highly unlikely. The Knights and Squires of the Body were a different matter, but the domestic servants of the royal households would merely be deployed in attending to the comfort of their masters behind the lines of battle.

I felt, however, that there was no need to disclose this fact to Amice and continued to bask in the warmth of her concern. As none of the other seamstresses was, at that moment, looking our way, I possessed myself of one of her hands and, lifting it to my lips, gently kissed it. She glanced up, startled, blushed fiercely, then went very pale and removed her fingers from my grasp. Her earlier coquettish air had quite deserted her. She jumped when the head seamstress raised her voice.

'Amice! If you have finished the Yeoman's tunic you are

wanted over here. We need your skill on this altar cloth. No one can set the more difficult stitches as well as you can.'

'Coming, Mistress Vernon.' Amice sent me one last upward glance from beneath her lashes, then turned and hurried towards the little group of women at the far end of the table.

She refused to look my way again and there was nothing left for me to do but return to my duties and my problems.

Chapter Eleven

No one complained about my prolonged absence, or if they did, I did not hear them. I caught one or two resentful murmurs when I finally presented myself for duty to the head Yeoman of the Chamber, but nothing was said overtly; a fact which, on reflection, I found a little disturbing. Was there a feeling among my fellow workers that I was somehow different? Not truly one of them? A sense that I was there under false pretences? If so, was our would-be assassin also alerted to the possibility that I was not what I seemed? And would he therefore suspect my real purpose? I tried not to think about it and to throw myself so whole-heartedly into my duties that all such suspicions would be stillborn.

I encountered no difficulty in securing the honour of waiting upon the duke at supper that evening, other Yeomen being only too pleased to exchange the boredom of office for a few hours of leisure in which to do as they pleased. And I was presented with an extra bonus when I discovered that Humphrey Nanfan and Stephen Hudelin had also been chosen to attend His Grace. If Matthew were right, and Ralph Boyse, Jocelin d'Hiver and Geoffrey Whitelock were present as well, I should have them all under my eye at once, which would at least give me an hour or so's ease of mind as far as our five chief suspects were concerned.

As Humphrey had promised, the officers of the household ate an hour earlier than the duke and his guests and this afternoon, as usual, we were seated, according to our proper stations, at the tables in the great hall. The two which ran along the north- and south-facing walls had been augmented by extra trestles in the centre of the room in order to accommodate the Duchess of York's servants as well as her son's. As we sat down to supper at four o'clock, my eyes searched the ranks of Duchess Cicely's women for a glimpse of Amice Gentle. I saw her at last, at a table lower than my own, and raised a hand in greeting. She inclined her head in acknowledgement of my salute, but even at that distance I gained the impression that she would rather I had not made it. She turned away quickly to speak to the girl sitting beside her.

Feeling rebuffed, my eyes came to rest on one of the handful of household women who had come south in the Duke of Gloucester's train: a girl of commanding presence and lovely to look at. It was not possible to make out her colouring, but I could see that the face framed by the snow-white hood was a delicate oval and the mouth full-lipped and sensual.

Humphrey, who had stationed himself next to me on the bench and who seemed to have constituted himself my guardian angel, dug me in the ribs with his elbow. 'That's Berys Hogan,' he hissed, 'nursemaid to the Lady Katherine, His Grace's bastard daughter. The child has come to pay a visit to her grandmother and will return with the duchess to Berkhamsted after we've sailed for France.'

I knitted my brows. 'Berys Hogan,' I repeated. 'Why does that name sound familiar to me?'

The servers were coming round with our meal: being a Friday, it was fish.

Humphrey, picking up his knife and spoon, chuckled. 'Well, it wouldn't be surprising if the gossip had reached your ears, even in such short space of time as this. The beautiful Berys is betrothed to Ralph Boyse, that fellow sitting over there among the Squires of the Household, but she's cuckolding him with Lionel Arrowsmith. Lionel's one of the duke's four Body Squires and is easily spotted. He's the one who looks as if he's been to the wars already.'

I did not bother glancing in Lionel's direction, but instead divided what attention I could spare from my plate between Ralph Boyse and Berys Hogan. Ralph, as far as I could tell, was a slender young man, about the same age as the duke and myself, with very black hair and a sallowish complexion. Even had I not already been told that his mother was French I think I should have suspected the presence of foreign blood in his veins, for he was too swarthy to be wholly English. His expression was close and secret, the handsome face set in sullen, unsmiling lines. But then, in response to a remark from his neighbour, he laughed and was suddenly transformed, reminding me forcibly of the duke himself, whose natural severity of feature could be lightened beyond all expectation by a moment of humour.

So now I could recognize Ralph Boyse and it only needed Matthew Wardroper to identify the other two this evening. I suppose I could have asked Humphrey Nanfan there and then to point out Jocelin d'Hiver and Geoffrey Whitelock, but I had no wish to arouse his curiosity by displaying an unnecessary interest in them. Besides, I was content for the present to observe Ralph Boyse, who in his turn was watching the exchange of glances between Berys Hogan and Lionel Arrowsmith without apparently seeming to do so. Several times during the course of the meal Lionel raised his beaker in Berys's direction, whereupon she cast down her eyes in what could have been mistaken for maidenly confusion had her shoulders not been shaking with ill-concealed merriment. Furthermore, she was not averse, I noted, to sending him looks that could only be described as encouraging, a sly smile curving the sensuous lips. I recalled Timothy's admonitions of Tuesday night and his warning that Lionel was playing a dangerous game. And now that I knew, as I had not known then, that Berys was one of the maids in charge of His Grace's daughter, I felt that Lionel was being even more foolhardy than I had previously thought him. If trouble flared, he would incur the duke's wrath as well as that of Ralph Boyse.

The meal was drawing to an end and the servers were already waiting impatiently to clear the tables (and put away the extra trestles) preparatory to laying them again for the duke and those people who had been invited to share his supper. As we were hastily swallowing the last morsels of food and gulping down the dregs of our wine, the steward rose and fussily banged on the floor with his wand of office. When he had everyone's attention he addressed us.

'Tomorrow night, His Grace the Duke of Gloucester and Her Grace, the Duchess of York, will give a banquet and masquerade in honour of Their Highnesses King Edward and Queen Elizabeth, His Grace the Duke of Clarence and other esteemed guests. All Squires and Yeomen, without exception, will be required on duty and everyone will be expected to give of his best. You will assemble here, in the great hall, tomorrow morning before breakfast, to receive your instructions.' And with that, the steward nodded majestically and quit the hall with a slow and measured gait.

As soon as he had disappeared from view there was a general groan of dismay.

'A pre-embarkation feast and entertainment,' sighed Humphrey Nanfan. 'We might have guessed. Well, I suppose we did, but hoped that either the king or my lord Clarence would play host instead.'

'What does it mean?' I asked in my ignorance.

Stephen Hudelin, rising from his place just across the board from us, spat into the rushes. 'It means damned hard work, that's what it means,' he said.

I glanced at Humphrey, who nodded gloomily. 'We'll be run off our feet,' he confirmed. 'Meantime, we'd better get on and see that everything's in order for His Grace's supper. No good worrying about tomorrow until it arrives.'

The sleeping quarters for the Duke of Gloucester's Yeomen of the Chamber was a narrow, stuffy room in one of the towers. Here, eleven of us, the ten who had come with His Grace from Middleham and myself, slept close together on straw palliasses and kept our worldly goods – razors, soap, clean shirts and so forth – in linen bags which we stored beneath our pillows. Such spare time as we had was spent, therefore, in close proximity to our fellows, so it was just as well that our duties kept us busy. (Humphrey Nanfan assured me that normal sleeping conditions at Middleham or Sheriff Hutton or any other of the duke's seats of

residence were better than our temporary lodgings here at
Baynard's Castle; but nothing he said inspired in me the
wish to give up my chosen life for the transitory importance
of counting myself among the personal servants of a royal
household.)

Finding that I had a few free moments between my own
supper and that of the duke, and having drunk too much
wine, I went to the privy to answer nature's call. Then, the
dormitory being near at hand, I decided to change my shirt,
the day having been hot and sticky and my activities
strenuous. I entered the room expecting it to be full of
those Yeomen not on duty, but the warm weather had
tempted them out of doors to savour the coolness of late
afternoon. All but one, that is, and that one was crouched
low over the mattress where I slept and was rifling through
the contents of my bag. So intent was he upon his task that
he did not hear me enter, so I crept up behind him and laid a
hand on his shoulder. Stephen Hudelin let out a yelp and
sprang clumsily to his feet.

'I thought,' I said grimly, 'that you were still in the great
hall, helping Humphrey Nanfan. Instead I discover you
here, looking through my things. What was it you were
hoping to find?'

'N-nothing,' he stuttered. 'That is ... I thought you'd
gone to the garderobe. That's what you said.'

'So you decided to take the opportunity to search my
bag. I repeat, for what reason? What did you think you'd
find?'

'I ... I need a shave and I've mislaid my razor. There was
... no time to ask anyone's permission and ... and so I
thought you wouldn't mind if I borrowed yours.' A little of
his confidence returned with what he considered to be a

fairly plausible explanation and he added belligerently, 'You don't, do you, chapman?'

'A chapman no longer,' I answered calmly, ignoring the bait. 'No, I don't mind. Here!' I stooped and picked out the razor from the pile of belongings which had been emptied on to the floor. The last thing I must do was to feed Stephen's suspicions by even so much as hinting that I disbelieved him. 'Take it and welcome. You'll just have time to shave before we're needed on duty. Do you have soap? I've some of the cheap, black, Bristol kind if you want it.'

He shook his head and the eyes beneath the shock of red hair seemed to burn, just for a second, with the same bright colour. I proceeded to strip off my tunic and change my shirt while he stood irresolute, swaying slightly on the balls of his feet, my razor clutched in one hand. He was trying desperately to guess what was going on inside my head, baffled by my apparent acceptance of his story and my good-natured reaction to it. Finally, he threw down the razor with an imprecation and muttered that he had, after all, decided not to shave. He stomped out of the room, flinging over his shoulder, 'You'd better hurry! It's almost five o'clock!'

I threaded the last of my shirt laces through the corresponding eyelets in the top of my hose and wondered exactly what Master Hudelin had thought to discover? Proof that I was not really a chapman but an agent of the duke? (If that were so, then, ironically, he was both wrong and right at one and the same time.) And what else had he hoped to report to his Woodville masters? That somehow, somewhere, someone had got wind of their plot to murder Duke Richard?

But would the queen's family be so foolhardy in the first place as to try to arrange the duke's death? Would they dare risk forfeiting the king's bounty and goodwill on which all their prosperity depended? And if so, what reason could be powerful enough to make them do so?

That one question, 'why?', haunted me, for its answer held the key to our killer's identity. The need for the Duke of Gloucester's death – and his death, moreover, before the Eve of Saint Hyacinth – would unlock the door to the mystery. I replaced my tunic and laced it slowly, but no sudden illumination came to lighten my darkness.

I followed in Stephen Hudelin's wake and ran down the twisting staircase which led to the minstrels' gallery above the great hall. On the landing half-way down, I had to flatten myself against the wall in order to allow three men-at-arms to pass me. They ascended leisurely, according me no more than a cursory glance, and indifferent to the fact that they were keeping me waiting. Behind me was a door, giving access to a small chamber which opened off the landing; and it was only when the first man, a huge fellow with broad shoulders, came abreast of me and I was forced back even further, that I realized it was ajar. It creaked inwards a fraction, causing me to stagger and cling on to the latch-handle for support before I could regain my balance. The leading man-at-arms sniggered and the other two grinned, but I was barely conscious of their amusement. I was only aware of the sudden quiet caused by the cessation of urgent, sibilant, conspiratorial whispering, which I must have been listening to for the last few moments without realizing that I was doing so. All sound had stopped abruptly with the movement of the door and I could almost hear the breath-held silence within the room behind me.

Foolishly, as it turned out, I waited for the men-at-arms to disappear around the bend in the stairs, before pushing the door wide and entering the chamber.

The room was empty. Small as it was, it boasted a second door, set in the opposite wall. I reached this in a couple of strides, flinging it open, but there was no one to be seen. Another staircase, no wider than the shoulders of a slender man and unlit by even the faintest gleam of torchlight, descended into the bowels of the castle. Turning sideways, and with my hands splayed against the roughness of the wall, I cautiously eased myself down three or four twisting, slippery steps before deciding that I had embarked upon a fruitless errand. Wherever they led, I should not find my quarry now. The two people who had been in such earnest consultation would have mingled with their fellows, lost in the ant-hill of activity which was Baynard's Castle.

I retraced my steps, pausing only to cast a brief and unhopeful glance around the chamber. But apart from a single chair there was nothing in it. The floor was innocent of rushes and a coating of dust lay everywhere, indicating that the room was rarely, if ever, used and I remembered how the door hinges had creaked beneath my weight. I stood, racking my brains, trying to recall some word or phrase which might have penetrated my consciousness, but nothing came. All that remained was an impression of urgency and, above all, secrecy, borne out by the rapidity with which the whisperers had vanished when threatened with discovery.

Had it been two men talking? A man and a woman? Two women, even? (No, not the last. Of that I was certain without knowing exactly why.) Of course, it might have been a wholly innocent meeting between two members of either household. But then, if so, why had they so precipitately fled? I sighed. With nothing resolved, but possessed of the strong conviction that had I been quicker to enter the room I should have discovered something of the greatest importance, I descended to the great hall to take up my duties at the supper table.

I was abstracted during the meal, failing to perform my duties properly and, on several occasions, incurring the wrath of the head Yeoman of the Chamber. Twice at least, I encountered Duke Richard's quizzical glance, the faint arching of the thin, black eyebrows, but he made no comment, not even when, on bended knee, I offered him a dish of prawns in mustard and then withdrew it before he had had time to take any. It was only Humphrey Nanfan's horrified gasp, and the Lady Katherine Plantagenet's gurgle of delighted laughter, that brought me to my senses. Red with embarrassment, I quickly rectified my mistake and withdrew to the back of the dais to await the arrival of the next course from the kitchens. Nevertheless, I thought, I must try to have an urgent word with Timothy Plummer. The duke should be told to treat me as he would the other servants, or their already burgeoning suspicion would flower into certainty.

In spite of my frequent errors, however, I could not stop cudgelling my brains for some sentence, phrase or even word, that surely must have left an imprint on my mind whilst I was listening to that whispered conversation. But what remained was the sense of urgency, of secrecy and, above all, of conspiracy which told me plainly that it had been no ordinary confabulation between two friends or fellow workers. The more I thought about it, the more I was convinced that I had been within seconds of discovering our would-be killer and cursed myself accordingly for my tardiness of action.

A line of servers emerged from behind the screen which separated the great hall from the kitchens. As I watched them process down the length of the room towards the dais, bearing aloft their silver salvers, the scents and smells of the next course wafting deliciously about our nostrils and making me hungry all over again, I became aware of Matthew Wardroper hovering at my elbow.

'Over there,' he muttered through barely moving lips, 'standing beneath the torch to the left of the archway. That's Jocelin d'Hiver, thought by Master Plummer to be in the pay of the Burgundians. And approaching the duke's chair now, Geoffrey Whitelock, probably employed by the king to spy on his brother.'

Matthew moved away again, leaving me to study the two young men. Jocelin d'Hiver was small and thin, with sharp, birdlike features in which brilliant black eyes darted here and there with an avian swiftness, watching everything and missing nothing. Geoffrey Whitelock, on the other hand, was as fair-haired as the other was dark; tall, slim and comely, with an attractive air, easy manner and a regularity of feature that was almost patrician. Of all the Squires of the Household on duty that evening, he seemed most at ease with his master, his head bent gracefully over the back of the duke's chair, his full lips curled in appreciation of whatever it was that His Grace was saying.

Humphrey Nanfan gave me a nudge as the servers filed on to the dais, and it was time once again to present the duke and his guests – who, tonight, were only the senior officers of his household – with pike in galentyne sauce and a side-dish of onions, garlic and borage. (I could not help thinking that the latter would produce such a blast of stinking breath as would put paid to all but the most ardently amorous advances during the coming hours of darkness.) This time I managed to keep my mind on what I was doing and discharged my duty without error.

Finally the meal was over, the covers drawn and the tables removed, so that the duke and his mother could better enjoy the evening's entertainment. Tonight the talent was home-grown, with the household minstrels providing music for dancing and the duke's own troupe of acrobats causing the seven-year-old Lady Katherine to double up with laughter until, loudly protesting, she was carried off to bed by her nurse and two attendant nurse-maids. Berys Hogan, however, was not one of them and I noticed that she remained in the hall with the rest of us.

Duchess Cicely, still, at sixty, displaying the remnants of a beauty that had in youth earned for her the nickname of the Rose of Raby, was speaking to her son. The duke listened, nodded, kissed her hand and turned to scan the ranks of his retainers. Finally he found the face that he was seeking.

'Ralph!' he called. 'A song. Her Grace particularly wishes to hear again the one you sang the other night. The Trouvère song from northern France. Do you have your instrument there or do you need to fetch it?'

'I have it with me, Your Grace.' Ralph Boyse beckoned to one of the pages who hovered close at hand, probably hoping to be sent on some errand or other in order to alleviate the tedium of inactivity. The boy advanced and handed Ralph his flute.

I immediately ceased to take any interest in the proceedings for, as I have stated before, I have no ear for music. To me it all sounds much as a tomcat does when serenading his lady-love on the roof-tops; a sad loss, I've no doubt, for they say that music is the food of the soul, in which case I've known only a lifetime of starvation. But there again, they also say that what you've never known you never miss and I can testify to the truth of that observation. I leaned my back against the wall, closed my eyes and let my thoughts drift once more to that sibilantly whispered, definitely sinister-sounding, overheard conversation.

Like a bubble forcing its way to the surface of a pond a single word now rose and burst among my crowding thoughts. 'Demon.' I let it float for a moment or two inside my head, considering it from every angle; but in the end it failed to convince me that that was what I had really heard. Who would be talking so urgently about a spirit of darkness? Or was the word 'demesne'? Had my whisperers been discussing something to do with demesne lands and the disposition of property? Or was my mind simply playing tricks on me, feeding me false information so that it could get some rest from my incessant probing?

Instinct warned me that Ralph Boyse's song was coming to an end and I readied myself to join in the general applause. Even my unreceptive ear, now that I gave him my full attention, could tell that he had a fine and powerful voice, interspersing the words of chorus and verse with echoing runs of notes upon his shawm. He played a final trill upon the pipe, then his voice soared, clear and unaccompanied.

'It is the end. No matter what is said, I must love.'

There was a moment's silence before the Duke of

Gloucester and his mother led the outburst of enthusiastic clapping. I joined in as a matter of course, but with furrowed brow, for I had just been presented with yet another puzzle. Why were those last words familiar to me? Where had I previously heard them?

Chapter Twelve

Of course! Lady Wardroper had hummed that same tune and sung those very words to me three weeks ago at Chilworth Manor. It was a Trouvère song, she had told me, called *C'est la fin*. Was it coincidence that I had also heard it again this evening? Perhaps. But perhaps not, in which case there was probably more than one perfectly reasonable explanation for such an occurrence. Matthew Wardroper could have taught the song to Ralph Boyse since his arrival in London. On the other hand, the greater chance was that Ralph, being half French, knew it already.

It seemed that the entertainment was drawing to a close, with the duke and his mother debating whether or not to recall the tumblers or to request the minstrels to play one last melody in order to round off the proceedings. In the event, however, it was decided that enough was enough and Duke Richard, always concerned for the welfare of his servants – a fact largely responsible for the majority's unswerving devotion to him – reminded us that tomorrow would be busy and that we should take what repose we could this evening. He then rose and escorted Duchess Cicely from the hall, leaving the rest of us to go about whatever remained of our duties, before seeking the sanctuary of our beds.

Once the senior officers of the household had dispersed, however, the younger ones were less inclined for sleep, indulging in some general horseplay and working off high spirits still unquenched by a hard day's work. Humphrey Nanfan and one of the duchess's Squires began to wrestle, while the onlookers each backed his favourite and bet excitedly on the outcome of the contest. In duty bound, I felt obliged to wager on Humphrey and cheered him lustily as he and the other lad fought amongst the rushes, both, with a great deal of grunting and groaning, striving to get the upper hand.

'More bottom than science, the pair of them,' said a voice behind me and, turning, I saw Ralph Boyse standing at my elbow. He swooped suddenly as they rolled towards us and I saw that his pipe had toppled off the chair, where he had placed it for safe-keeping, and fallen among the rushes. 'You young fools,' he shouted angrily, 'watch what you're doing! You could have broken my bombardt!'

A bombardt! Lady Wardroper had referred to such an instrument, and in the very same breath as she had discussed the song which Ralph had so recently sung. A second coincidence? How could it be otherwise? Yet coincidences always make me uneasy, in spite of the fact that they do happen, and that, frequently.

Nevertheless, I could not resist turning to Ralph Boyse with a question. 'Surely,' I said, 'I'm not mistaken in thinking that to be a Breton bombardt? It's smaller than our English shawms.'

He nodded, but made no attempt to return my smile. 'It has, for me, a sweeter sound,' he answered. His interest momentarily quickened. 'Do you have some knowledge of music?'

'No, indeed! I've no ear for it at all. But I thought I recognized the instrument. In fact, I heard it mentioned recently in connection with that self-same song you entertained us with this evening.'

He shrugged, stared, then narrowed his gaze. 'Aren't you the new Yeoman of the Chamber? The one who used to be a chapman, but who has now been given a place in His Grace's household in return for some service he once rendered the duke?'

I gave a little bow. 'I have that good fortune. I didn't realize, however, that my fame had spread.'

Ralph Boyse merely grunted, subjected me to another penetrating look, then turned to speak to someone else. Meantime, the wrestling bout between Humphrey Nanfan and his opponent had come to an end without producing an outright winner and several other couples were engaged in similar trials of strength. But people were beginning to drift away, either to their beds, conscious of the extra work to be done on the morrow, or to take a stroll in the soft summer twilight. For my own part, I felt a quiet walk in the upper air might help to clear my head, so when I had mounted the stairs to the Yeomen of the Chamber's dormitory I continued upwards until I reached a door set in the outer wall, giving access to a narrow walkway between two towers.

Below me I could see the river with all its traffic, still thick despite the lateness of the hour. Ships careened and skimmed across the shimmering water whose surface was stained now pink, now orange in the rays of a dying sun. A long ridge of emerald downs bounded the horizon, veined by trailing blue shadows. Clouds sailed serenely above me, their underbellies iridescent, pearled by the fading light. I leaned against the cold, grey stones of one of the towers and closed my eyes, thinking with pleasure of the night ahead and the peace of that little death which God sends at the end of every day, so that we can face afresh the trials and tribulations of the next.

I was so tired that I nearly went to sleep where I stood, only jerking into full consciousness again when my chin fell forward on to my breast. Forcing myself away from the wall, I walked over to the opposite side of the parapet and found myself looking down into a small inner courtyard where the castle bakery was housed. Smoke poured through the holes in the roof and lights blazed in every window. While most of us took our rest, the bakers were preparing tomorrow's loaves; and tonight they would also be preparing the cakes and tarts, the pastry coffins and sugar subtleties for the next day's banquet.

It was almost dusk by now, the summer's day drawing gently to its end. A movement in one corner of the courtyard suddenly attracted my attention and from out of the shadows there emerged Lionel Arrowsmith and Berys Hogan. She was supporting him around the waist, carefully avoiding his broken arm, while on the other side he bore most of his weight on the crutch and his uninjured leg. As they made their slow and painful progress towards a door set in the courtyard wall they stopped every now and again to exchange a lingering kiss and to embrace as well as they were able. I could not but admire the Body Squire's single-minded determination, which made him surmount all personal difficulties in order to keep an assignation with Berys Hogan.

I continued to watch, drawing back a little behind the

parapet, in case either of them glanced up and saw me. I need not have worried, however; the lovers seemed far too absorbed in one another to care what was going on around them. Finally, they reached the door in the wall, but before Berys lifted the latch, she and Lionel said a fond farewell, both her arms entwined about his neck. Freeing her lips, she laid a cheek against one of his, so that she was looking backwards, across his shoulder. Suddenly, she stiffened, rearing up her head as though she had seen someone lurking in the shadows. Avoiding another attempt by Lionel to kiss her, she opened the door and urged him through it as quickly as she could, then carefully latched it shut behind her. I dared not abandon my cover to obtain a better view and could only wait in the hope that the mysterious watcher, if there was one, might eventually show himself.

For a moment or two the courtyard appeared to be devoid of human life, except for the occasional baker's boy, who came to one or other of the bakehouse windows to cool himself and inhale some of the evening air. I was just about to abandon my vigil and return to the dormitory, having decided that I had misinterpreted Berys's actions, when a man prowled forward into my range of vision, crossed the courtyard and disappeared, like the other two, through the door in the wall.

I recognized the man immediately. It was Ralph Boyse.

Once again, as four nights earlier at the Saracen's Head, I lay wakeful and restless on my pallet, while all around me my fellows snored and muttered in their sleep.

Vainly I tried to interpret what I had seen that evening. Ralph must have been a witness to the meeting between his betrothed and Lionel Arrowsmith, yet far from being consumed by jealous rage and rushing headlong to separate them, he had seemingly been content to do nothing. But why? And had he happened upon them by chance, or had he suspected that he was being betrayed and set himself to spy on Berys? Furthermore, if I were right and she really had observed him, what would she do now? Would she seek him out and try to excuse herself? Make up some story about being sorry for Lionel in his present injured state? (But no man would be foolish enough to believe such a blatant lie! No, no! She could, and probably would, do better than that. In my experience women are cleverer at deception than men.) Maybe Berys had seen nothing, only sensed that she and her lover were being watched, in which case she would most likely hope for the best, eventually convincing herself that she had imagined the whole. As for Ralph, it could well be more satisfying to dream up some deep-laid plan of revenge rather than to take instant action. I must try to warn Lionel, put him on his guard, and persuade Timothy to knock some sense into his head about Berys Hogan. Tomorrow, I reflected, tossing and turning, might well prove to be an interesting day, provided I could stay awake long enough to play my part.

I resolutely closed my eyes and willed myself to sleep, with such success that the next thing to wake me was the head Yeoman of the Chamber beating loudly with his staff of office against the wooden door and shouting, 'Every man rise! Every man rise! Daybreak! Daybreak!' And indeed he was right. Dawn was already filtering through the narrow, unshuttered slits of windows.

All around me, fellow Yeomen pulled themselves reluctantly to their feet, stretching their arms until the bones cracked, or rubbing the sleep from their still half-closed eyes. There was much cursing as we groped around in the semi-darkness for boots and shirts and tunics, coaxing into them limbs which felt as though they were made of lead. As always, there were arguments as to which garment belonged to which man, and accusations of taking one another's property, but in the end it all got sorted out with surprising amity and we were ready to face a new day. But as we waited in line to use the castle privies, then descended to one of the inner courtyards to douse our heads beneath the pumps and hack the night's growth of beard from our chins as best we could with icy water, I was recalling a dream which I must have had just before waking, and which still clung about me with the persistence of a cobweb.

I had been standing in the woodland clearing north of Chilworth Manor, experiencing yet again that all-pervasive sense of evil, when Timothy Plummer had suddenly appeared, walking towards me through the trees.

'Is the word "demon" or "demesne"?' he had asked me angrily. 'It's important for His Grace's sake that I should know.'

'Neither,' I had answered confidently. 'It's . . .' But there the dream had ended abruptly.

It was in vain that I racked my brains for the missing word. Deep inside me I must know exactly what it was that I had overheard, but it had eluded me sleeping as it now eluded me waking, no matter how hard I tried to conjure it up.

The great hall of Baynard's Castle was awash with light, every torch and cresset lit, the candelabra of latten tin, suspended from the central rafter, ablaze with burning candles of scented wax. During the course of a long day the floor had been thoroughly swept and garnished with fresh rushes and armfuls of flowers, which had been scattered across the flagstones. The kitchens had been a hive of activity from early morning, and the smell of cooking meats, turning slowly on their spits, had been making everyone's mouth water uncontrollably. Tapestries had been brought to line the walls, their glowing colours adding an unaccustomed warmth to the normally sombre stone, and the tables, spread with fresh linen, groaned beneath the weight of gold and silver dishes.

The duke and his mother, the former magnificently attired in crimson velvet and cloth of gold, the latter resplendent in black silk damask, the senior officers of their respective households grouped about them, waited on the steps of the inner courtyard to receive their guests, who were then conducted by the steward to their places within the hall. From my position next to Stephen Hudelin, wedged against one of the sideboards which was loaded with different wines and cold side-dishes, I was able to observe their various entrances, and smiled secretly to myself at the jostling for precedence and the arguments with the steward over seating arrangements which went on. Every man present wished to stress his own importance, and every wife was insistent that he should do so.

Most of these early arrivals were, to me, just faces to which I could put no names. One set of features, however – swarthy skin, a high, arched nose, eyes like glossy chestnuts and a bush of curling black beard split by a wide and toothy grin – attracted me enough to ask Stephen Hudelin to whom they belonged. And that was the first time I ever heard of Edward Brampton. Born Duarte Brandao, a

162

Portuguese Jew, he had come to England to make his fortune, converted to Christianity, lived for a while in the House of the Convertites in the Strand and had chosen the baptismal name of Edward in honour of the king, who had stood godfather to him at his christening. He was still, at this time, plain Master Brampton, for his knighthood would not be conferred on him until many years later by Duke Richard, after the duke himself had become king. But, although I did not know it then, our paths were destined to cross in the future because of our mutual devotion to the House of York and in particular because of our undying love for one man.

That man, a-shimmer in crimson and gold, was now, to the braying of trumpets, leading in his most important guests. Duchess Cicely was escorted by her daughter, Elizabeth, and Elizabeth's husband, the Duke of Suffolk, a surly, brutish man who, oddly enough, was great-grandson, through his mother's line, of the gentle, humorous poet Geoffrey Chaucer. Next came a clutch of Woodvilles, led by Anthony, Earl Rivers, eldest of the queen's twelve brothers and sisters. I had heard him spoken of as a very learned man, who was so deeply religious that he constantly wore a penitent's hair shirt beneath his gorgeous robes; a man neither so grasping nor so greedy as his numerous siblings. Indeed, there was a kindness about the mouth and in the eyes which was absent in the rest of his family. He displayed, also, an air of patient resignation, which made me suspect that he would accept without demur whatever life brought him, be it for good or ill; not, by my reckoning, a man who would seek to interfere with the workings of that fickle damsel, Fate, by trying to usurp her function. Perhaps I leapt too rapidly to conclusions, but

163

in my experience a lot may be gleaned from first impressions, and nothing I ever heard or knew of Anthony Woodville in later years caused me to revise that original opinion of him. I made up my mind there and then that no danger threatened the duke from that quarter, although what his brothers and sisters were capable of I was far less certain.

Chief among the magnificent throng who entered the hall just before King Edward and his consort was George of Clarence. He was unaccompanied by his wife, having left the sickly Duchess Isabel at home in Somerset. I had never seen the duke before and studied the big, florid, handsome face with interest. Deep lines of discontent grooved the corners of his eyes and there was a sulky pout to his mouth which spoke of bitterness and disillusion. A fine tracery of small red veins marred the once youthful smoothness of his cheeks and his laughter was over-loud and over-hearty, his general demeanour being that of a man who felt that life had not dealt fairly by him. His dislike of the Woodvilles was poorly concealed and as the evening wore on, and he sank deeper in his cups, it grew yet more glaringly obvious; but it was a dislike just as patently returned.

The trumpets sounded yet again, stridently and more insistently, as King Edward and Queen Elizabeth were conducted, amid much pomp and ceremony, to their seats beneath canopies of cloth of gold in the centre of the dais. The king's likeness to his brother George was immediately apparent. Both stood over six feet and were of splendid physique, with the reddish-gold hair and startling blue eyes of the typical Plantagenet. Once known as the handsomest man in Europe, Edward was, however, now starting to run to fat. Sybaritic by nature, he had for years denied himself no luxury that his body craved and, encouraged by his wife and her relations, had created a court which was a byword for hedonism. His waist had begun to thicken, his jaw was heavily fleshed and his roving eye – for he had never been the most faithful of husbands – a little bleary. Nevertheless he was still a good-looking man, a fact to which the simpering smiles and encouraging glances of all the women present testified.

Beside her lord, glittering with jewels, sat Edward's queen, her famous silver-gilt hair shaved right back from the high white forehead and completely concealed by an embroidered cap, over which towered the twin peaks of her wired gauze headdress. The mouth, with its full underlip, was carefully painted and the skin stiff with a maquillage of white lead and rose water. Her chin was soft and rounded, like a child's, but the blue eyes, which stared with almost unseeing arrogance across the crowded hall, told me that here was a woman high-stomached and pitiless. Stories concerning her and her family's rapacity, and also about their lust for revenge, abounded. One such tale, oft repeated at that time, was of the terrible retribution visited upon the head of Thomas Fitzgerald, Earl of Desmond and sometime Deputy Lieutenant of Ireland. Ten years earlier, around the time of the queen's coronation, the earl had visited England and been asked by the king what he thought of his choice of a bride.

'Sire,' Desmond is reported to have answered, 'the lady's beauty and virtue are well known and deservedly praised. Nevertheless I think Your Highness would have done better to marry a princess who would have secured you the benefits of a foreign alliance.'

Such disastrous honesty did the earl no harm with the

king, who sent him back to Ireland loaded down with gifts. But two years later, when John Tiptoft, Earl of Worcester and nicknamed the Butcher of England, became Deputy Lieutenant of Ireland in Desmond's stead, he had had the earl arrested on some trumped-up charge, condemned and beheaded before any of his English friends, chief among whom was the Duke of Gloucester, had time to intervene. That was bad enough, but far, far worse was the brutal murder of two of Desmond's young children, a crime with which Tiptoft was taunted by the London mob when it was his own turn to mount the scaffold. At the heart of this story, however, lay the persistent rumour that the king knew nothing of the deaths of Thomas Fitzgerald and his offspring until it was too late; that the queen stole her husband's signet to seal the death warrants herself.

Now, whether that particular aspect of the story was true or not I have no means of knowing and am still ignorant to this day, but it was certainly one that was often repeated in taverns and ale-houses whenever the queen's name was mentioned (together with the rider that the Duke of Gloucester had been beside himself with grief and had sworn that however long he had to wait, he would be revenged for the death of his friend and his friend's two children). Be that as it may, watching Elizabeth Woodville that evening, looking at the contemptuous curve of that little rouged mouth, noting her dismissive attitude towards servants and courtiers alike and the condescension she displayed towards her mother-in-law, her superior in every way, I felt I could believe her capable of any infamy, even that of plotting her brother-in-law's murder if such an act would advance the cause of her family by the slightest degree.

And it was at that precise moment that I saw her half turn her head and beckon to someone who had been hovering near her chair. Stephen Hudelin glided forward and sank to one knee, as though ready to serve the queen. But his hands were empty. I left my station by the sideboard and edged a little closer, and through the haze of torch and candle smoke I could just make out the movement of their lips. The conversation was brief and, as far as I could tell, unremarked by anyone besides myself, it being only a moment or so before Hudelin rose and moved back into the shadows. All the same, I was convinced that he was indeed in the pay of the Woodville family and might well be the source of the threat posed to Duke Richard which had been nosed out by members of the Brotherhood.

The company was still settling itself, waiting for the banquet to begin, raising goblets of exquisite Venetian glass in pledges of friendship and goodwill. Thoughts of the coming conflict in France made for a more sombre mood than might otherwise have prevailed, but the atmosphere was lively enough and there were cheers when the minstrels in the gallery struck up with the Agincourt song.

> 'Our king went forth to Normandy,
> With grace and might of chivalry!'

'And so we shall soon have cause to sing again, cousin!' called out a young man who, I later learned, was the Duke of Buckingham, as he drank the king's health in the best malmsey wine.

All the men were on their feet then, roaring their agreement so that the music was quite drowned out. King Edward, a slight, somewhat enigmatic smile playing around

167

the corners of his mouth, waited for the uproar to subside before raising his own goblet in return.

'My lords, I thank you,' was all he said, making no effort to get up or make a speech.

I could see that this apparent apathy puzzled and disappointed a good many of his loyal subjects who, after a moment's embarrassed silence, sank back into their seats muttering to one another. I also saw Duke Richard give his brother a quick, questioning glance, which the king seemed determined not to meet, hurriedly turning his eyes away.

'Let eating commence!' he ordered and immediately, at a sign from Duchess Cicely, the trumpets brayed again as the first course was carried into the hall.

Chapter Thirteen

At last the feast was over. The various dishes – broth, jellied eels and crayfish, duckling, roast kid and sucking pig, a boar's head, chickens, roast heron, cokyntryce, venison with frumenty, doucettes and junkets, pancakes and fritters, nuts and cheese, dates and raisins, and a magnificent swan, drawn, plucked and cooked, then re-assembled in all its plumage, a collar of diamonds about its neck – had come and gone, and all washed down with a vast quantity of wines. (I cannot remember at this distance of time more than a tithe of what was consumed that evening, but of one thing I am certain: it was enough to feed a hundred common men such as myself for a year or more, and to feed them well.)

The guests lolled in their chairs or slumped on their benches, faces red and shiny in the guttering torchlight, hands clasped over distended bellies. Every now and then a beringed finger would indicate to some sweating server that its owner's cup was empty. The babel of noise which had filled the hall during the earlier part of the banquet was muted now, as energy waned with repletion. Occasionally someone was sick into the rushes, or heaved his heart up all over the table, but no one seemed to mind. Most of the men were, in any case, too drunk to care.

The only two who appeared sober and in possession of all their faculties were the king and the Duke of Gloucester; the former, I suspected, because he had a strong head for wine and could sink great quantities without showing serious ill effects; the latter because he was naturally abstemious, eating and drinking very little whilst making the pretence of doing so. As I have said before, Duke Richard, for all his love of show and finery, had a deep-seated puritanical streak to his nature which did not endear him to his robuster fellows.

Suddenly, the steward and the marshal rapped for silence with their staves, and it was seen that King Edward had risen to speak, towering over his still-seated guests. When, finally, the noise had died away, except for the occasional cough or hiccup, he flung wide his arms in an all-embracing gesture.

'My friends! My loyal friends and subjects!' Someone raised a ragged cheer which was swiftly hushed. 'In less than four days we cross the Channel to our stronghold of Calais, from whence we shall mount the greatest invasion of France that Europe has ever seen!' There was another cheer, unchecked this time. The king continued, 'We have more men, more cannon, more siege machines, more horses than any previous English ruler has ever before had at his command.' At this point several people started to bang enthusiastically on the table with their fists. King Edward smiled indulgently and his deep, pleasant voice rose in a crescendo. 'I say to you that we shall do such deeds as will diminish even those of Monmouth Harry and his beleaguered band!'

The drunken apathy of a few moments before had vanished. Women, as well as men, were on their feet, shouting and cheering and embracing one another in a fervour of English pride. As the king sat down again, the Duke of Clarence reached across the queen, pinning her in her seat, to clasp his elder brother's hand.

'We'll show 'em,' he said, with a slight slurring of his words. 'We'll show the bloody French! What d'you say, Dickon? We three! 'T'll be like ol' times again!'

From where I was standing I had a clear view of King Edward's face, and although he smiled and nodded, I thought his look was strained and that he returned his brother's clasp somewhat perfunctorily. He also exchanged a brief glance, so fleeting as to be barely perceptible, with a man seated further down the board who, I later learned, was John Morton, his Master of the Rolls. Meantime, Duke Richard, with a restraint which only served to underline far more effectively than Clarence's boisterous enthusiasm his eager readiness for the forthcoming fray, was also offering his heartfelt congratulations.

'If we have the largest invasion force ever gathered, it's entirely due to your unstinting efforts, Ned. You've been tireless in raising both men and money.'

'Nonsense!' The king flung himself back in his chair, while his queen continued to look daggers at the Duke of Clarence, angered by his recent affront to her dignity. 'You've worked just as hard as I have. Your Yorkshiremen are an army in themselves. Enough of this!' He addressed Duchess Cicely, smiling fondly. 'Madame Mother! Is there to be no entertainment for us?'

'Of course!' The duchess turned to her master of ceremonies. 'Let the masque begin.'

Everyone relaxed a little. Yeomen of the Chamber, Squires of the Body, servers, stewards and cup-bearers leaned thankfully against walls, wiped the sweat from their eyes and drew a deep breath as the centre of the hall was suddenly filled with a gyrating mass of masked tumblers and dancers. I was too tired to follow the story they were telling, but realized that it had to do with the animal kingdom, for every player wore the head of a beast – fox, sheep, goat and chanticleer. A farmyard piece, I thought sleepily, closing my eyes, with Reynard as the villain, up to his old tricks as usual. Perhaps the retelling of one of Geoffrey Chaucer's tales as a compliment to his great-grandson.

My eyelids started to droop and it took an enormous effort of will to force them open. But the heat of the hall, my restless night and lack of the fresh air that I was used to, were taking their toll; my limbs felt dull and heavy. Twice, Stephen Hudelin, who had resumed his place beside me at the sideboard, nudged me, but both times my senses reeled and I again lost consciousness. Then a sudden raucous burst of laughter from the assembled company jerked me awake to stare stupidly about me, not quite certain for the moment where I was or what was happening. Hudelin had vanished and as I peered about through the reddish, smoky haze of spluttering torch- and candlelight, I could see no one immediately recognizable from Duke Richard's household.

Where was Stephen? Where was Humphrey Nanfan? Jocelin d'Hiver? Ralph Boyse? Geoffrey Whitelock? A sudden sense of urgency seized me that I must locate them. And then, suddenly, I saw Geoffrey, tall, fair-haired, blue-eyed and graceful, standing just behind the king and almost leaning against his chair. His head was thrown back and he was laughing immoderately at the antics of the mummers.

Even as he did so, the king turned to speak to him, laughing also; and the resemblance between them at that particular moment was so marked that I could not help but hit upon the truth. Geoffrey Whitelock was most certainly King Edward's son; one of his many bastards, watched over and provided for during childhood years and eventually acknowledged and taken into the royal household. No doubt Lady Whitelock, wife of a Kentish knight, had, like so many of her peers, bestowed her favours upon the king, probably with a complaisant husband's blessing, and Geoffrey had been the result of that liaison. Little doubt, either, that the lad knew the truth about his parentage, judging by the way he dared to lay a familiar hand on King Edward's shoulder. In all probability, that distinctive height and those handsome, golden features were often to be seen in the royal palaces, amongst the king's numerous retainers.

In this particular case, however, Geoffrey had been found a place in the Duke of Gloucester's household, doubtless for the very reason surmised by Timothy Plummer. He was a spy for his royal father who, no matter how much he trusted Duke Richard, nevertheless liked to be apprised of everything that went on in his brother's household. But that the king would use Geoffrey as an instrument of murder against his own uncle was surely impossible. It had seemed to me from the beginning that King Edward would never prove to be the fountain-head of this particular plot; and now that I had realized the truth of his relationship with Geoffrey, I decided that Timothy Plummer and Lionel Arrowsmith could cease to consider the young man as a potential assassin.

And I was shown to be right almost at once, and in the most dramatic fashion.

* * *

One of the many gallants who had been making their way to
the queen's chair, in order to pay court to her during the
course of the evening, was just rising from his knees, at the
same time fervently pressing his lips to the back of the white
hand graciously extended to him. Such conversation of the
queen's as I had been able to overhear whilst performing
my duties had been liberally sprinkled with French words
and phrases; a habit of hers, so Timothy informed me later,
in order to stress her maternal family's connection with the
royal House of Luxembourg. Now, as she smiled coyly at
her departing admirer, she murmured, '*A demain! A
demain!*'

Demain! The realization burst on me like a lightning
stroke. Not 'demon', not 'demesne', but '*demain*'. That
was the single word which I had heard with any clarity the
previous afternoon; the word I had been struggling to
identify. The whisperers had been speaking in French, an
added reason why practically nothing of their conversation
had made any sense to my English ears. Those two
syllables, however, had been uttered with a stressful
urgency which, later, I was imperfectly to recall. *Demain!*
Tomorrow . . .

But tomorrow was now today! Whatever the subject of
that sibilant and anxious colloquy, whether or not it boded
trouble, whether it was or was not of sinister content, it had
certainly been about something which was due to take
place today. It might already have happened; some purely
innocent action now safely in the past. Yet I could not bring
myself to believe so. I felt in the very marrow of my bones
that evil had been hatched and was still to break out of the
egg. There was no logic for this reasoning, and God knew

that my instincts were not always sound, but with His guidance I usually, in spite of my own foolishness, managed to arrive at the truth.

My eyes were drawn towards the mummers, sweating inside their heavy masks, whose comedy was reaching its climax. The shawms of the minstrels, aloft in their gallery, sounded their high-pitched notes as the rest of the cavorting animals surrounded the fox, brandishing the rope with which they intended to hang him. Everyone's eyes were on the cornered Reynard, some of the onlookers noisily encouraging their favourite to get away, others whooping and screaming out hunting calls, as though they were in very truth witnessing the chase instead of merely watching a play. The king and queen were as vociferous as any, the former commanding Reynard to make his escape, the latter banging the table and yelling for death. Behind them, Geoffrey Whitelock was clapping his hands with glee and even Duke Richard, his dark eyes glowing, was caught up in the general excitement.

Then suddenly I noticed that one of the players, wearing the cockerel's mask, had separated himself from the mêlée about the errant Reynard and was edging slowly towards the dais where the king and his two brothers were sitting. If others remarked him, they no doubt thought it to be part of the action and indeed, for a moment I made the same mistake myself. But there was something about the manner in which Chanticleer fingered the dagger at his belt that caught my attention and, as he began to draw it, I saw the jewels in its hilt wink and sparkle in the light from the candles . . .

This was no make-believe weapon of wood and paint! This was the real thing, a gentleman's poniard, and the

175

blade glittered with menace as it was inched from its sheath. *Demain!* That tomorrow which was now today! Surely there could be no further doubt that what I had overheard had been our assassin receiving instructions that the time had come for him to strike?

But there was no more time to ask myself questions, nor to try to reason out the answers. With a shout of warning to the duke I leapt on to the board, treading on plates and scattering goblets of the finest Venetian glass with a sublime disregard for the havoc I was causing. I was but vaguely aware of the outraged invective which followed my progress as I jumped to the floor again on the opposite side of the table. Even so, I was not quite quick enough. Before I could reach him, Chanticleer just had time to divine that his intent had been discovered. He rammed the dagger back into its scabbard, turned and ran, taking advantage of the general bewilderment and chaos to vanish through the door set in the wall of screens which separated the hall from the servery.

I struggled to overtake him, but was hampered on all sides by people crowding forward to find out what was happening.

'Let me through!' I yelled. 'Let me through!'

Timothy Plummer suddenly materialized at my elbow, issuing orders with all the considerable authority at his command. 'Stand back! Stand back there! In the name of the duke!'

He followed me into the servery, where the fugitive's path was plainly visible by the overturned trestles and plates of broken meats littering the floor. Coagulating pools of left-over gravy and half a dozen different sauces were seeping into the rushes. Several of the servers had been knocked to the ground during our quarry's headlong flight and were dazedly nursing their various injuries.

'Which way did he go?' I cried, before I realized that there was only one way possible: through the archway in the southern wall.

Timothy Plummer had come to this conclusion faster than I had, and pushing past me, was already mounting the twisting staircase beyond. As I caught him up, he stumbled and fell, cursing volubly.

'What is it?' I demanded; and for answer he disentangled from his feet what I could just make out, in the wisping flame of an almost burnt-out wall-cresset, to be Chanticleer's mask.

I thrust it under my arm, helped Timothy to his feet and proceeded upwards. But the delay had cost us dear and by the time we reached the top, which gave us access to a corridor stretching in both directions, there was no sign of anyone anywhere along its length. To make matters worse, scores of people were now pushing up the stairs behind us, jostling and shoving and asking questions.

'I'll go one way, you go the other,' Timothy hissed in my ear, adding with a contemptuous dismissal of some of the highest and greatest in the land, 'Ignore this rabble.'

I had to smile, albeit grimly, as I turned to my right, leaving Timothy to explore the left-hand side of the passageway. This nonplussed our following for a moment and by the time, still vociferously demanding answers, the leaders had decided which one of us to tail, I had managed to enter and glance around the first two rooms I came to. But both were completely bare of furniture or hangings, offering no means of concealment.

At this end of the corridor a small flight of steps led down to a landing and a curtained alcove. Roughly I tugged back the leather curtain, its metal rings rasping against the wooden pole, and saw the scattering of clothes dropped anyhow over the floor of the window embrasure. There was still enough light remaining in the summer sky for me to recognize them as the upper garments of Chanticleer's costume. But far more important was the body of a young man, clothed only in his undergarments, lying face down, the hilt of a black-handled kitchen knife protruding from his back, its blade embedded in his heart.

'God's teeth!' breathed an awestruck voice behind me. A dozen necks craned to peer across my shoulders. Then the same voice whispered, 'Who is it?'

I made no answer because I had no way of knowing for certain. But I could guess. This, surely, must be the body of the mummer who should have played the part of Chanticleer in the evening's entertainment. Unfortunately for him, our murderer had needed the costume and so had been forced to kill. He dared not risk anyone pointing the finger of suspicion at him once the deed was done. He had failed in that, but succeeded, I reflected bitterly, in preserving the secret of his identity at the cost of an innocent's life.

The Duke of Gloucester was angry with all the irritation of a man who knows his anger to be unjustified.

The guests and representatives of the law had finally departed and the grieving band of mummers had borne away the body of their fellow to mourn his death and give him burial. The murderer had not been found, even though the sheriff's officers had questioned as many of the duke's and Duchess Cicely's retainers as they could. But in the end, with the moon paling into insignificance and the world edging once again towards dawn, the sheer impossibility of their task defeated them. There were too many people in too many places, too much movement and general activity on such an occasion, to yield a great deal of reliable information.

Apart from the guests, some persons were definitely accounted for. I myself was able to swear that Geoffrey Whitelock had been standing behind King Edward's chair and therefore could be exonerated of masquerading as Chanticleer. Some hundred or so others had also been noted and were above suspicion, but the whereabouts of the majority relied solely upon their own word. There was, moreover, a feeling amongst the sheriff's men that the death of a single mummer must not be allowed to interfere with great and momentous events of state and that the invasion of France was too imminent to justify a protracted investigation.

Long before their arrival at Baynard's Castle, Timothy Plummer and I had received instructions from the duke, conveyed urgently and secretly to us by his secretary, John Kendall. Nothing must be revealed of any known plan to assassinate him; my pursuit of Chanticleer had been simply because I saw a man drawing a dagger from its sheath and, with so many of the high and the mighty gathered beneath one roof, had feared for their safety and acted accordingly.

We had both been careful to obey these commands to the letter, but it had not prevented the vials of Duke Richard's wrath being emptied upon our heads. I had never seen him angry before and at first was inclined to be cowed. But after a minute or two my own anger rose at the unreasonableness of his upbraiding.

'My lord,' I said, when he finally paused for breath,

179

'these reproaches are unjust!' I heard Timothy give a stifled gasp, but took no notice. Raising my head, I looked the duke straight in the eyes. I felt my jawline harden. 'You accuse me of acting in a bull-like manner; of attracting everyone's attention. What then would Your Grace have had me do? Anything less than what I did and you would most likely have been dead before I could have reached you.'

'And the murderer caught! He could never have hoped to escape in those circumstances.'

I gave an exasperated sigh, which again brought a sharp intake of breath from Timothy. Once more, I ignored it. 'We can't know that, my lord. He must have thought it worth the risk, hoping to get away in the general confusion. But, in any case, he would have achieved his purpose – and that of his masters, whoever they may be.' I had already been so bold, that I decided I could lose nothing by being even bolder. 'Are you so tired of life, Your Grace, that you would wish to lay down your life in order to trap a murderer? I think not.'

There was silence for several seconds. Timothy and I were closeted with the duke in his private chamber and outside the narrow window the first flush of another warm and sunny July day was gilding the rosy darkness. Had I gone too far? Was I to be ordered a beating? My services dispensed with? And I realized with surprise that I no longer wished to be quit of this tiresome problem until it was resolved, and that, satisfactorily. Two men were now dead, both of a knife wound through the heart, and one of them an innocent bystander.

The duke's face was suddenly transformed by his sad, sweet smile. His body, still in its evening's finery, slumped against the cushions of his chair. 'Thank you, chapman. You do well to take me to task. I am in the wrong, I freely admit it. But for your prompt action tonight I might well have been killed.' He made an apologetic movement of his hands and the candlelight coruscated across the many jewelled rings he wore. 'I'm tired and apprehensive, as any man facing the unknown must be. And war is always the unknown. Furthermore, it entails a man leaving his wife and children and everything that he holds most dear.' He pulled himself together with a visible effort and straightened his shoulders. 'But the people have put their trust in us. They have parted with more of their gold and more of their young men than ever before. It is up to us now, the princes of this realm, that we do not fail them. That we give them the glorious victories that they look for, no matter at what cost to ourselves.' He sighed, then continued, 'Timothy, let me know immediately if your inquiries bear any fruit. But mark you, it is not to be shared with the sheriff's men, who will undoubtedly be snuffling around amongst us until we embark on Tuesday.' He nodded dismissal.

I lingered for a moment longer. 'Your Grace, are you absolutely sure that you know of no reason why your enemies should wish to kill you?'

The duke shrugged, the skin beneath his eyes looking bruised and heavy with anxiety and lack of sleep. 'All men of power have enemies,' he answered quietly, adding wryly, 'Which is why we set our spies about one another. Each of us needs to know what the others are doing and even thinking. And I could conjure up half a dozen reasons, I suppose, why my death might benefit certain persons. But in answer to your question, no! I know of no one good reason why, at this particular season, anyone should be anxious to encompass my death. And now—' he dragged himself to his feet, fatigue making him appear pale and strained '—we must get ourselves to bed for what remains of the night.'

Chapter Fourteen

An outward calm pervaded Baynard's Castle after the dramatic events of the previous evening. All members of the duke's and his mother's households had been bidden to attend Mass without fail that morning in order to pray for the repose of the young mummer's soul. But beneath the surface everyone was agog with feverish speculation and rumours of a plot to kill Duke Richard ran like wildfire throughout the building. Little knots of people huddled together in every corner, drifting apart whenever the eye of Authority was bent upon them, but regrouping again as soon as it was safe to do so.

It had not surprised me to be summoned to a meeting with Timothy Plummer and Lionel Arrowsmith in the tower room where we had first met on Tuesday night. The latter, still encumbered by sling and crutch, looked ashen-faced, blear-eyed and half-dead from fatigue. Timothy on the other hand was spryer than usual, relieved that the matter was now out in the open.

'I always thought it better that the plot should be made public,' he said. 'At least now there will be others besides ourselves keeping a watch over the duke to ensure his safety.'

'If he lets them,' Lionel grunted. 'He's already putting it

about that it was just some madman who had somehow got past the castle guards and who is therefore unlikely to disturb his peace again. All talk of a conspiracy against his life is to be strictly discouraged. I have my orders and so have you. He is relying on the fact that we quit London for Dover at dawn tomorrow to give another direction to people's thoughts.'

'Dawn tomorrow?' I echoed hollowly.

Timothy nodded. 'Aye. We told you! The king and his brothers embark on the first favourable tide a day or so from now to join the rest of the army at Calais.'

'Yes. Of course. I had forgotten it was so soon. And it's certain we go with the duke?'

'You and I will most certainly be accompanying His Grace, chapman. Lal will remain here until his bones are mended. He's no use to man nor beast at present. So!' Timothy's tone became brisker. 'What conclusions may we draw from the events of yesterevening?'

With an effort, I forced myself to abandon all thoughts of the forthcoming journey to France and tried instead to answer the question. 'Geoffrey Whitelock is not our assassin. He was in my sight throughout the mumming, but I cannot vouch for the other four. Did either of you notice any one of them immediately before or during the attempt on His Grace's life?'

Timothy slowly shook his head. 'Not with any certainty, no. The hall was too crowded, and by then the smoke from the torches had made it difficult to see across the room. Lal, what about you?'

'I might have seen young Humphrey Nanfan talking to someone, but I can't be sure.' Lionel hunched his shoulders. 'Well, at least we know that Geoffrey is blameless.

But there are still at least four others who could have been wearing Chanticleer's mask instead of its rightful owner. Anyone could have slipped from the hall before the mummers' entrance and lured one of them to that alcove. Did none of the troupe see their fellow led away?'

'Apparently not.' Timothy rose and began to prowl restlessly about the room. 'They had been given one of the chambers opening off that corridor for changing into their costumes and were already masked by the time they were called upon to appear. One of them did recall that the lad playing the part of Chanticleer was tardy and had fallen behind. And he was late, it seems, joining the rest of them for their entrance into the great hall. When asked where he'd been his excuse was that he'd got lost in the maze of passageways, but being muffled by the headdress no one recognized that his voice was unfamiliar.'

'So,' I said, 'someone lay in wait, hidden by the curtain of that embrasure, seized the latecomer as he hurried to catch up with his fellows, despatched him swiftly and cleanly with a knife through the heart, put on his costume and followed the rest of the troupe downstairs.'

Timothy grunted assent and ran a hand through his thinning hair before throwing himself down once more on the window seat. 'Whoever it is is a ruthless man. He's already murdered twice in the course of trying to carry out his mission. The mummer who was killed was a slender lad, but the mask and costume would easily disguise a person's natural shape and make him appear taller than he actually is. Which means that we've very little to go on. Well,' he sighed, 'we know Geoffrey Whitelock to be innocent, but that is all.'

185

'Not quite all,' I said, and two heads turned swiftly towards me. 'Don't raise your hopes too high,' I begged them. 'What I am about to tell you may have no substance in it. Listen and make up your own minds.'

I proceeded to give an account of the whispered conversation I had overheard, of my struggle to identify some word or phrase which might have lodged in my mind and of my final realization that one of the words uttered had been '*demain*'.

'My conclusion therefore is that the conspirators were speaking French, which is why most of their talk was beyond my comprehension.'

But neither Timothy nor Lionel shared my sense of the incident's importance.

'It seems to me that you are making altogether too much of it, chapman,' Lionel said, and Timothy nodded in agreement.

'Nevertheless,' I insisted stubbornly, 'it is worth remembering that the very next day an attempt was made to murder His Grace.' I thought for a moment, then asked, 'Does either of you know where Ralph Boyse was the evening Thaddeus Morgan was murdered?'

Lionel flushed painfully. 'He was with Berys.'

I recollected the conversation between him and Matthew Wardroper, here in this very room, and swore in frustration. 'You're certain of that?'

Lionel shrugged. 'Berys admitted it when I questioned her. Why,' he added bitterly, 'should she not? She was, after all, doing no wrong. She is betrothed to Ralph.'

'But can you trust her word?' I asked. 'Would she lie for him if he needed her to do so?'

'She might, I suppose, but it wasn't necessary. Several

people saw them together during the time we were all at the Three Tuns ale-house.'

Timothy leaned forward, resting his elbows on his knees, one hand thoughtfully stroking his chin. 'We should have considered this circumstance before. It means that Ralph could not have murdered Thaddeus Morgan. Therefore we can acquit him of being the man we want. And now I come to think more carefully on past events, there is no possibility that Ralph might even have got wind of Thaddeus's visit to me at Northampton, for the duke had granted him leave of absence the previous day to visit a sick uncle in Devon. He didn't rejoin us until almost a month later and was waiting for us here in London when we arrived from Canterbury.' Timothy, drumming with his fingers against one cheek, was silent for a moment before sitting upright again. 'I think we must now all agree that, as well as Geoffrey Whitelock, we can exonerate Ralph of being in any way concerned in this fiendish plot.'

'You're right!' Lionel spoke with an enthusiasm which seemed to me to betoken relief and I regarded him curiously, recalling other fleeting but unreadable expressions of his which I had noticed whenever Ralph's name was mentioned.

Timothy continued with satisfaction, 'I never thought the French likely to wish for Duke Richard's death, nor indeed that of any member of the king's family. Therefore we may now whittle our number down to three: Humphrey Nanfan, Stephen Hudelin and Jocelin d'Hiver. And of them, only the last speaks French.'

'But that doesn't make sense either,' Lionel objected. 'The Burgundians are our allies. They would have no reason that I can see to wish for His Grace's murder. It's far more likely to be brother Clarence or the Woodvilles.'

'Or neither,' I put in quietly. 'We must not overlook the fact that maybe none of these three, or indeed any of the five we began with, is our assassin.'

Timothy shook his head. 'Chapman, we are only human and cannot perform the impossible. There are limits to our powers. All we can do is try to discover the innocence or otherwise of those remaining whom we know to be spies within the household. We have between us proved that two of the five are not our assassin, so let us trust that with observation and patience we may do the same by the other three.'

'And if none of them turns out to be the murderer?'

Timothy grimaced. 'We must think again. But by that time the Eve of Saint Hyacinth may well have passed. And in any case,' he continued, 'I'm more sanguine than I was of being able to protect His Grace from harm. All his people are now alerted to the fact that he is in some kind of danger, however much he may attempt to throw dust in their eyes.'

Lionel and I agreed with this and we were about to disperse when the chamber door was thrown open noisily and Matthew Wardroper appeared, a little out of breath and full of righteous indignation.

'I guessed I should find the three of you here,' he said reproachfully, 'when Mistress Hogan told me that Lal was meeting with Roger Chapman and Timothy Plummer.' He turned on his cousin. 'I do think you might have included me, for it's been as much my adventure as yours. Anyone would think you didn't trust me!' And the youthful face flushed with anger.

Lionel hauled himself to his feet, impatiently fending off

all offers of assistance, and with his free hand clapped Matthew on the shoulder. 'Steady, lad, steady! I've told you, you're too young for me to let you run your head into unnecessary danger. As I said before, how should I answer to my aunt and uncle if any harm befell you?'

Matthew's soft lips pouted and the dark eyes, fringed by their even darker lashes, wore a sulky expression. 'I'm not a child,' he protested sullenly, his demeanour in many ways proving the opposite. He added defiantly, 'You were quite willing to make use of me when you had need.'

'That's true enough.' Lionel glanced at Timothy. 'It would be only fair to tell the lad what conclusions we have reached.'

'Oh, very well,' came the grudging answer. 'But be quick about it. It's time we returned to our duties and used our eyes and ears.'

Matthew listened docilely while his cousin made him free of our deliberations and then eagerly offered to keep watch over his fellow Squire of the Household, Jocelin d'Hiver.

Timothy, after the briefest of reflections, once again gave his consent. 'It will give Roger all the more freedom to study the movements of Stephen Hudelin and Humphrey Nanfan. Lionel, in case we don't meet again before our departure at dawn tomorrow, get well soon and join us in France as quickly as you can. Meantime, both Roger and I will keep an eye on your young kinsman here. And to you, Master Wardroper, I say this. Be very careful in your dealings with Jocelin d'Hiver. Until there is proof to the contrary, think of him as an extremely dangerous man.'

I doubt if Timothy Plummer would have approved my

immediate action after quitting the tower, which was to seek out Amice Gentle in her sewing-room.

She and her companions were not engaged with their needles today, but had been granted permission to begin packing up some of their work in readiness to leave with Duchess Cicely for Berkhamsted in three days' time. So Amice told me in the first rush of pleasure at seeing me again; a pleasure all the more freely expressed because of the absence of Mistress Vernon, the head seamstress.

'I've come to say goodbye,' I said, holding her little hand in mine. 'We're off at first light tomorrow.'

'I know.' She nodded solemnly, drawing me to sit down beside her on a bench, while her companions giggled and gossiped low amongst themselves, glancing frequently in our direction. 'Take care of yourself,' she added, shyly pressing my fingers. 'I . . . that is, we . . . were all very proud of you last night for the way that you saved the duke's life.' While I muttered an uncomfortable disclaimer, the large hazel eyes lifted questioningly to mine. 'Is there really a plot to kill His Grace, as some people are saying, or was it just a madman, as others insist, who managed to find his way into the castle?'

'I don't know,' I lied, sending up a short prayer for forgiveness. 'But it will behove all of us to watch over Duke Richard with extra care.' I took a deep breath. 'When I get back from France, may I come to visit you at Berkhamsted?'

The eager light died out of her eyes and once again I sensed that withdrawal which had rebuffed me at supper two days earlier. After a moment she said regretfully, 'No. It would be to no purpose. I am already betrothed.'

I felt for a moment as though I had been winded by a

blow to the stomach, but at last I managed to stutter, 'I see. I – I'm sorry. I – I didn't know. Your mother, when I talked with her in Southampton, gave no hint of such a thing.'

'It was arranged, with Her Grace's approval, the day before we left to come to London. My mother and father know nothing of it yet, for I've had no time to send a message to them since it happened.'

'You . . . love him, this man you're betrothed to?'

She answered quietly, 'I like him. Very much. Robert's a good man. He's one of Duchess Cicely's grooms. He'll be kind to me and Her Grace will give me a greater dowry than my father can afford.' Amice freed her hand from mine, smiling tremulously, and lifted her chin. 'I shall be contented enough and that's surely as much as most of us can expect in this life.'

'Perhaps . . . Then this is indeed goodbye.' I leaned forward and kissed her gently, full on the lips.

Tears welled up slowly in the hazel eyes and ran down her face unchecked.

'Yes.' She stroked my cheek and I felt the coldness of her touch. 'We hardly know one another. Why, then, does it feel as though I'm saying farewell to a friend?'

I did not answer but kissed her hand and the icy little fingers clung to mine. In the end I had to force myself away. Once outside the sewing-room I propped my back against the wall, breathing deeply until my emotions were once more under control. Amice was right: we barely knew each other. It was foolish to feel so bereft. And yet I found that I had been thinking of her constantly throughout the past few days; that her face had been always somewhere at the back of my mind. Ah well! It was not to be. I should soon forget her, I told myself angrily. There were plenty more fish in the sea and I had often fancied myself sick with love in the past, only to recover swiftly. Why then should this time be any different?

I squared my shoulders and ran downstairs to the bustling courtyard. There was too much else to occupy my thoughts for me to waste them on Amice Gentle.

We set out the following morning in a chill, grey mist, the harbinger of a hot summer's day. As the seemingly endless procession clattered across London Bridge, on through the sprawling suburb of Southwark and out on to the Dover road, the damp, pungent smell of the still-wet earth tickled our nostrils. Birds, wakened all too soon by the tramp of many feet and the thud of horses' hooves, started up their plaintive chorus; and as the hours passed trees, their leaves trembling with dewdrops as big as diamonds, swam up out of the milky haze which was beginning now to disperse.

In every village and hamlet through which we passed people left their work and came running to gawp at the brilliant cavalcade and at the three royal brothers who, in all the glory of martial display, with tuckets sounding and pennants flying, rode at its head. Each prince was surrounded by his most senior officers, while far behind followed the hordes of lesser servants and the rumbling baggage wagons.

Never having been a soldier, and knowing nothing of battles, I was astonished to discover how many and how varied were the numbers of retainers necessary for the maintenance of a lord's comfort in wartime.

'It won't all be fighting,' Humphrey Nanfan informed me, proudly displaying his superior knowledge of these matters. 'There's bound to be a great deal of feasting, jousting and suchlike when the king and his brothers entertain the Duke and Duchess of Burgundy at Calais.'

'It seems to me a funny way to conduct a war,' I grumbled.

We were sitting on the tailboard of a cart packed with napery, enjoying the warm sunshine and resting our weary legs. The head of Duke Richard's procession was now miles in front of us and would reach the night's halt at Rochester while we lesser mortals were still on the open road, where we would content ourselves with such shelter as we could find. I could only trust that Timothy Plummer was taking all precautions to ensure His Grace's safety; for with Lionel Arrowsmith left behind in Baynard's Castle, and with the necessity for me to keep watch over Humphrey Nanfan and Stephen Hudelin, an even greater responsibility had fallen upon his shoulders. At least Matthew Wardroper would be keeping Jocelin d'Hiver under his eye.

Idly I watched a man pause in his haymaking to hone his scythe, then take a drink from the leather bottle on the ground beside him. Women were moving slowly, bent almost double in the noonday heat, separating the stalks of already-cut grass in order to ensure that they dried out properly. Others were raking between the swathe lines, making certain that none of the morning's scything was wasted. It was a peaceful, harmonious scene, repeated at that time of year all over England, and I wondered how these men and women would feel if they thought that a foreign army was about to invade their world and trample down their crops. And, not for the first time, I fell to wondering what had decided King Edward to make war on France at this particular moment.

193

No doubt the more practical of his advisers had encouraged him to do so for the perennial reason of previous English kings: victories abroad discouraged dissension at home and that could only work to the ruler's advantage. Others, more idealistic, had probably pressed England's two-hundred-year-old claim to the French throne through Isabella Capet, wife and queen of the second Edward. Yet from the little I had seen of King Edward the fourth, I suspected that neither of these arguments would weigh very heavily with him. There was a scarcely veiled cynicism in that still handsome face which, to me at least, made his apparently motiveless decision all the stranger.

I hinted at these thoughts to Humphrey Nanfan, who was quick to counter with his own solution. 'It's to keep brother George from making more trouble I reckon. There's been a powerful lot of bad feeling between him and the queen's family these many years past; indeed, ever since she married His Highness.' Humphrey lowered his voice and wriggled closer to me on the tailboard. 'Years ago, when Jacques de Luxembourg, Her Grace's uncle, came to this country for her coronation, it was Duke George who dubbed him Lord Jakes. And whenever the poor fool went out riding in the London streets the crowds would pursue him, shouting things like "Here comes the Keeper of the *Privy* Purse" and directing him to the public privies in Paternoster Row. He didn't know what was going on, did he, poor sod? He'd smile and nod and thank 'em, and all the time my master would be doubled up with laughter. But the Woodvilles, they took it badly, especially as Duke George had protested one of the loudest against what he called his brother's misalliance.'

'You called Clarence your master just now,' I accused him.

Humphrey looked uncomfortable for a fleeting moment, then smiled guilelessly. 'My late master, I should have said, for at that time I was a page in Duke George's household. I told you,' he added defensively, 'that I fell out with a fellow servant and wished for another place. His Grace persuaded his brother of my usefulness.'

'I remember. It was the manner in which you spoke of my lord of Clarence, as if you still regarded yourself in his service.'

'Nonsense!' Humphrey tried to change the subject. 'Sweet Saviour, it's hot! I could do with a drink of ale.'

'Where were you the other evening,' I asked, 'during the mumming, when the attempt was made on Duke Richard's life?'

He turned his head sharply, regarding me with a sudden curiosity which he had not displayed before. I could see his suspicion deepening and the swift calculations going on behind his eyes as he pieced together certain incidents of the past six days, the days since I had become one of Duke Richard's servants.

'What does it matter to you?' he asked abruptly. 'You don't suspect one of the duke's own people, surely? His Grace has explained what happened. A madman got in from outside.'

I shrugged in an attempt to appear unconcerned. 'No reason. Just interest, that's all.' I forced a smile. 'You take me up too quickly, Humphrey.'

He stared hard at me for a moment longer until, apparently satisfied of the innocence of my intent, he too hunched his shoulders. 'Why shouldn't I tell you? It's no

195

secret after all. I was talking to Stephen Hudelin. You can ask him if you wish. He's only over there, walking alongside the cart containing His Grace's silver.' He raised his voice. 'Stephen! Come here! You're needed.' And when the older man had quickened his pace to catch up with our wagon, Humphrey continued without wink or nod or any change of expression that I could see, 'When that madman tried to kill Duke Richard where was I? Our friend Roger Chapman wants to know.'

Stephen glanced at me in his usual surly fashion. 'He was talking to me,' he said. 'But what does it have to do with you?'

Chapter Fifteen

We were on dry land once more, in Calais.

The great fortresses of Guisnes and Hammes frowned down upon us as we landed, but the town itself was in festive mood to welcome ashore King Edward and his two brothers. The summer weather had smiled upon us during our crossing of the Channel, and the richly decorated houses of the wool merchants hemmed us in on either side as the royal procession made its way to Saint Nicholas's Church to give thanks for our safe arrival.

Some of the thousands of advance troops who had lined the harbour to voice their greeting were already encamped on the marshy ground beyond the ditch outside the town, and it had been my expectation that, along with Stephen Hudelin and Humphrey Nanfan, I should be consigned to these miles of tents and baggage wagons which stretched as far as the eye could see from the double walls encircling Calais towards the friendly territory of the Duke of Burgundy. But I had hardly regained my land legs or settled my stomach after the heaving motion of the ship when I was summoned to a house which faced on to the market square, and which had been put at His Grace's disposal by an obliging merchant (who no doubt considered future patronage worth present inconvenience). There I discovered Timothy Plummer pacing up and down the parlour floor like some caged animal.

'Is this wise, sending for me so openly?' I asked as, at a gesture from him, I carefully shut the door behind me.

It was a pleasant room with a fine oaken table in the centre, a large carved armchair and several joint stools. The family plate, an impressive array of silver-gilt and pewter vessels, was displayed in a corner cupboard, rich tapestry hangings decorated the walls and an elaborately ornate staircase led to the upper storey. Our absent host was obviously a very rich man, but that was hardly surprising. As members of the chief English Wool Staple for the rest of Europe, the inhabitants of Calais were in general extremely wealthy.

Timothy spun round to face me, answering snappishly, 'I've had enough of caution. The Eve of Saint Hyacinth is now only six weeks distant and time is pressing. I cannot be everywhere at once and without Lionel, you and young Matthew Wardroper are the only two people in whom I can really trust. Have you anything to tell me?'

I seated myself, straddle-legged, on a stool and folded my arms. 'Only that Stephen Hudelin and Humphrey Nanfan claim to have been in conversation on Saturday evening at the moment when the duke's life was threatened. Each told me so independently of the other and I had no sense of collusion between them. Nor can I see any good reason why they should support one another's story if it doesn't happen to be true.'

Timothy was silent for a moment, grimly staring into space. When at last he spoke, it was to tick off a list of names with one hand on the fingers of the other. 'Geoffrey

Whitelock was within your line of vision when that attempt was made and as we know for certain that Ralph Boyse could not have killed Thaddeus Morgan, therefore we also know that he cannot be our man. And now Stephen Hudelin and Humphrey Nanfan would appear to be innocent, unless of course they are in this plot together. That leaves either Jocelin d'Hiver or . . .'

He broke off and I finished for him, 'Or someone else beside these five, which we have always feared might be the case.' Timothy nodded and lapsed once more into silence. 'So?' I prompted finally.

He glanced down at me thoughtfully. 'So we have to concentrate our main effort, from now on, on protecting His Grace's person. I shall therefore speak to the duke tonight and ask him to release you and young Matthew Wardroper from your household duties. I shall say that your services are required by me.'

I grimaced. 'And will His Grace oblige you, do you think? Or will you find yourself at the sharp end of his tongue?'

Timothy shook his head ruefully. 'I'll have to make him listen to me. It's for his own good when all's said and done.'

I grinned and rose from the stool. 'Rather you than me, my friend. And how will you explain my sudden rise in importance to my fellow Yeomen of the Chamber?'

Timothy shrugged. 'I shan't. For the truth is, chapman, that I'm past caring about anything except His Grace's safety.'

'Nevertheless,' I protested, 'we haven't yet fully considered the possibility that Jocelin d'Hiver could be our assassin, or that Stephen and Humphrey might be working together. Let me make some inquiries amongst the other members of the duke's household who have accompanied him to Calais. If we are to throw caution to the winds why shouldn't I question people more openly? Let me go to the camp. It's possible that someone might be able to confirm or deny their story.'

'Very well. But I want you to return here tonight. With your height and bulk, you'll prove a formidable addition to those guarding His Grace's slumbers. You may offer that as an excuse if you like to anyone wanting to know why you are so privileged.' He added wearily, 'Take no heed of what I said a while ago. We must still exercise a little caution.'

Half an hour later I was outside the town and being directed to that section of the camp where the less important members of Duke Richard's household officers were quartered. At least they had tents, whereas the foot-soldiers and camp-followers were condemned to sleeping in the open on the rough, bare ground. Skilfully avoiding both Stephen Hudelin and Humphrey Nanfan, I spent the rest of the day asking among the other Yeomen of the Chamber, pot-boys, servers – everyone, in short, who had also been present in the great hall of Baynard's Castle on Saturday evening and who had now been brought to wait upon His Grace in France – whether or not they had seen Humphrey and Stephen talking to one another round about the time when Chanticleer had made his attempt on Duke Richard's life.

My progress was naturally slow, for every question had to be put in such a fashion as to arouse as little suspicion as possible. And in the end I got small satisfaction, for no one seemed sure of having noted the pair in conversation. I was disappointed but resigned, it being only natural that all eyes had been fixed originally upon the mumming and subsequently upon the real drama unfolding in front of them. One server said that yes, he had seen Stephen and Humphrey talking together, but at exactly when in the night's proceedings he would not care to hazard. It was insufficient testimony for my purpose and when I returned to the house late that afternoon, just in time to help prepare the table for His Grace's dinner, I had to report failure to Timothy Plummer.

'No matter.' He sighed philosophically. 'As I said before, our chief efforts must now be concentrated on protecting His Grace's person. You've told the others that you will be staying close to the duke in future?'

I smiled. 'And can't pretend that I elicited much response to the news except envy. However, I'm not as sanguine as you are that such a course is the best, if not the only answer to our dilemma. We shan't remain in Calais for very long, that's for certain, and what happens once the campaign begins in earnest? It will be far more difficult then to protect His Grace.'

The worried frown once more creased Timothy's brow and I could almost have sworn that his hair was turning greyer by the minute. But all he said was, 'We must take each day as it comes and hope that God will grant us a miracle.'

I woke with a start from a dreamless slumber and heard the bells of Saint Nicholas's Church ring for Matins. Even then, after more than four years, I still found it difficult to sleep through the night-time office.

For a moment or two I could not recall where I was nor place my surroundings; then I recollected that I was lying fully clothed on a pallet bed in the narrow corridor outside the Duke of Gloucester's bedchamber. I had watched by his door until midnight, when I had been relieved by one of his Squires of the Body, who was still standing at his post, his right hand resting on the hilt of his sword, ready to draw it at the first hint of danger. A candle in its holder, placed on a shelf above our heads, gave out a faint but steady radiance.

'You sleep lightly,' the Squire whispered as I roused myself and sat up, rubbing my eyes and yawning.

'The bell woke me.' I shivered. 'I must find the privy.'

'It's in the yard at the back of the house.' As I got to my feet the lad eyed me approvingly. 'You're a stout fellow and no mistake. We could do with a few more of your girth.'

I made no answer, but tiptoed towards the head of the stairwell. Facing it, a narrow window, its shutters set wide to let in a cooling breeze and ensure that those who should be awake did not grow too drowsy in the summer heat, gave on to the market-place. As I passed, I glanced out at the ghostly shapes of the other dwellings around the square – and then froze into stillness. For the street door of a house immediately opposite had opened and a second or two later three men, cloaked and hooded, emerged. There was something furtive in their demeanour; in the manner in which they glanced about them and in the stealth with which they proceeded on their way. They walked in single file, each man hugging the wall of the nearest building and keeping well within its shadow. But their desire for secrecy was thwarted by the light from a three-quarter moon which penetrated between the overhanging eaves and illumined the cobbles. Before I could alert my companion, however, they had vanished into the all-pervading darkness of a convenient alleyway between the houses, so for the present I held my tongue.

I descended through the sleeping house to the courtyard door at the back, where two of the duke's faithful Yorkshiremen stood sentry. 'I need the privy,' I told them when they challenged me.

'What, another of you?' grunted the taller of the pair. 'You're the second in as many minutes. Too much guzzling before bedtime, that's the trouble.' He opened the door. 'Knock three times when you wish to come in again. And tell that other fellow to hurry.'

As I slipped outside I took a deep breath of salt sea air, then glanced around to locate the privy. It was at that precise moment that I became aware of a shadowy figure crossing the courtyard towards me from the direction of the outer gate.

'I was just checking that all was properly barred and bolted,' said a familiar voice, and to my astonishment I recognized the speaker as Ralph Boyse. What was he doing in the house when I had thought him safely in the encampment outside the town? 'Good-night,' he added, rapping softly three times on the door and being readmitted by the guards.

I looked after him thoughtfully before going across to examine the two four-inch-thick, iron-studded oaken leaves set in the high wall which bounded the property. Had Ralph left the courtyard? I doubted it somehow. Firstly, the top bolt of the gate could not be reached except by standing on a ladder or a mounting block. (A swift inspection of my surroundings told me that there was such a block in one corner, but it proved too weighty to be moved by one man on his own.) Secondly, bolts of that size would make a lot of noise when released or shot home, but I had heard nothing. And thirdly, Ralph could not afford to be absent from the house for longer than it would normally take him to use the privy without arousing the suspicion of the guards.

He must have been standing by the gate when he heard the courtyard door open and saw me. Had his presence there really been innocent? Had he truly been doing what he said? And it was in that instant that a voice, speaking barely above a whisper and talking rapid French, sounded close to my ear.

'Who's there?' I hissed, spinning round in bewilderment, unable to locate the source of the noise.

Then I saw that there was a crack, perhaps an inch or so wide and some two inches long, between the jamb of the gate and the wall, where plaster had become dislodged. Whoever had spoken was standing on the other side of the wall and I heard the rasp of his indrawn breath followed by the urgent slap of feet on cobbles as he hurried away. I cursed myself for a clumsy fool, but there was nothing I could do to remedy the situation. I used the privy and returned indoors. Any desire for sleep, however, had fled. My instinct was to seek out Timothy Plummer at once, but I had no idea exactly where within the house he was lodged and dared not risk disturbing others for fear of also rousing the duke. Instead I lay wakeful on my pallet until such time as it was my turn to resume the watch outside His Grace's door.

Had that whispered message been intended for Ralph Boyse? It seemed most probable. But who knew that he was here in the house and when had the assignation been arranged? And did it have anything at all to do with the plot against Duke Richard's life?

Timothy, when I put the question to him next morning, dragging him from his mattress in a quiet corner of the counting-house, was unwilling, to begin with, to pay much attention to my story. Ralph Boyse was innocent, for we had not only established that he could not possibly have murdered Thaddeus Morgan, but in addition he had been unaware of Thaddeus's visit to Northampton, having been in Devon at the time, visiting a sick relative.

'Why is he sleeping beneath this roof?' I asked. 'Why is he not in camp with the others?'

'The duke needs some servants about him,' Timothy reproved me. 'And Ralph both plays and sings well as you know. His Grace sleeps badly and sometimes finds music soothing before he retires for the night.'

'His Grace sent for Ralph?'

Timothy hesitated a moment before admitting, 'N-no. Now you mention it, I believe Ralph entered the town just before curfew yesterevening and himself suggested that Duke Richard might have need of his services. I was present when his message was delivered. Until then, young Matthew had been singing, but his voice is not so fine as Ralph's.'

'And then, of course,' I added thoughtfully, 'Ralph had to stay the night. Did he know where His Grace was lodging?'

'He would only have had to ask, once he was inside the town. But he would have no previous knowledge of the house nor of its peculiarities. Are you sure you didn't imagine this voice? That you weren't still half dreaming?'

'I haven't yet told you everything,' I answered. 'Do you

know who lodges in the house immediately opposite this one, on the other side of the market square? It has a very high, pointed gable.'

Timothy looked surprised. 'Aye. It's normally the residence of the Mayor of Calais, but for tonight, and for as long as he remains within the town, it is being occupied by His Highness.'

I frowned. 'The king sleeps there?'

'Yes. Why do you ask?' But when I had finished my tale, it was Timothy's turn to frown. 'Could you have been mistaken in the house? The Duke of Clarence is lodging next door and I'd put nothing past him, not even midnight assignations.'

'I made no mistake, of that I'm certain.'

Timothy thought for a moment, then shrugged his shoulders. 'Perhaps it was necessary for King Edward to have consultation with his captains. There are many secret moves and counter-moves in time of war.'

'It was two o'clock,' I cavilled. 'The dead time of morning. And why would the king hold military talks that did not include his brothers? His two most senior commanders.'

'How should I know?' Timothy spread his hands. 'But you can be sure that it has nothing to do with us. So, what did this voice say to you from the other side of the wall?'

'I've told you, it spoke in French and I know only a little of that language. It was rapid and low, barely above a whisper. Maybe I shall recall a word or two later, as I did on the previous occasion, maybe not. But it seems significant to me that this is the second time in the course of this affair that I have heard French spoken. We must remember that it is Ralph Boyse's mother tongue.'

206

'And also that of Jocelin d'Hiver.'

'He was not present in the courtyard.'

'Many people in the town speak French,' Timothy objected after a moment's consideration. 'They have to, in order to deal with their neighbours beyond the Pale. And many of the nobility use an old-fashioned, bastard version of the Norman tongue on occasions.'

'But who creeps about in the dead of night to speak to people through a crack in a wall? And why here, where it is known that the Duke of Gloucester is lodging?'

My persistence was beginning to convince Timothy that he must take a more serious view of the information I had laid before him. All the same, he was reluctant to accuse Ralph Boyse, a man we thought we had proved innocent of any fell intent towards His Grace. Moreover, the greatest impediment still remained – that until we knew the reason for a plot against Duke Richard's life, it was wellnigh impossible to point the finger of suspicion at anyone. We parted company, miserable in the knowledge that in over a week we had progressed very little, and that such assumptions as we had made were probably built on sand.

Later that day I accompanied the duke to the camp, where he had called a muster of his captains, and left him, securely flanked by two of his Squires and with a third guarding the entrance to his tent, while I went in search of Ralph Boyse. The ranks of those who wore the Gloucester azure-and-murrey livery seemed endless, but I found him eventually inspecting the contents of one of the baggage wagons, looking for a small, portable organ which had been mislaid.

'It's a favourite instrument of the duke's,' Ralph was

saying peevishly to the baggage-master as I approached. 'And he has particularly requested it tonight when I sing for him.'

'You're honouring us with your company again then, Master Boyse,' I said, quietly coming up behind him.

His head jerked round and I caught the flash of hostility in his eyes before it was swiftly veiled.

'I am, Roger Chapman. And it seems that you, too, have found favour with the duke. You appear to be a great deal in his company since we landed in France.'

I laughed. 'Only because the attempt on his life has unsettled him, although he'd never admit to it, and I'm bigger and stronger than most men.'

'That's true.' Ralph turned back to the wagon where a shout of triumph from the baggage-master announced his discovery of the organ. It was held aloft, its painted pipes gleaming in the sunshine, then Ralph wrapped his arms about it, hugging it against his chest. 'Are you returning to the town now? If so, we might as well walk together.'

'No, I'm attending upon the duke and must await his pleasure. He is in conference with his captains.'

Ralph took a firmer grasp upon the instrument he was holding. 'A pity,' he remarked. 'You might have given me a hand with this cumbersome object. We could have taken turns in carrying it. Never mind. I'll walk with you as far as His Grace's tent if you'll allow it.'

This sudden familiarity demonstrated more clearly than anything else could have done that Ralph was no longer in any doubt as to the true reason for my presence in Duke Richard's household. I was not a humble Yeoman of the Chamber but a privileged person, and one of whom to be wary. Every now and then he darted a watchful glance at me from the corner of his eyes, but his manner remained polite, although it could scarcely be described as friendly.

'I should be glad of your company,' I answered.

We threaded a path through the teeming mass of men and their equipment: armourers, bowmen, cooks and messengers, foot-soldiers, grooms, arrowsmiths and chand lers, all scurrying about like ants, and all trying to serve the interests of their own particular lords at the expense of all the others. Twice I had to assist Ralph over uneven ground when the weight of his burden made him less nimble than he might otherwise have been at avoiding obstacles; and more than once I was forced to lift bodily out of our way some argumentative fellow who was disputing our passage. As usual, my size discouraged any argument.

'You're useful to have around,' Ralph said. 'How came you to be a chapman?'

'My mother intended me for the Church,' I answered cheerfully, 'but with the blessing of my Abbot I decided that I had no vocation and was released from my novitiate. I liked the idea of being my own master and the freedom of the open road.'

'What part of the country do you hail from? Devon?'

'No. My home was in Wells, although my motherless child lives with her granddam in Bristol.' I raised my voice a little so as to be heard above the deafening clamour all around us. 'But I have often been in Devon and know it well, as I believe you must do. I was told you have a kinsman there. Whereabouts in the county does he have his dwelling?'

My companion did not reply immediately, being concerned to avoid a pothole in the road. But, 'Near the city of Exeter,' he said when he had safely negotiated this hazard.

209

'A fine place to live.' I hesitated a moment before continuing, 'The earth there is such a remarkable colour, so white and chalky.'

Ralph grunted his assent and I noted that he was beginning to sweat. No doubt his burden was heavy.

We parted company close to the duke's tent, I to wait until I should be needed to accompany my lord back to Calais, Ralph to find some wagon going in the same direction, or else to trudge the weary way on foot. I watched him thoughtfully as he paused to exchange greetings with an armourer who had just finished hammering out a dent in a cuisse. It had been well worth the effort to seek out Ralph Boyse, if only to learn that he knew nothing of Devon and had never been there. He had no kinsman who dwelt near Exeter, for the soil thereabouts is the deep rich red that accompanies granite.

So where had he been, and what had he really been up to last May, while Duke Richard's levies had been encamped around Northampton?

Chapter Sixteen

We did not return to Calais for our belated dinner until close upon noon, by which time my stomach was rumbling with hunger.

The reason for the delay was the duke's insistence on visiting his levies, walking around that part of the camp where his own particular troops were mustered and following in my footsteps of earlier that morning. He displayed an interest in the comfort and welfare of his men shown by very few of the other commanders, asking pertinent questions and displaying considerable knowledge concerning the answers. (This should not have surprised me, however, because this young man, who was my own age exactly, had been Admiral of England, Ireland and Aquitaine by the time he was eleven years old.)

At last, however, the duke was ready to leave and return to the town, a decision I silently but heartily applauded, and not just because I was famished. The familiar way he moved among the soldiery, stopping to speak to the roughest and ugliest of characters, filled me with the greatest apprehension; and on more than one occasion I urged his Body Squires to stand closer to him, even presuming to mount guard over him myself. How easy it would be, I reflected, for someone to produce a knife from beneath his tunic and slide it between his victim's ribs.

Duke Richard gave no sign of noticing these manoeuvres, except for a slight lift at the corners of his wide, thin mouth. However, when at last he turned to go, back to where the horses had been tethered at the edge of the vast encampment, he brushed against me, murmuring so low that only I could hear, 'It's time I put you out of your misery, Roger Chapman.'

He and his Squires cantered leisurely over the paved causeway which led eventually to Calais's landward gate. The rest of us were on foot, swinging along at a vigorous pace, but unable, nevertheless, to keep abreast of the horsemen. I was relieved therefore to see a party of the duke's retainers, headed by the unmistakable figure of Timothy Plummer, riding out across the lowered drawbridge to meet us. I was also pleased to recognize Matthew Wardroper amongst the group. There was something reassuring about the sight of his slender, upright figure, mounted on a chestnut gelding. Moreover, it was good to know that here, at least, was one man free from the taint of any suspicion.

I was less pleased, a moment later, to note Ralph Boyse, still clutching the portable organ, standing in the crowd lining the roadside to watch the duke and his retinue pass. Why was he not safely in Calais by now? It was an hour and more since we had parted company; ample time for him to have reached and entered the town, even hampered as he was by his burden. I tried to keep him in view as my fellows and I drew level with the onlookers, but there were too many people milling around the edge of the causeway, and on more than one occasion he vanished from sight.

212

The two parties of horsemen had by now met and mingled, Timothy Plummer and his escort closing in behind the duke who, even at a distance, was patently none too gratified to see them. He was doubtless displeased by this public demonstration of concern.

Suddenly, above the general hubbub, there sounded a brief but piercing whistle. Almost immediately Duke Richard's horse careered off the track and began a headlong gallop towards the deep ditch which surrounded Calais's double circle of walls. For a moment nobody moved, unable to take in exactly what had happened, and then for a few short seconds after realization dawned we all waited for the duke, deservedly famous for his equestrian skills, to bring the maddened beast under control.

'Jesus!' breathed the man next to me, those of us on foot having slowed to a halt. 'His saddle's slipping. The girth's broken.'

'Or been cut,' I muttered grimly under my breath.

We all started to run, knowing full well that it was hopeless. We could never catch up. It needed another horseman, and a skilled one at that, to overtake and check the bolting thoroughbred, a high-spirited animal and difficult enough to handle at the best of times. The duke's entire mounted retinue was already streaming in pursuit, but I placed little faith in the ability of any one of them to prevent the tragedy so obviously impending. If the duke did not break his neck, he must, barring a miracle, be seriously injured in a fall.

The cumbersome ornamental saddle slithered first to one side, then to the other of the horse's back, and Duke Richard twice avoided being thrown by the merest hair's breadth and his own superb skill as a rider. But the ditch was getting closer by the second. Once the animal stumbled into that nothing on earth could save either him or the duke from an extremely dangerous tumble.

Then, with disaster looming, young Matthew Wardroper seemingly came out of nowhere, reaching his master's side at breakneck speed, leaning across to snatch at the runaway's bridle and flinging a steadying arm about the prince's shoulders. There was a moment of wild confusion when it looked as if both men and their mounts must plunge together down the steep, rolling slope into the bottom of the ditch; but at the very second when all appeared lost, Duke Richard wrenched his horse's head to the left and veered sharply away from the edge, taking Matthew Wardroper with him. The blown steeds came to a stop a furrow's length from the brink, standing docilely while the two men dismounted.

I was near enough by now to see that young Matthew looked considerably more shaken than the duke, who put up both hands to ward off a host of anxious retainers.

'I am perfectly safe. There is nothing to be alarmed about,' I heard him say, before he was blocked from my view by a sea of bodies.

And he was the only one of us who looked calm and unruffled as, twenty minutes later using a borrowed saddle, he rode over the drawbridge and into the town at the head of his retinue.

The following day I found myself, more by chance than design, wedged next to Timothy Plummer as the three princes, supported by their immediate household officers and friends, crowded into the market square of Calais to

214

await the arrival of Margaret, Duchess of Burgundy. After the formal greetings and exchange of presents, King Edward and his two brothers, accompanied by their sister, would withdraw for rest and relaxation into the Hôtel de Ville, where they would be able to discuss more intimate family matters.

Timothy edged a little closer and whispered in my ear, 'Have you been told that tomorrow my lord and the Duke of Clarence will escort the duchess back to St Omer?' I shook my head as he grinned, taking his usual pleasure at imparting unwelcome news. 'True, I assure you. And I have arranged with His Grace that you shall be one of his following. Can you sit a horse?'

'I have ridden, although not recently. Does Ralph Boyse go with us?'

'No. Nor Stephen Hudelin, nor Jocelin d'Hiver, nor Humphrey Nanfan. They will remain here under the watchful eye of young Wardroper. But we two must go with the duke just in case none of the four proves to be the guilty person and danger threatens from another quarter.'

I shifted my position slightly in order to obtain a better view of Duke Richard, straddling his horse beside his brothers in the centre of the square. I noticed that today he sat a different saddle. I spoke to Timothy without turning my head. 'I haven't asked if His Grace's girth was deliberately cut yesterday morning. I took it for granted.'

'And right to do so,' Timothy responded glumly. 'There was no possibility of a mistake. The leather was almost new and the break was clean. A knife, or some other sharp instrument, had been used to slice it through.'

'What did the grooms say?'

'Swore that all the harness had been closely inspected as

usual before the duke set out. They're good, sound Yorkshiremen. Been in the duke's employ for years, both at Middleham and at Sheriff Hutton. There's no cause to doubt their word or actions. Like all his northern levies, they're both zealously protective of his person.'

I shrugged. 'I don't doubt it for an instant. The horses were tethered on the outskirts of the camp for over two hours and more while the duke went about his business. Anyone could have got at them. Ralph Boyse was in the camp throughout that period, as I've told you. Have you inquired about Humphrey and the others?'

'The three of them were absent from the duke's lodgings all morning. This is attested to. Apart from that, however, their whereabouts are unknown. They could have been inside the walls, but no one can say for certain.'

'What do they say themselves?'

Timothy sighed. 'His Grace has strictly forbidden any general questioning of the household. It will only draw unwelcome attention, he thinks, to this threat upon his life.' Timothy straightened his back as the distant sound of trumpets echoed from the landward side of the town. 'Nevertheless, I have ventured to ignore his commands in the case of our particular friends.'

'With what result?' I prompted as everyone in the square now came to attention, the tips of bills and halberds glittering in the sunshine.

'Naturally enough, considering the circumstances – for rumour of the true cause of the mishap has spread like wildfire in spite of the duke's attempts to keep it secret – they all claim to have been in Calais about their own or His Grace's business.'

'That's nothing to their credit. The girth may well have

216

been tampered with before Duke Richard set out for the camp but after the animal left the stable. The leather could have been sliced almost through, but not quite, leaving the motion of the saddle on the homeward journey to complete our assassin's handiwork.'

Timothy shook his head decisively. 'The cut was clean. No part of the strap was frayed.' He was pleased with himself. 'You're not the only one, chapman, who knows what to look for, or what conclusions to draw from the things you see.'

There was no chance just then for further conversation. With the banners and pennants of Burgundy hanging limply above her head in the noonday heat, and with the sunlight gleaming on the ubiquitous collar of the Golden Fleece, Margaret, Duchess of Burgundy, rode into Calais and the crowded market-place.

In appearance, she was very like her two elder brothers, tall and big-boned with the florid Plantagenet complexion. When she had dismounted, she first made obeisance to King Edward before rising from her curtsey to be embraced more informally by all three men. From my position of vantage, with only a single row of halberdiers between me and the main players in this little scene, I noted that although the duchess warmly greeted both her eldest and youngest brother, it was George of Clarence whom she was most delighted to see. She held him longer in her arms, kissed him more soundly and clung to his hand more possessively when the royal party and the most privileged of their respective retainers finally moved inside the Hôtel de Ville.

Those of us left outside in the square immediately relaxed, the soldiers allowing their shoulders to slump and their grip on their bills and halberds to slacken. The rest of us began to disperse about our various business. Timothy rubbed the back of his neck, his short stature having made it necessary for him to crane over the heads of the guard of honour in order to see what was happening.

'Where's the *Duke* of Burgundy?' I asked. 'Why hasn't he come with the duchess?'

My companion snorted. 'You may well ask. He isn't called Charles the Rash for nothing. Apparently, he's gone dashing off to besiege some tinpot town called Neuss just because the Mayor, or Burgomaster, or however they term 'em here, has annoyed him. Our own lord's hopping mad, by all I hear, and even Duke George ain't too pleased about it.'

'And King Edward?' I asked. 'What does he say?'

'Strangely enough, he's not too bothered by all accounts. Mind you, it's not surprising, really.' Timothy smiled the superior smile of one who was in the innermost counsels of the high and mighty. 'I don't know as I'd worry too much about having Duke Charles constantly dancing attendance at my elbow. And I dare say His Highness'd rather have his brother-in-law's room than his company.'

I rubbed my chin thoughtfully, but made no further comment on the subject.

Instead, 'What do you think caused the duke's mount to bolt yesterday when it did?'

Timothy hunched his shoulders. 'Someone in the crowd let out a whistle. Didn't you hear it? Well then! There's your answer.'

'But it didn't affect the other horses.'

'Maybe they ain't so high-strung as that bay of the duke's. It's always been a funny-tempered animal. It was

218

why my lord of Clarence sold it to his brother in the first place. There was no one in his stables who could handle it, including himself.' Timothy glanced sharply at me with an arrested expression in his eyes. 'You don't think . . . ?' he began, then pulled himself up short, shaking his head. 'No. That was over a twelvemonth since.'

We had by now reached the house where the duke was staying and thankfully entered its portals, leaving the market-place to the burning midday heat and the wilting halberdiers and billmen: poor souls who must wait for the duchess to emerge from the Hôtel de Ville and then escort her to her overnight lodgings. I agreed with Timothy that he was probably right to discount the fact that the Duke of Clarence had been the bay's original owner and we separated just inside the door with a parting injunction from him to remember that I was riding with the duke tomorrow to St Omer. I nodded and watched his retreating back as he bustled away about his own affairs. It seemed to me that there were times when Master Plummer was far too complacent about his powers of reasoning for Duke Richard's safety.

I stood for several seconds, head bowed in thought, recalling the scene in the market-place. Had the duke been riding the bay this morning? I fancied not. He had been mounted on a chestnut mare, if memory served me aright, and I intercepted a scurrying page to ask if he knew where my lord was stabling his horses.

'In Pissoir Lane,' came the answer.

This I found without much difficulty, every local inhabitant knowing where the public urinals were located. The stables stood at the opposite end of the alleyway, next to the smithy, and my azure-and-murrey livery gained me immediate access. I was directed without hesitation to the half-dozen stalls reserved for the Duke of Gloucester's horses and the two grooms accepted me with the same lack of reservation. As Timothy had told me, they were plain, blunt Yorkshiremen, who addressed each other as Wat and Alfred, and I came straight to the point, knowing that I need not beat about the bush.

'What do you think caused my lord's horse to bolt yesterday?' I asked them. 'Master Plummer thinks the animal was frightened by a whistle from someone in the crowd, it being highly strung and therefore volatile.'

The man called Alfred snorted. 'I'll tell thee this for nowt,' he said, in an accent so thick that to my West Country ears it sounded almost like a foreign language. 'Great Hal's nay s' highly strung as that Master Plummer, flittin' in and out, hoppin' around like a flea on a griddle, askin' a hundred bludy questions and nay list'nin' to the answers. Here!' He led me to one of the stalls and opened the door, indicating by a jerk of his head that I should follow him inside, where the bay, Great Hal, was peacefully foraging in his manger. In spite of this I approached the hindquarters of the spirited beast with caution.

The groom named Wat now joined us and it was he, pushing his obviously younger colleague aside, who ran an experienced hand across the beast's left buttock, close to the tail.

'See here,' he urged. 'If you look carefully where my finger's pointing you c'n just make out a smear o' dried blood.' I peered closely and sure enough a tiny scab, no bigger than a pinhead, was visible among the short, stiff hairs of the glossy coat. 'That's what made him bolt, isn't it, old fellow?' And Wat caressed the horse's neck with a loving hand. The animal paused briefly in its feeding and whickered a soft greeting through its nostrils.

There was silence. Then I said slowly, 'You're telling me that someone deliberately goaded Great Hal into bolting? Well, it's no more than I expected. That shrill whistle alone is unlikely to have unsettled him, but a sharp jab in his rump would almost certainly have upset a mettlesome animal such as this. Did you inform Master Plummer of your find?'

'We would've, reet willingly, if he'd only stayed to inquire. But he were off, like a hare when t'dogs are after it, once he'd satisfied hisself that girth'd been tampered with. Seemingly that were all he needed to know. We hadn't properly examined Great Hal by then. And Master Plummer's not returned here since for any further answers.'

I thanked them and left, deep in thought. I was convinced in my own mind, although it would be a difficult thing to prove, that the whistle had been a signal. From Ralph Boyse perhaps? He had been amongst those who had lined the causeway and I was growing increasingly mistrustful of this son of a French mother who most surely had not been where he said he was during Duke Richard's sojourn at Northampton.

My mind went back to Berys Hogan and Lionel Arrowsmith. I recalled how everyone had warned Lionel of impending trouble, of Ralph's jealousy, if he persisted in paying court to her. Yet those warnings had proved false and Berys herself, who must know the temper of her betrothed as well as anyone, had seemed unconcerned by the threat of Ralph's anger. There was something about their actions that worried me, but it was like trying to see to the bottom of a pond through muddy water.

221

My thoughts harked back to the events of yesterday, coupled with what I had just learned. If the whistle had been a signal, then for whom had it been intended? Only someone close to the duke, someone in his immediate retinue, could have pricked the horse's rump and made it bolt. With a sinking feeling in the pit of my stomach, I realized that this presented me, and of course Timothy Plummer, with an entirely unexpected problem, for neither Jocelin d'Hiver, Humphrey Nanfan nor Stephen Hudelin had been amongst those riding behind Duke Richard.

As I approached, I could see that the market square was still full of people, the sweating soldiers still waiting for Duchess Margaret to emerge from the Hôtel de Ville. Red-faced Sergeants-at-arms, as weary and uncomfortable as their men, bawled conflicting orders, the horses neighed and stamped their feet, while the townsfolk irritably tried to get on with everyday living. High above, the sun shone down relentlessly, making this the one truly hot day we had had since our arrival in Calais. To my right a flag-paved courtyard was sliced in two by shadow thrown by the transverse section of a roof. A bench ran along one wall of the houses which surrounded this little haven of peace and silence and I noticed that the building facing me was a tavern. I became conscious of an overpowering thirst. Within minutes I was seated on the bench, out of the sun's glare, swallowing the contents of a mazer.

When I had drunk to the dregs, I wiped my mouth on the back of my hand, leaned my head against the wall behind me and gave myself up to despair. I was no nearer an explanation of events than I had been when first approached, more than two weeks ago, by Timothy Plummer. It was now the sixth day of July and the Eve of Saint

Hyacinth was more than five weeks distant. Long enough for desperate men to make a further, and perhaps this time successful, attempt on Duke Richard's life. Two had been made already and I was as far as ever from solving the all-important question – why? I stretched my legs out in front of me and, having assured myself that no one was watching, I began muttering to myself as I ticked off on my fingers such fragments of the puzzle as I possessed.

Of all the five suspects presented for my consideration, and known by Timothy and Lionel Arrowsmith to be working for other masters, one had been cleared by my own observation, while of the remaining four Ralph Boyse appeared to me to be the most definitely implicated. His whereabouts during the first attempt on the duke's life had never been established and, although this could also be said of the other three, it was only Ralph whom I had so far detected in a blatant falsehood. Why had he begged leave of absence from the duke in order to visit a sick kinsman in Devon when he had obviously never visited the county? No one who had ever seen that rich, red earth would agree with the suggestion that it was chalky. Yet even if Ralph were indeed in the pay of France, as Timothy, Lionel and now I myself all thought him, what possible reason could the French have for wanting Richard of Gloucester killed? From the beginning, Timothy had been at pains to point out the unlikelihood of any such wish. King Edward, perhaps, as the sole instigator of this projected invasion; but Duke Richard's death, like that of his brother Clarence, could surely avail them nothing.

I shifted my position on the bench, let my hands drop into my lap and closed my eyes. A ragged cheer from the market-place, followed by the renewed barking of orders, indicated that Duchess Margaret and her brothers had at last come out from the Hôtel de Ville, and that she was now ready to be conducted to her lodgings. I stayed where I was however. Tomorrow I should be one of those accompanying her back to St Omer. I should see all I wanted to see of the lady then. Meantime, there were other matters needing my consideration.

Chapter Seventeen

They were small things, really, not mentioned to Timothy
Plummer because, on the face of it, unconnected with the
threat to Duke Richard's life. Nevertheless, they bothered
me. The lack of any real enthusiasm for the forthcoming
war displayed by King Edward at last Saturday's banquet in
Baynard's Castle; the fleeting yet significant glance that I
had intercepted between him and John Morton, his Master
of the Rolls; his reported indifference to the fact that his
brother-in-law and chief ally, the Duke of Burgundy,
instead of coming to greet him and join in a council of war,
had dashed off to besiege the little town of Neuss; all these
things, for some reason, made me uneasy.

Added to them was the memory of that furtive party of
cloaked and hooded men leaving King Edward's Calais
lodgings the night before last. Who were they? And what
had been their mission? Above all, was there a connection
between them and the Frenchman whose voice I had heard
through the crack in the courtyard wall, imparting a
message which, I was fully convinced, had been intended
for Ralph Boyse . . . ?

'So this is where you're hiding!' exclaimed a voice, and
when I opened my eyes Matthew Wardroper was standing
in front of me. 'Master Plummer has sent me to look for

you. He needs, he says, to discuss the order of procession for tomorrow. He wants to make sure that you and he ride as close to the duke as possible.' The brown eyes twinkled suddenly and he sat down beside me on the bench. 'But I dare say the matter will keep a while. Let me buy you another cup of ale.'

'Thank you. But there's something I want to talk to you about first.' And I told him of my visit to the stables and the grooms' revelation. 'Which means,' I concluded, 'that someone in the duke's entourage must have pricked the horse's rump, causing him to bolt. You were there, Matthew, so think, lad! Think hard! Can you recall seeing anything at all suspicious?'

While I spoke, his eyes had widened to a horrified stare. 'I thought it was the whistle which startled Great Hal, but this puts quite a different complexion on the matter. You're right. Only someone riding behind His Grace could have been near enough to touch the animal.' He raised a hand and pushed back some strands of dark hair from his puckered forehead. 'Any one of us could have done it, that's the problem. We were all crowding close at his back, unfortunately all looking straight ahead and not at one another.' The inevitable conclusion suddenly struck him and his head jerked round. 'Does this mean that Stephen and Jocelin and Humphrey are all innocent? That we are looking for someone we haven't even thought of yet?'

I sighed. 'I wish I knew the answer, lad. But I'm convinced of Ralph Boyse's complicity, even though I can't prove it. I'm also sure that he's not alone in the plot. He has an accomplice. Maybe more than one?'

'I'll get you that ale and a cup for myself,' Matthew said, rising to his feet and walking towards the tavern.

As he reached it, Jocelin d'Hiver emerged in the company of one of Duchess Margaret's Burgundian retainers, whose presence had evidently not been required by his mistress at the Hôtel de Ville. When he saw Matthew, Jocelin's step momentarily faltered, then he gave a forced, brightly welcoming smile and made the necessary introduction. The Burgundian bowed politely and said something in French, to which Matthew just as politely responded before they pursued their separate ways.

'Good-day, Monsieur d'Hiver!' I called out as he passed me.

Jocelin started visibly at the sound of my voice and swung round.

'Ah! Roger Chapman! Good – er – good-day to you, too.'

But he did not stop nor make me known to his companion. Instead, linking one arm through his fellow Burgundian's, he hurriedly left the courtyard.

Matthew returned with brimming mazers, one of which he handed to me. A few drops of liquid spilt on the flagstones, but were immediately dried up by the heat. The shadows in the corner of the yard where we were sitting slowly receded, whilst lengthening in others, as the sun proceeded on its daily course across the heavens.

'Did you see that?' Matthew asked excitedly as he resumed his seat. 'Jocelin with one of Duchess Margaret's men.'

'I did,' I answered, sipping my ale and falling into an abstracted silence.

'You're very quiet,' my companion accused me after a few moments, during which time he fidgeted irritably like a thwarted child. 'What are you thinking about? Is it

227

d'Hiver?' And when I nodded he went on eagerly, 'Do you think it might have been he and not Ralph who gave that whistle? Jocelin insists he was inside the town yesterday morning, but Master Plummer says there's nothing but his word for that. He might equally well have been at the camp.'

'True,' I agreed, draining my cup and rising.

Matthew pouted when he saw that there was nothing more to be got from me, then laughed reluctantly. 'You can keep your counsel when necessary, chapman, I'll give you that.'

'Maybe, when there's any to keep. But at the moment I'm still floundering in the dark. There are tiny glimpses of light here and there, but not nearly enough of them to reveal the whole picture.'

He had been busy contemplating his long-toed boots of fine Italian leather, but now he glanced up, his liquid dark eyes snapping with sudden shrewdness. 'Something's going on in that devious mind of yours, Roger.' He lounged to his feet. 'I'd give a good deal to discover exactly what it is.'

'You'd have to dig deep then to make any sense of it,' I answered. 'Meantime contain your soul in patience and keep a close watch on Jocelin and the other three while Master Plummer and I are away. Make sure that Ralph Boyse especially doesn't sneak away from Calais and follow us to St Omer.'

'Oh, trust me for that!' Matthew grinned engagingly and dealt me a buffet on the arm. 'You won't be gone for more than a night or two at most, our Timothy assures me. You can both sleep easy, knowing everything here is in good hands.'

He swaggered off, humming a snatch of one of the lewd ballads popular with the men. I went in search of Timothy Plummer, my head in a whirl. There were even more things now that I did not understand.

In the event, we stayed three whole days and four nights in St Omer before returning to Calais on Tuesday, during which time Duchess Margaret lavished upon her two younger brothers all the hospitality for which the Burgundian court was so justly renowned. A tournament, fêtes and picnics were held in their honour, and they were loaded with costly gifts as the princess strove to make up to them for the discourteous absence of her lord. But all these festivities meant that our own lord was constantly surrounded by strangers, keeping his Squires of the Body, Timothy and myself in a perpetual state of agitation. They meant, too, that Duke Richard grew increasingly fretful, not just because of our intrusive vigilance, but also because there seemed to be no end to the delay in striking the first blow of the war.

'We came here to fight!' I overheard him complain one day to his brother. 'Instead, we waste our time in frivolities.'

'There'll be plenty of time for fighting later on,' Duke George admonished him. 'Meanwhile just enjoy yourself, Dickon. If you know how to,' he added, laughing.

'We've taxed people at home to the hilt to pay for this invasion,' Duke Richard snapped back, 'and in return we've promised them victories. Which we're not going to get by sitting on our fat arses!'

It was so unusual for him to swear or use common language – too pious and self-righteous by half, many people thought him – that his last remark was some indication of the strength of his feelings on the subject. After that, he and his brother moved out of earshot and I heard no more, but I guessed him to be the prime mover behind our return to Calais on Tuesday. Left to the Duke of Clarence, we might well have remained at St Omer another week, but what puzzled me was the fact that King Edward appeared content to let us do so. He came out to greet his brothers in the market square, but displayed no anger at their protracted visit to their sister. Even more curious, there still seemed to be no preparations to march into France.

Timothy and I sought out Matthew Wardroper.

'How has all been in our absence?' Timothy asked him.

Matthew made a discontented face. 'As calm and as quiet as the grave. Not one of them – Ralph, Jocelin, Humphrey, Stephen – made the slightest move to follow you or even leave the town. They haven't shown any inclination to visit their friends in camp and when not on duty have loafed around the ale-houses, drinking, dicing and whoring. It's been most disappointing,' he added candidly. 'All my plans to save Duke Richard single-handedly by my superior wits have come to nothing.'

'Superior wits, indeed!' Timothy snorted bad-temperedly and stomped away to make sure that his orders for the duke's safety were being properly carried out.

I grinned at Matthew. 'Don't take any notice of him,' I recommended. 'He's tired from constant vigilance; worn down by the continued uncertainty of what's going to happen next.'

Matthew nodded gravely. 'If only we knew the reason for this devilish plot.' He sighed. And when I failed to agree, he looked at me narrowly. 'Do you and Master Plummer know something you haven't yet told me?'

'I believe Master Plummer to be as much in the dark as ever,' I answered slowly. 'As for myself . . . well . . . As I've already told you, a glimmer of light is beginning to be visible through the murk.'

'And you're still not going to tell me what that glimmer is?'

I shook my head. 'Not yet. Until my ideas are more fully formed I shall say nothing to anyone. I'm as chary as any other man about making a fool of myself.'

Matthew stared at me sullenly for a moment, then his features broke into a good-natured grin. 'Quite right,' he agreed. 'I'd be the same.'

I had frequently noticed in him this ability to throw off bad temper, like a snake sloughing its skin; one moment he was a man, with all a man's anger and resentments, the next the happy-go-lucky schoolboy without a care in the world. It was an endearing trait, and one that contributed to his popularity amongst his fellows.

The next two days were quiet. The heat continued, but a thin, grey pall of cloud drifted in from the sea, obscuring the sun. A brooding silence hung over the town and a kind of apathy gripped men's spirits, making everyone listless and irritable. Now and then tempers flared, resulting in a little blood-letting with bouts of fisticuffs and sword-fights, but none of them lasted long. The protagonists were too indifferent to the outcome. It was as if, after all the months of preparation, of raising and equipping the greatest invasion force ever to leave England's shores, enthusiasm for the war had drained away as soon as the troops set foot in Calais. But I was convinced that the general malaise started at the very top with the king. His barely concealed inertia infected everyone.

Yet this loss of interest on His Highness's part was extremely curious for, as everyone kept saying, it was King Edward who had made the decision to go to war with the old enemy across the Channel, who had persuaded Parliament to make him large grants of money for the purpose, who had indefatigably travelled the country, cajoling and bullying his wealthier subjects into contributing substantially to the cause. Almost single-handedly he had fanned the spark of Agincourt fever still burning in every Englishman's heart, until it once more became a steady flame. So why, now, did he loiter in his stronghold of Calais, apparently content to wait upon the tardy arrival of his brother-in-law before making any move against the French?

But I was not the only one who found the king's motives hard to fathom. My lord of Gloucester was growing ever more impatient and critical of his eldest brother day by day.

'I must speak to my lord,' I said to John Kendall, Duke Richard's secretary.

He eyed me severely. 'Chapman, you grow too bold. I suppose we all know by now that you are not really employed by His Grace as a Yeoman of the Chamber, but neither have I received any intimation from the duke that you enjoy special privileges. I will inform him that you *crave the indulgence* of an audience, but you will have to wait until I send you word.'

'It's urgent,' I protested.

Again he merely shook his head. 'I have told you that I will let you know. But I warn you, even if he agrees to see you it will not be today. Nor, probably, tomorrow. The Duke of Burgundy arrives in Calais this morning.'

And with that I had to be content: I could see that John Kendall would not be moved. I went to find Timothy, only to be asked snappishly why I was not at my customary post of duty amongst His Grace's guards.

'The Duke of Burgundy's advance runners arrived not half an hour since, to announce that he himself will be here by noon.'

I had discovered Timothy in the ground-floor counting-house, a room which had been temporarily converted into a dormitory for some dozen of Duke Richard's personal retainers, Master Plummer and myself amongst them. By a lucky chance he was alone, an unusual circumstance with so many of us constantly coming and going. Quickly I closed the door.

'In heaven's name, what are you doing?' Timothy paused in the act of pulling on his best azure-and-murrey tunic, kicking his second-best one under his pallet bed. 'We must be ready to accompany the duke as soon as he leaves the house.'

'Listen,' I said urgently. 'I have an idea as to what might lie behind this plot to kill Duke Richard.' I had his attention now and proceeded, 'I may be wrong. I have as yet no proof of any kind, although if I'm correct in my thinking it can't be too long now before it's confirmed by events.'

'For God's sake, chapman, come to the point!' Timothy was rigid with impatience. 'What do you think you know?'

The door burst open behind me and we both jumped. To my relief it was Matthew Wardroper, but his message was that the duke was about to join his brothers in the market-place.

Timothy swore. 'We daren't stop now, chapman. There's a tavern just around the corner, tucked away in a small courtyard. Do you know it?' I nodded. 'Then meet me there this evening, after supper.'

Matthew asked sharply, 'What's going on? Has something happened?'

Timothy straightened his tunic. 'Roger thinks he knows what lies behind this plot against Duke Richard.'

Matthew exclaimed excitedly, clutching my arm, and I hastened to assure him that I had as yet no grounds for my suspicions and that only time would tell if I were right.

'In which case young Matt had best come to the alehouse too,' Timothy said, pushing past me to the door. 'Two opinions will be better than one, I reckon. Now for God's sake let us be going and, as always, stay as close to the duke as you both dare.'

Duke Charles of Burgundy, known as 'the Bold' to his friends and as 'the Rash' to almost everyone else, was a long-faced, haughty-looking man, dressed all in black, the Order of the Golden Fleece gleaming at his throat and his horse's harness hung with dozens of silver bells which jangled loudly each time that the unfortunate animal moved. He had one child, a daughter Mary, the progeny of his first wife, and seven years of marriage to our own Plantagenet princess had failed to produce any more; a constant source of barrack-room jokes among the Burgundian soldiery, or so Jocelin d'Hiver had told Matthew.

When Duke Charles rode regally into the market square at Calais I was standing some few paces behind Duke Richard, my eyes constantly flicking from one person to another in the crowd, on the watch for any untoward movement which might herald another attempt upon his life. I was therefore unaware for several minutes of the buzz of consternation which had arisen amongst the onlookers, or the signs of a heated altercation between the duke and his brothers-in-law. When at last I did realize what was happening I hissed, 'What's going on?' at one of my neighbours.

I recognized from his livery that he served under the captaincy of Louis de Bretaylle, one of the king's most trusted and highly thought-of lieutenants.

'Good God, man!' he exclaimed, laughing. 'Where are your eyes? Burgundy's brought no army with him; no men other than those few at his back. Our lords are furious, as well they might be.'

But when I glanced towards the knot of royal brothers it seemed to me that only the Dukes of Gloucester and Clarence were at all perturbed by the circumstance of their brother-in-law's dereliction. King Edward appeared to accept with equanimity the fact that, as it afterwards transpired, Charles of Burgundy, having abandoned the siege of Neuss, was off, for reasons known only to himself, to invade the dukedom of Lorraine. In a hard, grating voice, which I could hear from where I stood, he was haranguing King Edward and his brothers, but as he spoke in French I was unable to understand what was being said. Later, when the greetings and ceremonies, much muted in their tone, were over, and the lords had gone off to King Edward's lodgings for a council of war, I asked Matthew Wardroper for a translation.

He shrugged. 'Only something to the effect that the English army was great enough to sweep across Europe to the very gates of Rome itself without any help from him.

Also that he will be ready to join forces with us later, after he has finished pillaging Lorraine. Of course, he didn't put it quite so bluntly, but that's what he meant,' Matthew added with a grin, but sobered quickly. 'Tell me when you're ready to meet Master Plummer, won't you? I'm dying of curiosity to hear what it is that you've discovered.'

'I haven't discovered anything,' I protested. 'Matt, I know this is hard, but I want you to stay with the duke this evening.' His face fell ludicrously and he pouted defiantly. 'I'm sorry,' I said. 'It's a lot to ask, but I promise you shall know all presently. I need someone to keep an eye on Ralph Boyse. He's singing for Duke Richard tonight. I overheard one of the pages say so.'

He hesitated, but only for a second before his sunny nature reasserted itself. 'And you swear faithfully to tell me later? Oh . . . very well, then.' He smiled at me, and I had a sudden, vivid recollection of Lady Wardroper as I had seen her five weeks ago at Chilworth Manor. 'But what about the others? It won't be easy to keep watch on all of them.'

'Never mind the others,' I answered tersely and walked away, leaving him staring.

The rest of the day passed swiftly. The council of war came to an end and the lords returned to their various lodgings, the Duke of Burgundy remaining for the night with the king.

By the time I reached the tavern Timothy was already seated in the courtyard, waiting for me, two brimming mazers on the bench beside him and one in his hand. 'Where's Matt?' he demanded.

'I've persuaded him to stay behind and keep watch on Ralph Boyse who's entertaining His Grace this evening.' I sat down and drank some ale.

'Why Ralph in particular?' Timothy asked. 'What about the other three?'

'Because I no longer believe they're any threat to the duke,' I answered, a statement which caused my companion to raise his eyebrows.

'Why not? What information have you uncovered?'

'As yet nothing that you'd really call information.' I sipped my ale. 'Let that be for the moment.'

'If you know something,' Timothy began threateningly, then took a look at my face, paused and shrugged. 'Very well. For the moment. So! You say you know the reason for the plot against Duke Richard.'

I took another swig of ale before replying. 'I said I think I know. How serious is King Edward about this war do you imagine?'

Timothy choked as he swallowed his drink the wrong way. When he had recovered his breath he demanded incredulously, 'What makes you ask such a question? How serious! Deadly so, that's obvious to even the meanest intellect. The French, poor sods, have done nothing to invite it. It's the old, old story. He who is King of England should also be King of France. It's the same claim which has sparked all the wars of the last two hundred years. It goes back to Isabella Capet, the mother of the second Edward.'

I rubbed my chin thoughtfully. At the other end of the bench a young couple were staring soulfully into one another's eyes, those of the young man, slightly protuberant, shining like dark, ripe plums. In richness of colour they reminded me of Matthew Wardroper's.

'I believe the king to be playing a deeper game,' I said slowly. 'I believe him to be in touch with King Louis. To have been in touch with him for some long time. King

Edward needs more money than Parliament is prepared to grant him for the extravagances of his queen, her family, his mistresses and his court. King Louis wants England under his thumb. And how better for both men to achieve their aims than for King Louis to pay King Edward a generous annual sum of money on condition that he withdraws from France, never to trouble her borders again?'

Chapter Eighteen

Timothy said, 'I'd lower my voice if I were you. You're talking treason as well as nonsense. But even if what you say were true, do you think His Highness could persuade his lords and captains to agree? You know full well that Duke Richard, for one, would never be party to such a betrayal of the people's trust.'

'And that's my point,' I cut in swiftly, moderating my tone as Timothy had advised. 'But first, reflect upon the others surrounding His Highness: that noted turncoat and spendthrift, my lord of Clarence; the queen's brother, Earl Rivers, and her son, the Marquess of Dorset, reportedly profligates both and always in need of money; the king's bosom friend, Lord Hastings, yet another spendthrift by what I've observed of him; John Morton, a man who, to judge by his shifty glance, is eager to stir up trouble wherever and whenever he can; and all the rest of the court. Do you think any of them so high-minded that they could resist a bribe? Or, more importantly still, do you consider that any one of them has sufficient influence over the king to force him to change his mind once he's made it up?' Timothy slowly shook his head, his attention caught and held. 'Of course you don't. Except . . .'

'Except Duke Richard,' my companion whispered hoarsely.

'Duke Richard,' I repeated, 'who has remained totally loyal to the king throughout his life, whose opinion His Highness values, whose good regard, I suspect, is as necessary to him as breathing. And this same man is the very one who would try with every means at his disposal to persuade the king against the course he's set his heart on. King Louis would know this. How much easier, therefore, to remove, if possible, the obstacle in his path rather than trust to chance that King Edward will not heed his brother?'

Timothy chewed his bottom lip. 'But why by the Eve of Saint Hyacinth?'

I shrugged. 'How do I know? Maybe it is about that time, Saint Hyacinth's Day, that the two kings have agreed to reveal their hands.'

'Yes . . . You mean they'll both play out the charade of going to war for a certain period . . . ?' He broke off, spluttering. 'W— What am I saying? This is a farrago of nonsense from an overheated brain! Why am I listening to you?'

'Because I'm offering the only plausible explanation you've yet heard for the threat to Duke Richard's life.'

'Psha!' Timothy made a noise like a cat sneezing and waved his hands excitedly. 'What proof do you have?' But when I had given him my evidence he was even more dismissive than before. 'Is this all? It's nothing, chapman, and well you know it. There may be a dozen reasons for His Highness's behaviour.'

'Name one.'

'His health may not be as good as it usually is. The strain

of raising money for the invasion must have taxed even his great strength. Or it could be a woman. It's no secret that he's tiring of his present mistress, Elizabeth Lucy, and on the look-out for another. Perhaps the lady is proving more difficult to shake off than he imagined. Then there's the constant feuding between Clarence and the queen's relations. Keeping the peace amongst them all can't be easy for someone who likes domestic harmony. And then of course there have been two attempts on his favourite brother's life. Although I doubt but what he's accepted our lord's version of events: a foiled attack by a madman and an accident.' Timothy paused, casting around for anything else which might occur to him. Finally, he spread his hands and hunched his shoulders. 'Well, there are four sound reasons for the king's malaise – if indeed there is such a thing outside of your imagination.'

I finished my ale. 'You hired me,' I pointed out huffily, 'to try to solve this mystery, yet you dismiss the one sensible solution I've come up with as nonsense.'

'We-ell . . .' Timothy began, but I interrupted him.

'Listen, I have something more to say. Let us return to the murder of Thaddeus Morgan. Someone knew that he was to meet Lionel that night outside Holy Trinity Priory and followed him. There, that same someone learned of the following evening's rendezvous which was to provide Lionel with the name of the duke's would-be assassin. Now, think! Who among your five original suspects had the best means of access to your secrets? To the fact that you, as His Grace's Spy-Master, had become privy, through the Brotherhood, to the plot to kill Duke Richard?'

'Well, who?' he demanded petulantly.

'Ralph Boyse, of course. The man you have always been

241

sure was a spy for the French. He had a link directly to Lionel Arrowsmith. Berys Hogan!'

Once again, Timothy choked over his ale. 'Lionel wouldn't be so foolish as to talk to Berys Hogan about such important matters. You insult him. A good thing after all that Matthew isn't here to listen to such slurs against his kinsman!'

I sighed. 'A clever woman can wheedle anything from a man if she puts her mind to it. Think! Everyone kept warning Master Arrowsmith that he was playing with fire by courting Berys. She is affianced to Ralph Boyse, a man, you all said, of uncertain and violent temper. Yet Ralph showed no indications that I could see of jealousy, not even when he must actually have watched them together in a courtyard of Baynard's Castle.' And I told Timothy what I had witnessed. 'Therefore I believe Berys was only following her betrothed's instructions when she permitted Lionel's attentions. Any information she could glean from him was passed on to the man she is really in love with. Whether or not she knew the reason for what she was doing I have no means of telling and in any case it doesn't concern me. But there is your link between the French, the murder of Thaddeus Morgan and the plot to kill the Duke of Gloucester.'

I could see that Timothy was beginning to be convinced in spite of his natural disinclination to believe Lionel a prattling fool, or King Edward capable of such devious scheming as I had attributed to him. But neither could he deny that my arguments had a thread of reason and plausibility running through them, making sense of what had, until now, seemed a totally inexplicable problem. All the same, he refused to accept my explanation without a struggle and hunted around for further objections. After a moment or two he found them.

'I've told you before,' he said with relief, 'that Ralph could not possibly have killed Thaddeus Morgan. He was known to have been inside Baynard's Castle at the time. There are witnesses who saw him with Berys Hogan. Nor, and again I repeat myself, was he at Northampton when Thaddeus first sought me out. He could not have known of the visit.'

I ignored his first point and fastened on the second. 'He had no need to be apprised of the plot because he was already a party to it. What he discovered, through Berys, once he had rejoined the duke's household at Canterbury, was that you were also now in the secret. It was a sad blow for him, no doubt, but as long as you had no idea from whence the danger came, or why it threatened, he had nothing to fear. But what it did was to make his task far more difficult, as security about the duke was immediately tightened.' I added, 'Why did he tell Duke Richard a lie when he said he was going into Devon? He has never been there in his life. The interesting thing, therefore, is where he was, and what he was doing during his absence.'

Timothy wriggled uncomfortably on the bench, folding his arms across his chest and rocking himself gently from side to side. 'You still haven't explained Ralph's presence in Baynard's Castle the evening of Thaddeus's murder.'

'He has an accomplice,' I answered slowly. 'Ralph is not an assassin, he's a spy and needs to be kept in place by the French, who are unaware that you already suspect him. There were two men whispering together that day in Baynard's Castle. It was this second man who killed Thaddeus Morgan.'

Timothy swore softly, unlocked his arms and slewed round to face me. 'I suppose that's possible,' he admitted grudgingly.

'I think it more than possible. I think it highly probable.'

'But in the name of the Virgin, who is it? Jocelin d'Hiver? I've never trusted those Burgundians and Flemings. They're rightfully liegemen of King Louis. If the French hadn't arranged for the murder of Duke Charles's grandfather fifty years and more ago I doubt there would ever have been any rift between them. They say that the English entered France through the hole in John the Fearless's skull.'

'Maybe,' I replied. 'But I don't think our man is Jocelin.'

'Who, then?' My companion's voice was tense.

I hesitated for a second or two before I said with more assurance than I felt, 'Matthew Wardroper.'

Timothy drew a long, shuddering breath. 'Now I know you're mad,' he said feelingly, his tone lightening with relief. 'Young Wardroper came to us as innocent as a newborn babe of all that had previously happened. I'd stake my life that he's no more a French spy than you are. Than I am. By heaven, he's Lionel Arrowsmith's cousin!'

'Birth's no bar to a man committing treason, as has been proved often and often. Money is a powerful inducement in the game of treachery and double-dealing. The greed for gold has turned many a respectable coat in the past. Why should its lure be any less powerful in the present?'

Timothy peered into his mazer as if in need of sustenance, but finding it empty he leaned back against the wall and linked his hands behind his head. 'Go on, then,' he jeered. 'I'm listening. Tell me why you suspect young Matt.

This, I suppose, was your reason for preventing him from coming with you this evening.'

'I didn't reach my conclusions either lightly or easily,' I said almost guiltily. I spared a thought for Matthew's parents, the eminently respectable Sir Cedric and his beautiful wife, then put them resolutely out of my mind and continued, 'To begin with, as you already know, my footsteps were, by God's grace, directed to Chilworth Manor in the same week that Matthew joined the duke's household in London. I neither saw nor spoke with Sir Cedric, but I sold Lady Wardroper a pair of gloves. At one point during the course of our transaction she broke into song, humming a stave or two of the verse before giving voice to a snatch of the refrain. "It is the end. No matter what is said, I must love." You've heard it often enough.'

'Not I!' Timothy exclaimed. 'I've no ear for music.'

'Nor I, but I can recognize words when I hear them. Lady Wardroper told me that it was French, a Trouvère song called *C'est la fin*, especially affecting, she said, if accompanied by the little Breton bombardt.' I paused for a moment with raised eyebrows, but Timothy made no response. 'Ralph Boyse often sings it. It is one of his favourite airs and the instrument he plays is a Breton bombardt.'

'Well?' my companion demanded impatiently as once again I hesitated.

'The goodwife of Sir Cedric's shepherd mentioned to me that a travelling musician had passed that way the preceding month and had played for him and Lady Wardroper, lodging for the night in the guest hall at Chilworth Manor. The goody also mentioned that Matthew was then at home. "Kicking his heels" were her words, "and waiting to take

245

up his new appointment in the Duke of Gloucester's household."'

Timothy frowned. 'Are you saying...? Can you be saying that this travelling minstrel was ... was in reality Ralph Boyse?'

'It would have been about the same time that he was supposed to be in Devon, but his ignorance of the red earth around Exeter convinces me that he was almost certainly elsewhere. I think he was at Chilworth, close by Southampton.'

'For what purpose?'

'For the purpose of speaking to Matthew and giving him his instructions.'

Timothy wrinkled his nose like a dog with a suspect bone. 'You'll have to do better than that,' he demurred.

A party of drunken revellers emerged noisily from the inn, shouting bawdy ditties and laughing inanely as they wound an unsteady path across the courtyard. Timothy watched their progress with a jaundiced eye.

'They'll be worse than that as soon as they set foot on French soil,' he prophesied gloomily. 'There's something about foreign parts that brings out the very worst in Englishmen, however well-behaved and docile they are at home. They'll be committing rape and rapine in every town and village they pass through. Some'll be hanged, others flogged, but it won't deter the rest of 'em. However, that's not my problem, God be thanked. Go on then, chapman. Give me another reason for suspecting Matthew Wardroper.'

'The two attempts to maim Lionel were both made after Matthew arrived in London and after Ralph had learned, again through Berys, that the plot against the duke had been uncovered. The first try was a failure, Lionel only breaking an arm in the fall and being able to keep the rendezvous with Thaddeus outside the Priory. Somebody followed him that night and I'd be willing to stake my life that it was either Ralph or Matthew. Myself, I believe it was the former. Ralph would have had friends amongst the officers on the gates who would have let him in and out without too many questions asked.

'Had Thaddeus been able to supply a name there and then, I don't believe that either man would have lived to tell the tale, but unless absolutely necessary Ralph wouldn't have wanted to risk murder on the open highway. As it was, the pair of them had to be prevented from meeting again the following evening and the second attempt to harm Lionel was more successful. The fall this time broke his ankle and Matthew was sent to meet Thaddeus in his place. Whose suggestion was that? Do you remember?'

'Lal's,' was the prompt response. 'So you lose that argument, my friend. Matthew knew nothing of the plot until we took him into our confidence.'

'And played, quite by accident, straight into the conspirators' hands. I'm sure that had you decided to go to the warehouse yourself, in Master Arrowsmith's place, Matthew would still have got to Thaddeus before you. But you made things easy for him.'

Timothy digested this for a moment, then asked, 'Do you have any other reasons for accusing young Matthew? You haven't yet convinced me.'

I sighed, although I knew in my heart of hearts what he must know, too: that there was a great deal of guesswork and intuition in what I was saying, but very little substantial weight of evidence.

'Two things. Firstly, Thaddeus had not been killed cleanly, but had obviously managed to struggle with his assailant after the fatal blow was struck. There was a bruise on his jaw where someone had hit him. Later, when we were all together in that room in the tower – you, me, Master Arrowsmith and young Wardroper – I noticed Matthew rubbing the knuckles of his right hand as if they were sore, but then I thought nothing of it. Secondly, there was something which bothered me about the finding of Thaddeus's body. At the time, I was unable to decide what it was, and so, gradually, it faded from my mind. Recently, however, that unease has returned to haunt me and at last I think I know its cause.

'The murderer must have realized that his victim was not quite dead when he left him. Dying, most surely, but not completely devoid of life. Why did that fact not worry him? Why did he not make certain that Thaddeus was despatched before your envoy arrived for the meeting? For how did he know when that would be? Thaddeus might still have been able to whisper a name: the name of his killer and also that of the man appointed to slay Duke Richard. It was a risk he dared not take unless he was in a position to control events. So that man, by my reasoning, had to be Matthew Wardroper.

'The one thing he didn't, of course, foresee was the arrival on the scene of myself and Philip Lamprey, but even then his luck held firm. Thaddeus died in my arms without having uttered a word. And as,' I finished, 'for the two attempts so far on Duke Richard's life, who thought to inquire where Matthew was or check his movements during the masque? But we know where he was when Great Hal bolted. Riding behind His Grace.'

There was a long silence as my voice finally died away. The courtyard was quiet now. Only in the tavern itself were there sounds of conviviality and laughter. The shadows were beginning to lengthen as the sun sank behind the roofs of Calais and windows sparkled into life, lit by pale aureoles of candle-flame. In the west, the darkening sky was streaked with lakes and rivulets of clearest pearl, while far away beyond the walls could be heard the faint, bell-toned hushing of the sea.

Timothy stirred at last, reluctantly, as though returning to cramped and painful life after a deep and dreamless sleep. 'You've no shred of proof to back these assertions,' he said. 'There's nothing but what's in your head.'

'I know,' I admitted. 'But do *you* believe me? If so, then between us we might be able to think of something we can do?'

He got to his feet and reached down a hand to help me to mine. 'Against my better judgement, against all reason, I believe you. As you say, the thing now is to get some proof.' Another thought struck him, undermining his new-found faith. 'But it was young Wardroper who saved the duke when Great Hal bolted! Why would he wish to do that if he is our assassin?'

'I think that the person who saved the duke was the duke himself,' I answered. 'His own horsemanship. His own quick thinking. Oh, I don't deny it looked as though Matthew was the rescuer and I don't doubt but what it seemed that way to Duke Richard. But there was a deal of confusion as they neared the edge of the ditch; a lot of tugging and pulling. From where I was standing, Matthew could equally as well have been trying to force His Grace over the brink. I wanted to get the duke's own opinion on the matter, but John Kendall denied me an audience this morning because of the Duke of Burgundy's arrival.'

'And also,' Timothy said drily, 'because he thinks you grow too bold and forget your station.'

I grinned. 'That, too, I'm sure.' I stretched my arms above my head. 'By the saints, I'll be glad when this is finished and I can get back on the open road again.'

We walked back to the market square and turned our feet in the direction of the duke's temporary lodging.

'You'd give up a roof over your head, regular meals and pay, for the chancy existence of a pedlar?' Timothy asked in disbelief.

'Willingly,' I answered. 'You may enjoy this world of gossip and intrigue, where everyone spies on everyone else, where no one trusts any other, where the smiles are false and solemn words and promises are given only to be broken, but that's not for me.'

Timothy shrugged. 'Each to his own taste.' He laid a restraining hand on my arm as we neared the street door of the merchant's house. 'Not a whisper,' he urged, 'to anyone of the doubts and suspicions you've voiced to me tonight. I refer particularly to your thoughts concerning the king's intentions. If you are right, you would do well to let His Highness reveal them himself in the fullness of time. For if you are wrong you could be arrested for the crime of *lèse-majesté*.'

'I shall be discreet,' I promised. 'I value my skin as much as you do.'

'And where is young Wardroper this evening?' Timothy asked grimly as we crossed the threshold, having produced the password and been acknowledged as friends by the sentry guarding the door.

'I instructed him to keep an eye on Ralph Boyse.'

'You did *what*?' Timothy spluttered. 'Knowing all you believe you know about the pair of them?'

'His Grace is surrounded by his friends and at least three of his Squires of the Body,' I soothed. 'He'll be safe enough until bedtime. I don't imagine either Ralph or Matthew will do anything in the open unless forced to it. No murderer ever wishes to be caught. His own life is too precious.'

We could hear singing drifting down the stairs from one of the upstairs rooms. Ralph's voice was uplifted in a gentle, pleasant air.

Timothy growled, 'At least his mother was a French-woman. What will be young Wardroper's excuse I wonder.'

I noted that my words had not, as I had originally feared, fallen on stony ground, but had found fertile soil and put down roots. In that case God grant that I was correct in my assumptions and had not vilified innocent men, including King Edward.

'What do we do now?' I asked Timothy. 'Without more evidence there can be no arrests. It would be no more than my word against theirs at present.'

He nodded. 'We stick as close as a burr to His Grace and put as much distance between him and those two as we dare without arousing too much suspicion. Meantime, we think, and think hard, for some way to resolve the problem. Some way to prove to all the world that they are villains.'

I was shaken by a momentary doubt. 'And if I am proved to be mistaken?' I demanded.

'Then no harm done, if much time wasted. You've told no one but me? Very well. No need to worry. You're a good man, chapman. And one I'm proud to name as my friend. I shan't betray you.'

251

Chapter Nineteen

The Duke of Burgundy rode out of Calais the following morning, and the results of his previous day's council of war with King Edward were soon circulating amongst the troops. Duke Richard was to accompany his brother-in-law, along with some of the other lords and captains, back to St Omer, then bear south to join the king and the Duke of Clarence, who were meanwhile to advance with their levies upon St Quentin, its defender, the Count of St Pol, having offered to surrender the town.

Timothy and I were to travel with the duke wherever he went.

'I had a private audience with His Grace as soon as he was dressed this morning and he's agreed to it,' Timothy said. 'I've also requested that he leave Ralph Boyse and young Wardroper to follow on with the rest of the household, although I haven't told him why. It'll give us a night or two's respite from their company and a chance to think. By the way, John Kendall told me that Duke Richard will see you now if you're still of a mind to speak with him.'

The rooms set aside for the duke's private use were even more than usually crowded as iron-bound chests full of clothes, books and music were carried downstairs to be loaded on to the baggage wagons. In a day or two, when the remaining officers and servants had also left, accompanying the king, the house would grow quiet again, a decorous gentleman's residence awaiting the return of its rightful owner.

Duke Richard was today partially armed in breastplate and gorget, with rerebraces on his upper arms and cuisses on his thighs, giving a military aspect to his amber velvet. For the first time since our arrival in Calais ten days before, it seemed as if we might indeed be going to war and not idling our lives away on some eternal picnic. Yet again I felt a momentary qualm; that uneasiness in the pit of my stomach as I confronted the fact that I might be wrong in my assumptions.

'Well, Roger?' The duke raised his eyebrows. 'You wished to see me?'

'To ask you a question, my lord.'

'I'm listening.'

I hesitated, uncomfortably aware of his quizzical gaze but, plucking up courage, proceeded, 'My lord, when young Matthew Wardroper—'

'Wardroper again,' he murmured. 'That's the second time this morning his name's been mentioned.'

I ignored the interruption. 'When he rode after you, the day Great Hal bolted, did ... did you feel that ... that he was trying to rescue you or ... or drive you into the ditch?'

The eyebrows climbed a little higher. 'Blows the wind from that quarter?' the duke said softly. 'A very odd question, you must agree, but I'll try to give you an honest answer. What you make of it I have no wish to know, you understand me? I trust this affair will soon be resolved, and

254

with the least possible fuss. And let it also be clearly understood that I want no man accused of anything without positive proof.' He fingered his chin consideringly for several seconds, then continued, 'Until this moment I have thought Matthew my rescuer, but I admit that your query raises certain doubts in my mind. My whole attention was naturally focused on bringing Great Hal under control and I cannot remember the incident with any clarity, but . . .'

'But?' I prompted eagerly when he paused.

'But the truth is,' he finished flatly, 'that I am no longer sure what happened. That is all I can tell you.'

I would have pressed him further, but there was a look in his eye which forbade it. I hoped he would inquire into the reasons for my question, but he curtailed the audience, turning away to greet John Kendall, who had just entered bearing a sheaf of papers for the duke to read and sign, and I had no choice but to bow and quit the room. Nevertheless, I had achieved something. His Grace, far from dismissing my suggestion as arrant nonsense, had as good as agreed that it might have merit and I could not help but see that as a confirmation of my suspicions.

Two hours later Timothy and I rode out of Calais in Duke Richard's train, leaving Ralph Boyse and Matthew Wardroper behind us. But not for long. Soon we should rejoin them and the rest of the levies on their march to St Quentin.

'They must surely make another attempt then,' Timothy muttered. 'If you're right about the meaning of Saint Hyacinth's Day, they haven't much time left. We must be ready for them.' His brow puckered fretfully. 'I should have thought better of young Wardroper. Lionel will be appalled when the truth gets out. He recommended his cousin to the duke's service and will feel responsible for Matthew's treason.'

I said nothing. Above our heads the banners of England and Burgundy flapped and mingled in the summer breeze, while behind us stretched all the panoply and might of two proud countries caparisoned for war. And on either side of us people went about their daily business as though we did not exist, sharpening scythes, bringing in the hay, tending their bees. It was as much as I could do not to leap from my nag and join them. Duke Richard was not the only person who trusted that this affair would soon be brought to its conclusion.

The rain sluiced down on the field of Agincourt, turning the ground into a sea of mud, the trees dripping mournfully on the encamped English army. It was almost sixty years since Henry of Monmouth had led his decimated troops across that ground to crush the might and chivalry of France and win for his country one of the most resounding victories of all time. But no such glory awaited the present English host as the army took its rest on that famous field.

We had waited in St Omer, entertained by Duchess Margaret and kicking our heels in frustration, for over two weeks, daily expecting a messenger from Calais to say that the king had at last set out for St Quentin. There were murmurings amongst the men about the strangeness of the delay, but for me it only strengthened my conviction that my reasoning was correct: King Edward was playing a deep and devious game. Finally, however, word arrived that the army was at last on the move and that Duke Richard was to join his brothers on the field of Agincourt.

Why King Edward had selected this particular rendez-vous I could only guess, but I suspected that it added colour to his bellicose intentions and helped to allay any growing fears that his commitment to the war was less than whole-hearted.

As soon as camp had been made, the duke's tents pitched alongside those of his brothers, fires for the men started and shelter scouted for in the neighbouring countryside, Timothy and I went in search of Ralph and Matthew, leaving strict instructions with the Squires of the Body that one of them was to be in attendance upon His Grace at all times. To a man, they looked down their patrician noses and muttered darkly about teaching one's granddam to grope ducks, or the goslings wanting to drive the geese to pasture, but we departed, satisfied that they would not fail in their duty.

We found Matthew easily enough. He was already on his way, in the company of Jocelin d'Hiver and another Squire of the Household, to the duke's main pavilion, to present his devoir and resume his normal duties.

'Where's Ralph Boyse?' Timothy asked him, adding quickly, 'Duke Richard wants him.'

'No longer with us,' Jocelin answered before Matthew had a chance to reply. 'Fortunate devil,' he went on enviously, glancing around at the water-logged plain, the distant, rain-sodden woods of Tramecourt and the men huddled over smoking fires which offered no kind of warmth to their shivering limbs.

'What do you mean?' Timothy demanded sharply. 'Where's he gone?'

'He was sent home to England with a dozen or so others

who had developed dysentery,' Matthew explained. 'As Jocelin says, lucky devil.'

I forced myself not to look in Timothy's direction. 'Ralph seemed well enough to me when I last saw him.'

'That was weeks ago,' Matthew pointed out with reason. 'There was an outbreak of dysentery in Calais just after you left.'

The third man with them nodded. 'A lot of men were struck down. Some died. Mind you, I don't think Ralph was very bad. In fact until the night before the ship sailed I didn't even realize he was ill.'

'A man can suffer in silence, I suppose,' Matthew expostulated. 'Anyway, Master Steward was sufficiently convinced to send him home. I'll tell His Grace what's happened.'

'I'll do it,' Timothy said swiftly and turned back towards the tent. If Duke Richard denied that he had been asking for Ralph, Matthew might begin to wonder. Later, when the duke was at supper, the Spy-Master sought me out to inquire, 'What do you make of that, then?'

It had at last stopped raining, but the August evening was still dreary and overcast, an impenetrable canopy of cloud hanging low overhead. The ground squelched beneath our feet and there was a chill in the air which had caused my companion to wrap himself in a cloak. I was hardier, used to being out in all weathers, but even I found myself shivering every now and then.

'Ralph was never our assassin,' I answered slowly. 'He is separating himself from Matthew now that we are getting further from the coast and into France. He is no longer necessary to the plan. His French masters – whoever they are, and one of them certainly tried to contact him that night in Calais and has probably since succeeded – have told him to return to England. They wouldn't wish to jeopardize his position in the duke's household. Matthew is now on his own. If he should be caught, Ralph has no connection with him.'

'But we know better.'

'And would have difficulty proving it, provided both Matthew and Berys Hogan keep their mouths shut. But no one as yet, apart from the duke, knows of our suspicions. They still think us floundering about in the dark.'

Timothy stirred up a patch of mud with the toe of his boot. 'Will young Wardroper make another attempt, do you think?'

'I think it probable. Unnecessarily.' I anticipated his question and went on, 'I don't believe that even Duke Richard will be able to change the king's mind in this matter, but there's no way the French can be sure of that until His Highness finally shows his hand and successfully quells all opposition.'

Timothy sighed. 'Let's hope you're right. I worry all the time that perhaps we should be looking elsewhere for some other person.'

'Trust me,' I said with a confidence that frequently deserted me, especially in the long, sleepless watches of the night.

Strangely enough, I slept more soundly that night than I had done for weeks.

I had stood guard with the sentries outside the duke's tent until the hour of Matins and Lauds, when Timothy and two others had relieved us. I wrapped my cloak about me and, scorning the shelter of a baggage wagon, found myself a place beside a camp-fire in the company of half a dozen good Yorkshire fellows. One or two were snoring, lost to the world, but the rest were huddled over the flames, chatting desultorily, unable to sleep despite the fact that it was two o'clock in the morning.

I had no expectation of sleeping either, but I must have lost consciousness within a few minutes, for the next thing I knew I was standing by that empty shrine in the woods near Chilworth Manor where all sound of birds and insects was silenced, where the trees themselves seemed charged with menace. Coming towards me was the shepherd's wife, smiling and nodding.

'Just like his mother, you know,' she said as she passed me. I turned my head to look after her, but she had vanished and in her place was Amice Gentle.

She murmured, 'I'm ready to start stitching when I've measured you.' Then as she smiled, her features dislimned, taking shape once more as those of Lady Wardroper, who was holding a Breton bombardt in her hand. Raising it to her lips, my lady played a stave or two of *C'est la fin*, then walked past me into the trees where, like Millisent Shepherd, she too disappeared. I could feel the heat breaking out all over my body and someone was shaking my arm and shouting . . .

'Wake up, lad! Wake up! Tha's got too near the fire. Thee hose is alight.'

I awoke to a smell of scorching wool and was just in time to roll clear of the fire before it could do my leg any serious injury. Only a patch of sore red flesh was revealed once I had stripped and examined it.

'Tha wert ridin' the night mare,' one of the Yorkshiremen

said to me. 'Tha wert muttering in thy sleep like something's preying on thee mind.'

'It is,' I answered shortly, climbing back into my scorched hose and wincing at the pain in my leg.

'Tha wants a poultice of lettuce and house leek on that,' another man advised me kindly.

I barely heard him, but lay down again and covered myself with my cloak, which had got thrown aside during my tossings and turnings. Sleep had fled, however, and my dream went round and around in my head until I began to assemble order out of chaos. Things which had confused me for weeks suddenly began to make sense and I was able to see the path in front of me more clearly. At last, just before dawn, I fell into a dreamless slumber, awaking refreshed to a world still wet underfoot, but with the sun breaking through the clouds and the mist rising almost knee-high across the rain-washed plain. In the distance, the woods of Agincourt and Tramecourt smudged the horizon and the morning air was acrid with smoke as men everywhere tried to breathe life into last night's burnt-out fires in order to boil a pan of water. From the canvas pouches at their belts each man produced a handful of damp oats with which he attempted to make a little thin gruel. Refusing my companions' generous offer to share theirs with me I departed for the Duke of Gloucester's tents, looking for Timothy Plummer.

'Where's Wardroper?' I asked as soon as I found him.

'I saw to it that he was sent off with a party foraging for milk and eggs for His Grace's breakfast.' Timothy lowered his voice and pressed my arm. 'There's talk that we're to spend a second night here, despite the news brought in by scouts at five o'clock this morning that King Louis has raised the Oriflamme and is massing an army at Beauvais. The chivalry of France, by all accounts, is flocking to his standard. Our lord and some others are champing at the bit in frustration. They can't understand the king's delay. But it makes me feel more certain that you have come to the right conclusion, chapman.'

The day passed uneventfully. Matthew returned with the rest of the foraging party and from then on Timothy and I scarcely let him out of our sight. Both of us were glad of the excuse to avoid the company of Duke Richard, who grew ever more fretful as the hours wore on with no summons to a council of war by his eldest brother. Indeed the king had withdrawn into his pavilion with instructions that he was not to be disturbed; a command easily comprehended when one of the higher-class camp-followers was seen being ushered into his tent. A report to this effect reaching our lord's ears, his thin lips compressed until they almost disappeared and his temper for the rest of the day was extremely short.

I received my share of the duke's displeasure when he told me curtly to get myself a new pair of hose and not to enter his presence again in such a condition. I had forgotten the great hole scorched in one leg by the fire and went off, duly chastened, to find the Livery Sergeant. His Grace was in no better mood by nightfall, when he suddenly emerged, grim-faced, from his tent, two of his Squires at his heels, and headed at a brisk pace in the direction of his eldest brother's pavilion. I glanced inquiringly at my fellow guard, but this worthy merely shrugged and muttered that he would not care to risk the duke's anger by following where he was not bidden.

'Then I must go alone,' I said and, by running after my quarry, was able to catch up the duke and his Squires just as they entered the king's tent, and managed to slip in behind them without being noticed.

In the guttering torchlight which filled the confined space with a veil of smoke I could make out King Edward sitting at a table with some of his captains – Louis de Bretaylle, the Duke of Norfolk, the Earl of Northumberland and Lord Hastings. The Duke of Clarence was kneeling on the ground playing dice with Earl Rivers and the Marquess of Dorset, while the Duke of Suffolk stood a little apart, swigging wine from a leather bottle. Just inside the tent opening Lord Stanley and John Morton drew aside to allow Duke Richard's unimpeded progress, but neither man could have been flattered by the unseeing way in which he swept past them.

The conversation was turning upon that ever-fruitful topic, Charles of Burgundy.

'Shall I ever forget,' the king was demanding half-laughingly of Lord Hastings, 'his audacity in arriving in Calais with only a bodyguard, as coolly as if he had brought all the troops he had promised me . . .' He broke off at the sight of his youngest brother and Duke Richard's tense expression. He flung up a hand. 'All right! All right, Dickon! I know you've come to reproach me! But we are on the march again tomorrow. You have my solemn oath.'

The duke's set features relaxed a little. 'Not before time,' he murmured gruffly; and a moment or two later, after receiving further reassurances from King Edward, his sudden and unexpected sense of humour reasserted itself. When Louis de Bretaylle complained that Duke Charles had brought not one man of that vast army which was to have been Burgundy's contribution to the war he said, smiling, 'But my dear Louis, my brother-in-law admitted himself that we don't need him. And what he lacked in men he made up for in encouragement.'

The king and Lord Hastings began to laugh.

'Charles's self-esteem is so great,' the former grinned, 'that it's almost disarming. He had the effrontery to suggest that once I had crushed the French by sheer weight of numbers he would be happy to give me his advice on the trickier aspects of an Italian campaign.'

It was at this moment that I lost all interest in what His Highness was saying. I suddenly realized that Duke Richard had moved to one side of the tent, his back almost touching its silken wall, and was, moreover, standing in the full glare of a branch of candles placed on a small camp-table. From outside, his outline must be immediately recognizable to anyone who knew him well; for not only was he small of stature, but the long, swinging curtain of hair brushed shoulders which were not quite equal in size. (I had been told that as a still-growing child of eleven, fighting for his eldest brother, his right breast and upper sword-arm had developed faster than his left, leaving him with a very slightly lopsided appearance.) These three bodily characteristics, height, hair, shoulders, together made him easy to identify.

Even as I spotted the possible danger the thing which must have unconsciously attracted my attention to it in the first place happened again: there was a faint trembling of the silken wall, as though someone were creeping close to it outside. I plunged through the tent opening into the darkness, startling the king's sentries who were guarding the entrance. Before they had time to gather their wits or challenge me I had raced around the side of the tent and was just in time to see a shadowy figure raise an arm high above its head. I caught the gleam of metal and knew that the descending hand must hold a knife.

I was still too far away to grab our assassin and the only course left to me was to shout. After all these years I have no notion what I said, and probably had no clear idea then. But whatever I yelled, it was loud enough and fierce enough not simply to deflect our would-be murderer's aim as he plunged his blade through the ripping silk, but also to frighten him into instant flight. I was but vaguely aware of Duke Richard crying out, followed by a general uproar inside the tent, for I was already in full pursuit of my quarry as he stumbled away across the water-logged ground, his feet slithering all ways on the soaking grass.

'I'm going to lose him,' I thought desperately, as my own boots slipped in a patch of mud, nearly sending me sprawling. But I had reckoned without the commotion waking most of the surrounding camp. As men staggered to their feet, blinking owlishly through the gloom, I cried, 'Treason! Stop that man!'

By now, both sentries and most of the occupants of the king's tent had joined in the hunt, haring across the wet ground, cursing as they stumbled over sleeping men, calling for torches to be brought. Others had appeared from all quarters of the camp and I suddenly found Timothy Plummer at my side.

'Duke Richard,' I panted. 'Is he all right?'

'A nasty gash in his upper left arm, but nothing to signify. A clean wound, quickly mended.' He gasped in some air. 'Was it Matthew Wardroper you saw?'

'Until we catch him I can't say for sure, although in my

own mind I'm certain . . . There he goes!' I yelled at the top of my lungs. 'There he goes! Heading for the Tramecourt woods.'

But that fleeing figure had already been spotted by others and there was a sudden shout of triumph as the miscreant was brought crashing to the ground. As we all crowded breathlessly around, torches and firebrands were raised to illuminate the heaving, furiously writhing figure, and someone stooped, seizing the chin and twisting the contorted face up towards the light.

Timothy gave a grunt of satisfaction. 'Matthew Wardroper,' he said.

I shook my head. 'No, not Matthew. He's been dead and buried these many weeks.'

Chapter Twenty

Everyone stared. At last Timothy voiced the general question.

'What in God's name do you mean?'

'What I said. This isn't Matthew Wardroper. If my guess is correct, his body lies somewhere in a clearing in the woods near his home.' I stirred the figure on the ground with my toe. 'Am I right? I don't know how you killed him. With a knife, probably, that seems to be your favourite weapon. But he's buried near that empty shrine.'

The brown eyes stared up at me, full of malevolence, but there was no answer.

Lord Hastings, who had arrived with the king and a few other lords, demanded harshly, 'Then if this isn't ... well, whoever you thought he was, who is it?' He glared down at the prisoner. 'Speak up! Who are you? You might as well tell us because we shall get it out of you, one way or the other. Speak up, you miserable traitor!'

'I'm no traitor!' the reply came, hot with indignation. 'I'm Julien d'Amboise. My mother was English, but my father is the Comte d'Amboise and I'm a true liegeman of King Louis!'

'A likely story,' snorted the Duke of Suffolk. 'If that's

the case, why are you trying to murder my brother-in-law of Gloucester?'

I had been watching the king closely ever since the young man had revealed his true identity and now saw the sudden half-turn of his head towards his Master of the Rolls, who was standing just behind him. Immediately, John Morton stepped forward saying smoothly, 'This inquisition can surely be conducted elsewhere. His Highness must be wishful of discovering how my lord of Gloucester does – as indeed we all are – so let Monsieur d'Amboise, if that really is his name, be put under close guard and escorted to some safe place where he can be interrogated later.'

The king nodded his approval. 'Put Monsieur d'Amboise in chains until the morning, when I shall send my own men to question him. At once! Now then!' He flung an arm around Lord Hastings's shoulders. 'Let's go and find Dickon.'

I sat with Timothy Plummer in the Duke of Gloucester's tent, the two of us having been summoned by His Grace when the fuss had at last died down and the camp was quieter. On our way there Timothy had whispered urgently to me, 'Whatever other answers you give Duke Richard, you know of no reason why the French should want to kill him – that is, unless you wish to fall foul of King Edward.'

I understood his warning. If the king's future conduct precipitated a quarrel between him and his youngest brother that was one thing, but for a mere underling to cause strife on account of what might still prove to be wild speculation was quite another.

'You can trust me,' I assured him.

Duke Richard, stripped of his doublet, his upper left arm swathed in linen and the wrist supported by a strap, was sitting on the edge of his camp-bed, unattended except for one sleepy page. When Timothy and I were ushered into his presence he bade us draw up stools and make ourselves comfortable. The page was roused from his torpor to pour us wine, then allowed to return to his corner again and doze.

'You see, chapman,' the duke said with a smile, 'that I presume all danger is past, now that you have caught my would-be assassin. Once more, I am deeply in your debt.'

'I am always happy to be of service to Your Grace.'

'In that case satisfy my curiosity and tell me how you knew that Matthew Wardroper was dead and that an imposter had taken his place.'

I sipped my wine, warily eyeing the goblet of fine Venetian glass in which it had been served. I was afraid my clumsiness could easily destroy this beautiful object and I sympathized with the packers and porters whose job it was to transport such things.

'In order to answer that question, Your Grace,' I began, 'I must first describe how God directed my steps to Southampton and then to London.' And I filled in the background to my story as best I could. When I had finished the duke nodded and Timothy stirred impatiently.

I went on, 'There were several things, my lord, which should have made me suspect the truth from the start, if I'd had my wits about me. One of these was that the shepherd's dame told me how alike were Matthew and his mother. "Eyes, hair, features," she said. But whereas Lady Wardroper's eyes are blue, those of Julien d'Amboise are brown. Now, although I have never seen Sir Cedric Wardroper, I suspect that his, too, are of that same colour, for Amice Gentle remarked that although Matthew, as she thought him, had his mother's delicate features and dark hair, he had his father's eyes.'

'Continue,' urged the duke as I paused again to drink.

'While I was with Lady Wardroper she sang a few words of *C'est la fin*. She asked me if I cared for music, adding that she knew no man who did. Is it possible she would have said so if her own son both played and sang, as our false Matthew does?'

'Very unlikely,' Duke Richard agreed. 'Proceed.'

'One of the things which always puzzled me was the way Wardroper, or d'Amboise as I suppose we now must call him, sometimes gave the impression of being two different people. Mostly he appeared to be what he was meant to be, a light-hearted, somewhat feckless young man. But there were moments when he seemed quite otherwise: astute and far more worldly wise. I should have thought more about it and asked myself why.'

'I suppose d'Amboise could not prevent his own character from now and then showing through,' said the duke. 'But you judge yourself too harshly, Roger. You could not be expected to guess the reason.'

I shook my head and placed the precious goblet, now empty, carefully on the ground beside me. 'I cannot forgive myself so easily, Your Grace. All these things, together with the fact that I should have suspected him sooner of Thaddeus Morgan's murder, would have prevented you much unease.'

'When did you first begin to guess the truth?' asked Timothy.

I rubbed my chin. 'I think, but without realizing it, it was one evening in Calais, when the man I thought to be Matthew Wardroper and I were sitting drinking outside the inn. Jocelin d'Hiver and one of his Burgundian friends appeared and spoke to him in French, which he perfectly understood and replied to without any difficulty. Yet Matthew Wardroper, according to Master Gentle, the Southampton butcher, knew very little French.'

The duke frowned as he finished his wine and twirled the empty goblet between his long, thin fingers. The light of the candles made it glow with myriad rainbow colours. 'But how did King Louis's spy-masters know what Matthew Wardroper looked like?'

'Ralph Boyse,' I said promptly. 'It was his job to find that out, which he did by gaining leave of absence from Your Grace and going to Chilworth Manor in the guise of a travelling minstrel. It had to be before Matthew took up his position in Your Grace's household, but Ralph knew all his movements from Master Arrowsmith, through Berys Hogan. The day after he quit Chilworth where, amongst other songs, he had sung *C'est la fin* to Lady Wardroper, Ralph was in Southampton. Both the butcher and his wife made mention of him. Mistress Gentle said that the minstrel spoke in a Yorkshire dialect and Ralph Boyse came from that county. I suspect that he met with one of King Louis's agents and gave him a full and detailed description of young Matthew. He also informed him of the day on which Matthew would leave for London. The agent then re-crossed the Channel and reported to his masters, who at once looked round for a young man as like Matthew

Wardroper as possible, who was willing to undertake a dangerous mission. If a detail or two, such as the colour of his eyes, did not tally, it was of little consequence. Ralph knew that Lionel had not seen his cousin for many years and it was highly unlikely that in the short time between Matthew's arrival in London and Your Grace setting out for France either of his parents would visit him.'

The duke nodded. 'So! King Louis's spy-masters duly found their young man, who took ship for England. And then what happened?'

'He landed at Southampton, made his way to Chilworth Manor very early in the morning of the day that Matthew set out for London, followed him, probably caught up and fell into conversation with him in the forest and then, at the right moment, killed him and dragged the body deep into the undergrowth, where he buried it. I suspect that d'Amboise also buried the saddle and the horse's other accoutrements before turning the animal loose. It would soon be seized upon, most gratefully, by one of the woodlanders.'

There was a long silence inside the tent. Outside, sentries called softly to one another, a horse whinnied, the growl of muttered conversation disturbed the darkness as sleepless men tried vainly to take their ease.

At last the duke said slowly the one thing I had been dreading to hear, 'You haven't yet told me, Roger, why the French should desire my death.'

I heard Timothy's quick, involuntary intake of breath and it was all I could do not to look at him for guidance.

'Your...Your Grace,' I stuttered helplessly, 'I – er – I...'

Duke Richard's eyes never left my face, but suddenly he took pity on me and smiled. 'Peace, peace. I'm not going to ask you. It's not that I think you don't know, but I'm beginning to have my own suspicions. If I am right – although I pray to God that I'm not – then it is a subject better left alone. What's to come will be between the king and me.' He stared grimly in front of him, the jaw hardening, the eyes like steel. Then he roused himself and tried to smile. 'I've kept you both too long from your rest. Tomorrow we set out towards St Quentin. It will be a wearisome march.' He rose and held out his hand for us to kiss.

Once outside the tent, Timothy exhaled a long-drawn-out breath. 'Thank God that's done with. Trust His Grace,' he added proudly, 'to be in step and also to be wishful of sparing us embarrassment. What will you do now then, chapman? Your job here's finished. You're free to go. Not that you've ever been otherwise. No one would have kept you against your will, but you know that. Are you off back to England in the morning?'

I shook my head. 'I'll march with you as far as St Quentin and see what happens. I can't return home without knowing whether or not my suspicions have some foundation.'

'Yours and the duke's,' Timothy grinned, clapping me on the shoulder. 'Very well then, we'd better get some sleep. Let's find a good fire to warm us.'

Some days later, as the English army approached the walls of St Quentin, the city guns boomed out over the country-side, killing several of our men and horses. The Count of St Pol had apparently returned to his rightful allegiance. And

273

within the hour messengers arrived with the news that King Louis and his army had advanced as far as Compiègne.

That was on the eleventh day of August. Within the week, English and French ambassadors met at Amiens to talk of peace and the following day, the Eve of Saint Hyacinth, they returned to St Quentin with King Louis's propositions. In return for the prompt withdrawal of the English from France and a seven years' truce he offered King Edward an immediate payment of 75,000 crowns and an annuity of 50,000 crowns; the Dauphin and the Princess Elizabeth were to be betrothed; and finally both kings were to go to the other's aid if either was threatened in the future by rebellious subjects.

King Edward accepted and only two of his captains opposed him – the Duke of Gloucester and Louis de Bretaylle.

'Well, you were right, chapman,' Timothy said, as we strolled together around the walls of St Quentin, its guns now fallen silent. 'All hell's broken loose in His Highness's tent, with our lord and Captain de Bretaylle accusing him of breaking faith. As I passed the royal pavilion a while ago I heard one of them shouting that although in his time King Edward has won nine victories, this is a disgrace which will outweigh them all.'

'What about the other lords?' I asked. 'Does none of them condemn His Highness?'

'What? With King Louis scattering pensions and expensive gifts among them as liberally as leaves fall from trees in autumn? There's no chance of that. But he won't bribe Duke Richard and that makes all the rest of 'em furiously angry. John Morton's always hated the duke and he'll dislike him even more after this. Anyway, be prepared to move, lad. We're off to Amiens it seems, to be royally entertained by the French while the final details of the treaty are hammered out by the lawyers.'

'And Julien d'Amboise? What's to happen to him?'

Timothy's lip curled. 'Oh, he's to be treated as a prisoner of war and returned to his family. It wouldn't be politic to execute the son of the Comte d'Amboise. But messengers have already been despatched to London with orders for Ralph Boyse's arrest. He, poor sod, won't escape the hangman's noose. But that's the way the world turns, chapman, as you well know.'

I nodded. 'And as I predicted, it was all for nothing. King Edward won't be influenced on this occasion by his brother.'

Nor was he swayed by the arrival of a furious Charles of Burgundy, who thundered into the camp the following day and accused His Highness, in tones so loud that everyone could hear, of perfidy and ended by taunting him with the victories won by former English kings over the French. Crécy, Poitiers, Agincourt were names tossed into the bright summer air. Then the duke departed, refusing to have anything to do with the peace.

We marched to Amiens where, outside the town, the inhabitants, acting on their sovereign's orders, had set up hundreds of tables laden with food and drink. We all fell on the food like ravening wolves and then lay about in the meadows for the rest of the day, our bellies distended, and more than half-drunk. The whore-houses were also opened up to the English troops and a long procession of men staggered in and out of the main gates until they closed at curfew. I hasten to record that I wasn't one of them. Brothels and their inmates have never tempted me. You can catch too many unpleasant diseases from them and I need to be fit.

No one bothered me or expected me to perform any duties. All those in attendance upon Duke Richard knew by now that I was not really of his household and would be quitting their ranks very soon. The duke, his face ravaged by disappointment and anger with his eldest brother, called me to his tent and asked what he could do for me, but he already knew the answer.

'Nothing, Your Grace. I'm happy as I am.'

'If you won't join my service or allow me to help you in any other way, at least let me make you the gift of a horse. You could travel further, sell more, on horseback.'

I considered the offer for a few moments, but then declined. 'Your Grace is generous, but I prefer my own two legs. They're more reliable.'

He laughed, but the sound was forced, as though he and mirth had become strangers. 'In short, you refuse to be beholden to me.'

I regarded him steadily. 'I prefer to be my own man.'

He sighed. 'And I respect you for it. If only,' he added bitterly, 'more men thought as you do. Do you tarry long enough to go to the bridge at Picquigny tomorrow?'

'Picquigny, my lord? Where's that?'

'A little village near here, on the banks of the River Somme, where King Louis and my brother will meet to sign this inf— this treaty.'

'And will you go, my lord?'

'No, but those of my men who wish to may do so. It might be a spectacle worth seeing and I should not wish to prevent them.'

'Perhaps I shall go as well then. God be with Your Grace, now and always.' I knelt and kissed his hand. The fingers were as cold as ice.

'And God be with you, Roger my friend. I trust that our paths will cross again in the future.'

On King Louis's orders a covered bridge had been built across the River Somme at Picquigny, divided in half by a wooden grating through which he and his fellow monarch could parley; a device which lessened the threat of assassination at the hands of the untrustworthy English. (For every Frenchman worth his salt knows that we all conceal devils' tails beneath our tunics and hose.) King Louis also took the added precaution of ensuring that his approach to the bridge was from open ground, while our king was forced to advance along a narrow causeway between marshy flats. In addition, four Englishmen were stationed on the French side of the bridge and the same number of Frenchmen on the English, further hostages against misfortune, and neither sovereign was accompanied by more than a dozen attendants.

Amongst his following King Edward had chosen the Duke of Clarence, the Earl of Northumberland, Lord Hastings and John Morton. In King Louis's retinue several of his men were dressed exactly like him in order to confuse any would-be assassin, with the result that the French looked a far shabbier company than the English. This was because the outward trappings of kingship seemed to mean nothing to Louis, who was robed in a motley assortment of old and faded garments which would have put a mountebank to shame. King Edward, on the other hand, was wearing cloth-of-gold lined with red satin and a black velvet cap in which sparkled a diamond fleur-de-lys as a compliment to his host. No greater contrast could have been imagined than between these two men, one so tall and still handsome, even if running a little to fat, the other stooped and ugly, with glossy, protuberant eyes and an overpoweringly large and bulbous nose.

Timothy Plummer, who had come with me to Picquigny, whispered, 'Duke Richard kept his word, then. There's no sign of him anywhere.'

I shook my head. 'Nor will be. He'll have no truck with anything that smacks of betrayal.'

It was a lovely summer's morning, voices carrying well on the still, clear air; and so it was that from our position near the bridge we could hear something of what was being said. Both kings made speeches in French, then someone on our side spoke up in English, saying there was an ancient prophecy which foretold that an honourable peace should be made at Picquigny between the two countries.

Timothy muttered in my ear, 'We've always got a bloody prophecy whatever the occasion. That's something you can bet on.'

I begged him to be silent as I wanted to listen, but the two monarchs were now embracing one another through the wooden bars of the grille and speaking in French. A missal was brought, together with a fragment of the True Cross, on which both men swore to keep faith with the articles about to be concluded between them; and a parchment containing the terms of the treaty being duly signed, the Peace of Picquigny was thus safely concluded. The two kings then withdrew to Amiens to talk in secret, but only after King Louis had made some jest which set the English in a roar and which I later got Jocelin d'Hiver to translate for me. It seemed that King Edward had been invited to Paris to amuse himself with the ladies and had also been promised the Cardinal de Bourbon as his confessor, a churchman who would easily grant him absolution for any number of sins committed. King Edward had replied that he had always heard that His Eminence was a jolly good fellow.

And it was on that note of ribaldry that the greatest invasion of France ever embarked on by an English army came to its inglorious end.

After witnessing the events at Picquigny I took ship at Calais and made my way to London and Baynard's Castle, where I changed into my own clothes and retrieved my pack and staff. I lingered long enough to see the return of King Edward as, early in September, he and his brothers rode through the streets of London. Although everyone cheered, the huzzas were thin and mainly directed towards Duke Richard. I had heard sufficient mutterings among the people to convince me that they felt bitterly let down by what had happened.

The following day I set out for Bristol. My troubled conscience told me that I had been away from my little daughter for far too long and that she would grow up not knowing who I was unless I spent the winter with her. And the thought of winter quarters, of being cosseted and well fed by my mother-in-law, Margaret Walker, was not unpleasant. Already there was a chill in the air as evenings grew shorter and the darkness closed in. It would be good to sit by a fire again, my child on my knee, while the cold and the rain did their worst outside.

But not for too long. As soon as new life began to stir in

the earth, the trees to bud, the flowers to blossom, I should be off once more on my travels. I could not bear the confines of four walls indefinitely; I should be on my way, savouring again the pleasures of the open road, abandoning Elizabeth to her doting granddam. I was not proud of the fact, but I knew myself too well to be blind to my faults. I was as God made me, a wanderer – at least I was in those green years. Today it is a different story.